Lust

SEVEN DEADLY SINS

Compiled & Edited by
Ben Thomas & D Kershaw

Also available from Black Hare Press

DARK DRABBLES ANTHOLOGIES

WORLDS
ANGELS
MONSTERS
BEYOND
UNRAVEL
APOCALYPSE
LOVE
HATE
OCEANS
ANCIENTS

BHP WRITERS' GROUP SPECIAL EDITIONS

STORMING AREA 51
EERIE CHRISTMAS
BAD ROMANCE
TWENTY TWENTY

OTHER VOLUMES

DEEP SEA
WHAT IF?
KEY TO THE KINGDOM
BEYOND THE REALM

Twitter: @BlackHarePress
Facebook: BlackHarePress
Website: www.BlackHarePress.com

Lust, Seven Deadly Sins Anthology title is
Copyright © 2020 Black Hare Press
First published in Australia in February 2020 by Black Hare Press

The authors of the individual stories retain the copyright of the works
featured in this anthology.

*All characters and events in this publication, other than those clearly in the
public domain, are fictitious and any resemblance to real persons, living or
dead, is purely coincidental.*

All rights reserved. No part of this production may be reproduced, stored in a
retrieval system, or transmitted, in any form or by any means, electronic,
mechanical, photocopying, recording or otherwise, without the prior
permission of the publisher and copyright owner.

Paperback : ISBN 978-1-925809-47-3
Hardcover : ISBN 978-1-925809-48-0

Cover Design by Dawn Burdett
Book Formatting by Ben Thomas

A shuddering deluge whelmed your wake of yore :
You razed the halls of fatal Paris' sire :
Loaded the dice of Actium : lit the fire
Changing pale Magian to the Scarlet Whore,
Who Phrygian swine and Messalina bore,
And sterile spouses of the modern mire :
Your undertone jangles the lyric choir:
Your furtive fingers smear the lover's lore.

Mandrake, disgorged by grave of murdered Shame,
Clinging to dozing Trust with vampire lips,
Oily with fetid Sodom, or the wan
Gomorrah-sin the ages dare not name !
Seductive wrecker of immortal ships !
Serpent of Eden ! Brothel toad ! Begone ! 10 II.

Lust by Bernard O'Dowd, 1909

Table of Contents

Darkness Consumes by Terry Miller 13

I Want You by Nerisha Kemraj 19

The Council of Six and a Half by K.B. Elijah 21

Tortured Word Games by Michael D. Davis 37

Zantiel by G. Allen Wilbanks 43

The Selkie's Appetite by Jodi Jensen 53

Safe Word by A.L. King 67

Of Oyster Shells and Shit by Hari Navarro 73

Goodbye, Casanova by A.R. Dean 87

Flaunt by A.R. Johnston 95

The Fae's New Dawn by J.W. Garrett 101

Louve Garou by Blake Jessop 111

#IAmHuman by J.L. Royce 127

Poison Lust by Cindar Harrell 147

Truly Human by Clint Foster 151

Nice Face by D.J. Elton 159

Fair Game by Dannielle Viera 163

Sexcapades by Dawn DeBraal 263

Freedom by Eddie D. Moore 165

Primal Urging by Edward Ahern 171

Marionette by Erica Schaef 175

Chad by Gabriella Balcom 179

The Red Pierce Reunion Tour by J.M. Meyer 185

A Cup Full of Tears by James Dorr 197

Prey by James Lipson.. 203

A Matter of Perception by Jason Holden.................... 217

Mermaid at War by Jessica Chanese......................... 221

Aramis and Shelby by Catherine Kenwell.................. 235

L'amour L'mort by Jo Seysener 245

Lust for Life, or No Job for an Ordinary Woman by John H. Dromey 249

Lucifer's Lament by Lyndsey Ellis-Holloway............... 251

Sanguine Enamel by M.J. Christie............................. 261

Tiger Nut Sweets by Maura Yzmore.......................... 273

Unplugged by M. Sydnor Jr. 275

Taming the Beast by Maxine Churchman.................... 287

Blooming Day by N.M. Brown 295

My Girl by Nicola Currie 301

Local Girls Are Waiting for You by Raven Corinn Carluk....... 315

The Stranger by Rhiannon Bird................................. 321

Some Body by Robin Braid.. 331

Good Intentions by Sandy Butchers............................ 337

Digits of Doom by Serena Jayne 351

Damned by Stephanie Scissom 355

I Warned You by Stephen Herczeg............................. 363

I Got a Message for You by Sue Marie St. Lee 379

Podcast of the Dead by Mark Mackey....................... 395

Pi by Ximena Escobar.. 399

Coitus Interruptus by Thomas Kearnes....................... 409

Little Man of Apartment No 1610 by Tristan Drue Rogers.... 425

What Hears Your Prayers by Wondra Vanian 435

The Fallen: Lust of the Dragon by Zoey Xolton 441

Author Biographies 453

Acknowledgements 483

Darkness Consumes

by Terry Miller

I have always found inspiration in the darker things. The more I live, the more I find the truth in Shakespeare's words, "All the world's a stage." We've been cursed with sin and are naturally drawn to its inclinations. Those I find in the light, I more often discover, are merely attendees to a masquerade. I suppose this is the reason why I have always succumbed to seclusion. It gives me the opportunity to observe while never really getting personally involved. At least, that's what I once thought. One could argue that a person could never be uninvolved completely. Everything is a learning process and learning takes a certain level of involvement, doesn't it? At one time, I granted myself the luxury of depriving others from delighting in my suffering; and, suffer I have in my soul, my heart, and my mind. The few I have let in have proven me wise to consider a life of reclusion. It would be a lie to say I don't fear for my sanity, but who doesn't have such moments? This is life, perhaps not how it was intended to be, but what it has evolved to become. The truth be what it may, I understand that my reality is based upon my perception. So far, I believe myself to be correct in the majority of my presumptions, as evidence has testified.

I do not want to argue religion, faith, disbelief, or any other things pertaining to one's morality. I can only speak to what I know, and what I know comes from what I've seen. And while I'm on the subject, I could write volumes on what I've seen. Doing so, though, would only serve to bore you, the reader, and I wish you to keep reading. I want you to understand the darkness I've grown accustomed to. I know the darkness in others and have grown quite familiar with it within myself as well. With that said, it is only that which I find inside the crevices of my own mind with which I should be concerned. Even more so, I should be alarmed at the extent of my affinity for what some would only describe as macabre. People fail to see that horrors are all around us. Ones that I used to shy away from before she helped me understand the beauty in it. Hollywood feeds us vampires, werewolves, ghosts, and the like while true monsters walk in the daylight disguised in living flesh. That's not to dismiss the supernatural, no, not at all.

When I first met Miranda, it was love at first sight. Her eyes could hypnotise, and those lashes stretched to the ceiling, framing them in their perfection. Her smile, through thick, full lips, could only cause a man to dream of their touch. I found their touch. I found *her* touch. The weeks that followed were pure bliss. I didn't see it coming with its incognito methodology. It was slow, opportunistic, tracing a path through the crevices of a fractured and tormented mind. Past relationships had left me beyond jaded, far beyond helpless. I was the fertile soil for the seeds of a malicious sower.

Three months passed before I asked Miranda to move in with me. Her response was an immediate, enthusiastic yes. Every night she was insatiable. At first, I found myself grow weary, but my drive soon mimicked her insatiable appetite. We were like two beasts in the heat of our animalistic lusts. I quickly found myself consumed. I wanted nothing but more of her, which she was more than willing to supply. We were becoming one.

Miranda's silhouette upon the wall; I admired its writhing form. The shadows of her arms reached to embrace me, yet her hands were gripped firm on my ankles. I knew then that it was her darkness that took the true interest. With that being said, what's it say for me? Did it corrupt my innocence, or did it find, hidden somewhere, its dark companion? I am unsure. I gave myself freely, without excuse but my need for love, for purpose. My purpose was to love her, serve her.

There was a darkness in Miranda's soul, and when our hearts met, it crept into mine. Time passed and the dark roots began to grow, their vines drinking freely from my bitter cup. I found myself revelling in a newfound fascination for our co-inhabitant abyss. Her gift burrowed its way into my psyche without even a hint of its ill intent. This darkness was ours, and while I stared long into the abyss, it indeed stared back at me with a hunger likened to a stalking beast. That beast became me, and I relished in it. The parts of me that made me *me* slowly faded as we became one. My will was not my will but ours. It was a level of intimacy I had never known, and I was drawn to it like a moth to a flame.

I lost myself as days turned to nights and nights turned to days; melding, blending, they were all the same. The darkness within was the air I breathed, and the beloved fluids we exchanged fuelled our lust for that which grew both between us and in her womb. The weeks found us weakening as that which once fed us fed upon us. Our lust was its determination to be born, each copulation bringing it one step closer to our world.

It finally consumed us whole, turning us inside out and feeding upon our parts. Its plan had come to fruition and we exchanged realms, captive to its inner workings.

You're probably thinking that if this is true, how am

I capable of finishing this story now that I'm gone. You see, I'm not *gone* as you perceive it. I'm very much alive! Miranda is here somewhere as well. We exist here in the darkness. What you are unaware of, is that it was using us for far worse than just its entrance into our reality. My documentation of these events served to lure you, the reader, into its grasp. By reading my words, it entered your mind, slowing pulling you into itself in the process. How could you read these words if it were not true? The world in which you now dwell is not the world you knew when my story began. Sure, it looks the same to the naked eye, but be not fooled by the mere appearance of light. How great is a darkness that can disguise itself so that those therein perceive it not? If not for my role in its scheme, I would be just as unaware. You have been drawn within it, the same as I. If you look well enough, you will find me somewhere in this forsaken place. Beware the light by which you search, for things are not as they seem. What I fear the most is this feeling that it is not finished with us, like it still has plans; plans for us all.

I Want you

by Nerisha Kemraj

My fingers dance as they unwrap you,

eagerly exploring your volume.

I need to have you now.

My desire grows as you caress my lips.

My tongue automatically moves to lick you

before you melt inside me,

and my mouth waters as I take you in.

My hunger for you drives me crazy.

I want all of you, no sharing.

My body quivers with satisfaction

as the adrenaline pushes me beyond excitement.

You invoke new bursts of energy within me

as I feel you coursing through my body.

I scream out for more!

Is there such a thing

as too much of a good thing?

Satisfaction engulfs me

But my greed begs for more

Alas,

your empty wrapper lies on the floor

Until next time, my darling,

chocolate bar,

Another trip to the store,

will soon see me

indulging in you some more!

The Council of Six and a Half

by K.B. Elijah

I approached the building with trepidation. It had aged considerably in the last 50 years, with its stones coated in thick black pollution, and the carved gargoyles appearing wearier than the frighteningly fearsome visage they were intended to convey. I tried to recall if there had been flag poles the previous time I was here, but I couldn't remember.

I cleared my throat as I walked up the worn steps towards the doorman. He undoubtedly hadn't changed in 50 years: the same grey hair, the same sombre face and neat suit.

Presumably, the same forgettable name.

"Morning," I greeted him cheerfully.

"You're looking...quite modest today," the doorman said with disdain, and I glanced down in alarm.

"Er, you should see what I'm wearing underneath," I fired off hastily with a wink, thankful I'd at least remembered to wear blue, and he visibly relaxed. As he opened the door and I breezed past him, I fiddled with the top two buttons of my blouse.

After a moment, I undid a third. Couldn't be too careful.

The elevator to the penthouse corporate boardroom was quick to ascend, a smooth ride punctuated by a professional voice announcing my destination. The speed of the journey assured me that Sloth hadn't yet arrived.

As the doors slid open, I was warmly greeted by five backs turned firmly towards me. They were fussing over the back window, a glorious skyline vista that assured the occupants of the room of their dominance over the city. Spires and towers loomed in both the foreground and distance, sunlight glinting from their windows, while to the left, low hills grew ambitiously into peaked mountains. It was an old city, this one, full of history and character, but with an unquenched desire for more: more space, more height, more grandeur.

My stomach squirmed in a familiar sensation at the word *more*.

But the inhabitants of the room weren't admiring the view. They were arguing over the words stickered across the length of the glass in a pale looping font, the designer's attempt at sophistication and evidently, inspiration.

"The only sin is mediocrity—Martha Graham"

"It's a disaster," a tall man was saying. "Did no one check that this room was suitable?"

"I checked the photos," a woman in a green dress responded sullenly. "Didn't see this. Why did I have to book the room, anyway? I wanted to do the *catering*!"

"Obviously, I handled the catering," said a round androgynous person in a garish orange velour suit. "It's always been that way, and it just wouldn't make sense otherwise."

"Enough squabbling!" I, along with the others in the room, flinched at the thundering voice that erupted from Wrath. "We have a visitor."

All heads turned to me.

"Oh, hey, Lust!" The woman in the green dress swept towards me enthusiastically, raising her arms for an embrace. I returned Envy's hug, knowing what was coming.

"Oh, I love your blouse!" she cooed, unfolding herself from me and holding my shoulders at arm's length as she looked me up and down. "I wish I was allowed to wear blue. And those boots! I'd give anything to have a body like yours. I'm so *jealous*."

"You don't say," the tall man said, sweeping in to pump my hand and brushing Envy away with an arrogant flick of his wrist. "I just *have* to catch you up on everything I've been doing," he added, "although you've probably been following me on social media like everyone else."

"Er, I've been busy," I lied, offering Pride a small smile and turning hurriedly to Gluttony. "You're looking fatter than ever."

Gluttony grinned with the compliment. "And you are just deliciously delectable, aren't you?" They eyed my audaciously low blouse hem. "I could just eat you up."

"Maybe later," I laughed, comforted by the familiar banter.

Greed, as usual, was right on Gluttony's heels, her pudgy fingers reaching for mine as her blonde pigtails bounced around her cherub-like face. "Sit next to me today!"

"You will not!" Wrath boomed, his black eyes boring into us both. He loomed over us all, for looming was all he ever did, and it seemed as though a permanent storm-cloud aura clung to his thin frame, a sensation of foreboding and fear.

"But I want her to!" Greed hissed, digging her nails into my skin as she attempted to claim me for her own. "I want Lust!"

"You know your places," thundered Wrath. "Get to

them!"

We hurried to the circular table and I slotted myself between Pride and an empty chair.

"Sloth isn't here yet?" sneered Pride, his lips curling up in distaste and ruining his handsome face. "Don't tell me we have to wait for him...again."

"I'm here!" We all turned see the doorman from downstairs pushing a wheelchair across the floor from the lift. "Shan't be late this time!" mumbled the man in the chair, whose eyes were drooping shut even as he spoke.

"Wow," Envy said, an eyebrow raised. "You actually nearly made it on time."

Sloth yawned. "Been here since the last meeting. That way, there was no travel."

"You've been living in this building for 50 years?" I asked, wrinkling my nose as the smell of his unwashed body hit me, and trying not to gag.

The doorman pulled out the chair next to me and slotted the wheelchair into the empty space it left behind, before departing via the lift. The doors took a long time to close; it seemed Sloth had infected them like usual.

"Slept most of it," Sloth drawled. "I think they renovated a few times, which was a touch noisy, but it was comfortable enough. Just found a dark cupboard and had someone seal it shut so I wouldn't be disturbed. Oh look, they added an inspirational quote. That's terrible. Should do something about that."

He promptly started snoring.

"May they be dismembered while alive," Wrath intoned suddenly, and I jumped in my seat. We were starting, then.

"May they be boiled in oil," Greed added sweetly, twisting a pigtail around one finger.

"May they be dipped in frozen water," said Envy, wistfully staring at Sloth's wheelchair and glaring at her own chair in alternating moments.

"May they be broken on the wheel," Pride said, his chin held high.

"May they be smothered in fire and brimstone," I recited tonelessly.

I elbowed Sloth.

"Er, may they be thrown into a snakepit," he muttered, before the snores commenced once more.

"May they be fed rats, toads and snakes," announced Gluttony happily. "Including those in Sloth's snakepit."

Nobody reacted. They had tried that joke on every quinquagenary Council meeting since the first one, and it had grown old fast.

"Welcome," Wrath declared, and spread his arms. "Brothers and sisters, it is good to see you again at the

Council of Seven Deadly Sins. We meet here, in this central point of the ley lines, to prove how deep humanity falls into sin. The most depraved of vices, the wickedest of actions, the most—"

"Sorry," Gluttony said, "but I can't concentrate on a word you are saying with those letters behind you. Mediocrity isn't a sin! Do you see her sitting with us? No. Sins are *pure*. We worked hard to get this gig, and they're making out like she's worse than the lot of us put together!"

"Personally, I think there is some truth to the words," said Pride. "One should always strive for excellence so one can be proud of it."

"You'd be proud of mediocrity too," Envy snapped. "You're proud of everyone but me!"

"Well, I do have standards," he snarled.

"Guys, we're getting side-tracked," I pointed out. "We're better than this."

"We're really not," Greed laughed. "But I agree with Lust. Let's get to the fun part of this meeting."

"The morning tea afterwards?" Gluttony asked hopefully, but everyone ignored them and turned to Greed expectantly. She always had to go first for this stage of the meeting, as much as that annoyed Envy; Greed would be insufferable otherwise. There was only so much repetitive whining from that high-pitched and childish voice of hers that they could take.

"I have had many great achievements over the last 50 years," she commenced solemnly, looking each of them in the eyes in turn. "But the highlight was a decade and a half ago when I caused a man to lose $649,000, his wife, his mistress, his Labrador, his house, his career and his sanity, all with just a little nudge towards the casino one day after work. It was *beautiful*."

I clapped politely along with the others.

"Good work," commended Wrath. "A fine example of greed. My favourite moment was 32 years ago, when I assisted a man to kill six people in retaliation for his wife's death at the hands of a drunk driver, including the bartender who had served the drinks and the mechanic who had serviced the car two months prior."

"What about the driver himself?" I asked, and Wrath gave a cruel smile.

"Eventually."

The table cheered, and I forced myself to join in just as enthusiastically. Wrath dug around in the pocket of his red suit and pulled out a USB, which he tossed down in front of us.

"They made a movie about it, if you're interested."

"No way," Envy breathed. "That is so unfair!"

Wrath looked across at me. "Lust, you're up."

My palms were suddenly sweaty. I wiped them carefully on my skirt, trying to pull it higher up my legs as I did so. The doorman had been right: I was dressed far too modestly today.

"It's a good one," I said slowly, desperately racking my brains for a story to tell. Surely something worthy had happened in the last 50 years?

"Six months ago," I drawled, keeping it recent in case any of them had checked up on me in the half-century since our last meeting, "This girl goes out to a motel for a secret rendezvous, and the guy's already there. He has candles and rose petals laid out, and a bottle of Chandon chilling in the bar fridge."

Envy shifted in her chair.

"They spend all night together, and as the dawn rises, you know what she asks?"

The table is silent, staring at me with their mouths slightly open in anticipation.

"She asks," I said, getting excited, "whether he will *marry her*!"

There's more silence, and they don't seem to understand that it was the end of the story. And then it dawns on me what they're thinking.

"Anyway," I added hastily, "I'm sure Envy has some

great stories to tell—"

"That's not lust!" Pride said haughtily. "That's *love*! Have some pride, woman!"

The others, seemingly freed of their frozen states by Pride's outburst, make similar statements.

"What the hell, Lust?"

"Why didn't you stop them?"

"Have you gone soft in your old age?"

"I love love," Gluttony murmured happily, and I blinked at them. "Makes everyone so fat and comfortable. No one cares what they eat when they're in love."

"That's not the point," said Pride irritably. "You're not Love. You're Lust."

I squirmed in my chair. How had I thought I could get through this meeting without being found out?

"I misspoke," I mumbled, but Wrath slapped his hand on the table.

"Tell us the truth!"

I bit my lip. Dishonesty wasn't a sin, at least not one of our calibre, but it wasn't acceptable to lie to this table, and we had sworn oaths to our brothers and sisters long ago that we would be true in all things.

"I, er...I need help," I whispered. "These last few decades, I haven't been able to think straight. Sinful lust is no longer what gets me up in the morning; it's the warmth of love that I crave. Kind acts, generous gifts, pledges of eternity and beyond." I fought back the tears that threatened my eyes with their warmth. "What's wrong with me?"

"You've changed," Greed declared. Her voice was cold.

"Hey," Envy whined. "If Lust gets to change, why can't I? That's not fair!"

"Do you want to change? Become Mild Jealousy, perhaps? Or Not-Give-A-Damn?"

"No. I love me." Envy giggled. "It's so deliciously bitter."

"You are the heart of this Council!" Sloth drawled, and startled, I glanced to my left to find his bloodshot eyes open and fixed on me. "I rely on lust for procrastination and laziness, Envy needs lust for what others have, and Gluttony depends on lust for food! You can't abandon us now!"

"I don't think I have a choice," I said, trying to look miserable. "I've tried everything: therapy, self-help groups, going cold turkey, those new-age crystal things that supposedly help you adjust your aura. I'm *doomed*."

"You don't sound too upset about it," Gluttony commented.

I shrugged, attempting to hide my smile. "Love

makes me feel good. That's all I can say."

Wrath growled.

"It's not my fault!" I retorted. "Lust is losing its condemnation! They're teaching that it's acceptable to live for yourself, to fight for and take what you want. Casual sex is practically *encouraged*!"

"I hear you," murmured Sloth, rather unexpectedly considering the last words he'd sent my way. His eyes were shut again, but his voice was unusually clear. "I used to be the worst of all sins." There was disgruntled muttering at this statement, but he ignored them. "And now lying on the sofa binge-watching Netflix is as common as anything."

"There may be some truth to it," Pride muttered reluctantly. "Ever since participation trophies were introduced for children playing sports, pride is being shot off left, right and centre, and no one gives a damn about it. Social media posts are either a blag or a complaint, and bragging these days merely warrants a sigh and an unfollowing, rather than a sentencing to hell. It's getting a touch difficult to work with."

We all leaned back in our chairs.

"Well *I* haven't changed," Wrath snarled.

"Oh, really?" Envy asked, snorting. "Because I may have heard on the grapevine that you helped out a bunch of people the other day. One might even call it *saving their lives*?"

"That doesn't count! My wife had wrongfully accused them for our daughter's death, and she was going to-"

He fell silent, then cleared his throat. "Point. Taken."

"What are we going to do?" I asked, my voice echoing around the room. "If we are no longer considered the seven deadly sins, what does that make us? This Council?"

"Still pretty damn terrifying," Greed said, baring her little teeth. "So, the world is changing, and humanity's values are reforming around it, but we still all *matter*. We are still all deadly in some way or another. We may just have to...change along with it."

Gluttony coughed. "I did get a call the other day from Pollution, asking if he could join the Council."

"He's one of the Horsemen," Envy whined. "If he gets to be both, I should too!"

I clicked my tongue. "What about Racism? He's been on our backs for ages, and he's gaining a lot of support as a Sin."

Murmurs of assent met my words.

"I am terribly sorry ladies and gentlemen, but you only booked this room for an hour." We turned to find the doorman standing by the lift, holding the doors open with a pale hand. "If you could please descend to the ground level and move into the foyer, we have refreshments set out for morning tea."

Gluttony pushed back his chair and was racing towards the lift before he had finished speaking.

"We need more time," Wrath ordered, but the doorman didn't flinch.

"My apologies, sir, but the room is booked from 11am." His voice was pleasant and mild.

"By who?"

A faint smile slid up the doorman's mouth. "The quinquagenary Council meeting of the Heavenly Virtues."

We all groaned as one and followed Gluttony into the lift, who was sticking a pudgy finger into the 'close door' button before we'd even managed to cram into the small space.

The air was stuffy, and smelled like Sloth, whose 'a shower is too much effort' attitude made it difficult to breathe. I forced myself through the lift doors as soon as they started to open on the ground floor, and almost bowled over a slender figure with brown curls framing her pretty face.

"Ah, uh, hi, Patience," I stammered, caught off

guard. I hadn't met one of *them* for a long time. She winked at me, then blew a kiss to Wrath over my shoulder.

"Good morning, Lust. You're looking rather lascivious."

"Thanks for trying," I said, "but we both know that isn't true. Still, I appreciate the compliment."

She inclined her head and caught Wrath's arm as he passed. "Did you enjoy my little addition to the meeting room?"

"That was *you*? I'll…I'll…" Wrath's face nearly turned purple with rage.

Patience smiled and patted his cheek. "You'll get over it. Don't forget we're meeting Wayne and Beth at the restaurant at seven, darling."

Wrath looked at the floor, his anger abated. "I haven't forgotten. But you better not be late; all they do is talk about their pig farm. Five minutes late, and I'm divorcing you."

He kissed her on the lips and moved over to the plate of biscuits before Gluttony could consume them all.

I looked past Patience. "Where's the rest of your group?"

"Oh, it's just me and Kindness these days," Patience replied, waiting for the others to exit the lift without displaying even a twitch of irritability as Sloth's leisurely pace. "The world is running a little thin on heavenly virtues at the moment. Know anyone who might be interested? We've got plenty of spare seats."

I hid my smile as I grabbed a coffee from the refreshments table. If my lustful side didn't return, maybe I would think about taking on the job of Love full time. I tapped out a calendar reminder on my smartwatch, below 'buy milk' and 'book wedding celebrant'.

'Update resumé'.

Tortured Word Games

by Michael D. Davis

"P-L-E-A-S-A-N-T, pleasant. See what you can do with that, you dumb shit."

"Planes. Your turn."

"Staple. Back to you, dumb ass."

"Atlas."

"Peasant."

"Step."

"Planet."

"Tape."

"Petals. You running out of words already?"

"Of course not." Yes, I was. For the love of God why could I only think of the word pen? I had to beat him. Come on it's an easy word, plenty of letters to work with. Wait, I had it, "pasta."

"Took you awhile there, Glenny… Least."

I had to win, just once, I don't want to be the first to run out of words. "Pen."

"You are running out. Nasal. Back to you."

Shit. Think, think, P-L-E, no, S-T-A, fuck! I didn't want to say it, "I'm out."

"And another round to the champ. Pick a real stumper with the next word, won't you, Glenny?"

There was no time to think of one, no need. The door opened at the top of the stairs and the room was flooded with light. I tensed and crawled back towards the wall. Even Prescott lost his cocky attitude. I thought she was coming towards me, but then she veered off towards him. Prescott screamed some and fought little; after you've been here for as long as us, the strength—even the desire—for freedom dwindles.

As she dragged him off towards the workroom by his chain, I racked my brains to come up with a good word. I knew, however, that I'd have some time to work. Usually, she brings us back after a few hours too drugged up to feel any pain, more than often missing some sort of appendage or organ. The waiting is just as bad as anything she could do to us in the workroom; you never know when she'll come, and she leaves us here for days, feeding us only occasionally.

That's how the game started. It's a distraction, a way to get our minds off where we are, what's being done to us. It's simple, we take turns saying a word and you have to make up those words using only letters from the start word. Whoever runs out of words first loses. Prescott's never lost, I've never won. She has taken my right foot, my left leg below the knee, one eye, most of my fingers, and who knows what from inside of me. It's only time before she takes my life. And the one thing I want to do before I die is win a game, just one.

Prescott was unconscious when he was brought back. When he finally woke up, he had a large scar across his newly shaven head.

"Alright," I said, "let's start. I-M-A-G-I-N-A-T-I-O-N, imagination. Let's see what you got."

"Aiming."

"Magi." *I know I'm going to win this time*, I told myself; something was different.

"Amigo," said Prescott.

"Moaning."

"Nation."

"Mania."

"Tango."

He was weakening. He was taking longer pauses before his words. I had him, I could feel the win in my mouth with just a few more words, not just a craving. "Goat," I said.

"Gnat."

"Giant."

"Mango."

"Gain."

"Gait."

He didn't say a word. Seconds passed into minutes and we both sat there. The feeling grew within my body, fast like a forest fire. The fact that I'm going to die chained in a chamber hacked to pieces didn't matter now that I won the game. I was the champion. No more wasted hours wishing for victory, it was now upon me.

That's when his lips started to part. He was going to speak, ruin it all. I jumped away from the wall, going as far as the chain would let me. I gripped his head in my hands using the few fingers I had left and smashed him against the concrete. I couldn't hear it again, his voice, "Another for the champion, none for Glenny." I hit his head against the floor till it was nothing but mush, his new scar leaking red. His last words were whispered, I barely heard them, "Thank you, man."

When she found out, she really wasn't happy. However, she didn't kill me, which wasn't a blessing. A few days after she took out Prescott's body, a new guy was brought in and chained in his spot; Nathan was his name.

"Well, Nate," I said. "We're gonna be here a while. Wanna play a word game?"

"How do you play?" he said.

"Don't worry I'll teach you; I'm reigning champion."

Zantiel

by G. Allen Wilbanks

Jason Kant trailed his eyes across the tables and booths in the pub, observing the barflies scattered throughout the bustling business. It was a typical Friday night at The Blackthorn, with a constant flow of people shuffling to and from the bar, restocking on alcohol for themselves and their companions. Socialising was thirsty work, and the customers kept the two bartenders on shift that night busy mixing and pouring drinks. It was standing room only throughout most of the business, with no place available to set down a beer except for a couple of small tables that had been stripped of their chairs and pushed aside to make room for the foot traffic.

Usually, Jason considered this type of scene a "target-rich environment," as he would refer to it to his buddies. Tonight, however, most of the women he saw in the pub seemed already gathered into larger groups or worse, paired off with other guys. They may as well have been hiding behind the bars of a cage, as they were completely unapproachable to a solo bachelor like himself. He sipped his beer and continued to scan the room for likely companionship.

The evening so far didn't look good. Although the place was packed, he found very few options among the one or two girls he could see seated by themselves. They did not appear terribly friendly or eager for company. He spotted a few women paired up at various tables, but he decided against approaching them as well. Trying to separate friends could often get difficult if he decided he wanted to take one of them home with him.

Jason considered calling it quits for the moment. Maybe he could find a place to sit down and wait a while; see if the situation changed after an hour or so. Or, maybe he should just leave this bar and go find another more welcoming location. Before he could decide which route to take, he spotted something promising.

A girl perched alone on a stool at the far corner of the bar. Behind the constant crowd of people vying for the bartenders' attention, he had almost missed seeing her. She sat with her back to the edge of the long, wooden counter, scanning the room around her with a curious, hopeful expression. She looked to be a couple years younger than Jason's own twenty-five years of age, though not so young they would have had to turn her away at the door. Long, dark hair framed a teardrop-shaped face, and wide, expressive, dark eyes over a delicate, pointed nose gave her an air of innocence that Jason hoped was only skin deep. She wore little or no makeup, but she had a simple, unadorned beauty that appealed to his baser instincts. The low front on her blue and white striped, tank top didn't hurt his libido any either.

She did not seem to Jason to be waiting for anyone. She didn't have the anxious appearance of someone whose friend was late, or the angry, frustrated demeanour of a stood-up date. She watched the activity around her, smiling at passing strangers and giving off the universal signals that she was open to some human interaction if anyone proved courageous enough to join her. Jason figured that maybe he should be that person. As he wandered closer, he noticed that his luck continued to improve. The stool immediately next to her was currently available.

Jason slipped a hand into his pocket and felt the plastic card that acted as his hotel room key. He debated walking up to the girl and setting the key on the bar in front of her. But, no. That was a chick trick. Any slut looking to get slammed into a mattress could drop their room key into the lap of any stud in this place and they would be five minutes away from a naked good time. It didn't usually work the other way, however. Guys had to work a little harder than that if they expected to score.

It wasn't fair, Jason complained mentally to himself. The odds were stacked against the guys in this arena. Although, resting in his pocket right next to the room key, he had a little something prepared that he figured might just even those odds a little bit.

Jason moved close enough to the girl that she could not fail to notice his presence, and when they made eye contact, she did not immediately look away. Another good sign, he thought. Instead, she smiled, held his gaze for a long moment, then turned around in her seat to face the bar, her back to him.

He knew an invitation when he saw it.

Settling onto the empty bar stool beside the girl, Jason pointed at the empty glass on the bar in front of her.

"Excuse me, but can I buy you another one of whatever that was?"

"Appletini," she said, sliding the empty glass toward him. "I know it's silly, but I absolutely love the things. Thank you."

The girl's cheeks flushed pink. *Was she embarrassed?* Jason wondered. She certainly didn't look like a regular to this kind of setting, but she was also too pretty to be completely new to guys hitting on her. Maybe this was her first time trying to get picked up in a bar. Ah, well. No problem, he told himself with a small grin. He would be happy to break her in.

Jason had a momentary vision of him and this girl across the street in his hotel room with nothing between them except a layer of sweat. He liked the image his mind conjured and he felt himself reacting to it. He shifted on his stool, trying to hide the growing bulge in his pants, then thought better of it. *Maybe she'll like what she sees,* he told himself. *Hell, she'll probably get off on it. Girls love knowing a guy is interested.*

He caught the bartender between customers and ordered the appletini as well as another beer for himself. The bartender snapped the cap off a bottle and slid it toward him, then proceeded to mix the martini. When the bartender set the drink next to his beer, Jason tossed a twenty onto the bar with his left hand.

"Keep it," he said, and watched the bill disappear into an apron pocket.

Jason placed his right hand over the top of the martini glass, picking the drink up by the rim of the glass and allowing a few grains of white powder that he had palmed from his pocket to fall into the pale green liquid. He held up the glass and swirled the appletini in front of his new acquaintance, ostensibly to temp her to take it from his hand, but also to be sure the powder was fully dissolved in her drink before handing it over.

The girl giggled, accepted the drink from him, and took a long sip before setting it back on the bar in front of her. Sliding a finger along the rim of her glass, she stared straight ahead, avoiding eye contact with Jason. An amused grin pulled at her lips. He liked the way she looked. A dimple appeared in her right cheek when she smiled that Jason found adorable. He wanted to lean in and kiss it, but he resisted the impulse. There would be plenty of time for that later.

"So, now that you have your drink, can I ask you your name?" Jason commented.

"Zan," the girl replied, still gazing into her appletini.

"Zan. That's an interesting name."

"It's short for Zantiel. But I prefer Zan. Easier to remember, don't you think?"

Jason nodded. "It's a pleasure to meet you, Zan. My name's Jason."

Zan turned on her stool, letting her knee graze against Jason's thigh as she finally glanced up to meet his gaze. "Hello, Jason. So, what happens next? Are you going to get up and go find someone else to buy a drink for, like the philanthropic gentleman you seem to be, or are you sticking around for a while because you think that now I owe you something?"

Jason stammered for a moment, unsure how to reply.

This shy appearing girl was suddenly much more direct than he had expected her to be. It would take a few more minutes for the stuff he gave Zan to start working, and if she sent him away before then, someone else would reap the benefits of his handiwork. He needed to stay put a while longer; keep her talking.

"I…I guess I suppose you owe me at least five more minutes of conversation before I leave. That wouldn't be an unfair trade, would it? After five minutes, then you decide if we talk five minutes more, or I go away."

"Five minutes," Zan agreed. She pursed her lips and nodded as if reaching a decision. She took another long drink of her appletini, almost emptying the glass. "Okay. Deal. But I'm warning you, Jason. If you ask me what my astrological sign is, this conversation is over."

"Promise," he said, laughing and crossing his chest with a finger. "No sign questions. So, where are you from? I haven't seen you around here before."

"South. Way south of here, I suppose you could say."

Zan upended her martini glass and emptied the last of the contents, swallowing quickly. She ran her index finger around the bottom of the glass and slipped it into her mouth, sucking noisily.

"Damn, Jason!" she said, popping the finger out of her mouth and whistling a sharp note of appreciation. She slapped his shoulder playfully. "I don't know what you put in this drink, but it sure does pack a punch. I might have to go and get me some more of this stuff later."

"I don't know what you mean," Jason blurted out, too quickly.

"Of course, you do. I'm talking about the stuff you dumped into my drink before you handed it to me. You know, because you thought I was cute, and you wanted to fuck me while I was unconscious."

Jason jumped to his feet, but Zan caught him by the arm and pulled him back down next to her. She was strong. Much too strong for a person her size and Jason found himself dragged back onto the stool he had tried to vacate. When Zan was confident he would not bolt again, she released him. She placed a hand on his chest and patted him gently, almost affectionately.

"Oh, it's okay. I understand. You couldn't help yourself. But I have to say, rape…" Zan tsked a few times. "That's a nasty one. That's enough to send you to the bad place."

She waggled a finger in his face and sing-songed, "Naughty, naughty, naughty."

Jason tried again to stand, but a sudden tightness in his chest kept him from gaining his feet. The pain radiated out from under his ribcage, creeping up along the sides of his neck and down his left arm.

"What…what did you do to me?" he panted.

"You're having a heart attack, sweetheart," Zan purred. "At least, it's going to look like a heart attack to anyone who cares enough to cut you open and look. It's a big one, too. I'm afraid it's really going to hurt."

"You bi—" but, the pain flared brighter and Jason couldn't finish the pejorative.

"Don't worry. I know you feel bad that we didn't get much time together, but I promise we'll see each other again. I'm going to ask if I can oversee your assignment personally. I figure I collected you, it's only fair I get to keep you."

Jason slumped and fell from his seat, landing on his back on the sticky floor of the pub. He heard Zan in the background, yelling out to the crowd for help. As the pain in his chest became intolerable and his vision began to dim, she knelt beside him and cradled his head in her lap. She leaned in close to whisper into his ear.

"Isn't this nice? I'm going to be the last thing you see in this world, and the very first you see in the next."

The Selkie's Appetite

by Jodi Jensen

Ireland, 1688

Alastar's head broke the surface of the water as the full moon rose above the craggy shoreline. The men of Donegal were at sea, fishing to feed their families, and the children would all be sleeping by now.

He watched for a few moments to be sure the beach was deserted, then swam to an outcropping of rocks that jutted precariously from the waves. Hauling himself onto a relatively flat boulder, he was greeted by the welcoming barks of a harem of seals.

"Lasses," he murmured, shedding his seal skin to reveal his human form underneath. "Hush now, I'll tend to ye later." He glanced at the stretch of sandy shoreline again, then stuffed his pelt deep into a crack and covered it with smaller rocks, driftwood and shells.

Naked and unashamed, he made his way through the harem, patting one on the head here and there, smiling at the large doe eyes that followed his every move. Once on the other side of the tiny, rocky island, he gazed at the shadows of the village huts on the hillside and his smile grew. The women inside those huts were every bit as adoring, and had been for years.

He dived into the churning waves, eager for the pleasure that awaited on land.

Still donning nothing but his human skin, Alastar approached the first hut. A small candle sat in one window, its glow sending him an inviting message.

Rosaleen…

His male flesh stirred as his mind conjured images of the raven-haired beauty. He always visited her first. Always needed the urgent coupling she provided.

He'd raised a hand to knock, when the door opened.

With a lift of her eyebrow, Rosaleen's eyes swept over him appreciatively, then she dragged him inside by the arm.

Alastar gave her a wicked grin and pulled her into his arms.

"Not a thing about ye has changed," she whispered, smacking him on the shoulder. "Git ye in bed, lest ye wake the lads."

Never one to turn down an offer, he strode into the next room, certain her eyes were on his backside the whole way. When he turned, he was pleased to see he'd been right, for now, it wasn't his backside she was looking at.

Rosaleen's dark eyes widened and she licked her lips as she reached for the laces on the bodice of her woollen gown.

"No time for that." His body trembled with need and he nodded to her bed. "Bend over."

The woman, bless her, never even hesitated.

Lifting her skirts up over her back, Alastar took one look at the beautiful, creamy flesh of her thighs and was ready. In a single thrust, he was inside of her.

Half a dozen more, and he was finished.

"Ye always do that," she grumbled as she straightened and fixed her skirts.

He tucked a finger under her chin, charmed by the adorable pout on her luscious lips. "But ye have three lusty lads from me. That's more than anyone else."

Her expression softened. "Maybe this time ye gave me a wee lass."

"Maybe," he agreed. With a quick peck on the cheek, he released her and started for the door, his thoughts already on who he wanted to visit next.

Ciara? Elva? Ruth? Fiona?

Fiona, yes.

He skirted the edge of the village until he reached her hut and just as it had in Rosaleen's, a candle glowed in Fiona's window.

And once again, the door opened before he knocked.

The fiery redhead didn't say a word, merely grabbed him and kissed him.

Lips locked, Alastar pushed her inside and up against a wall.

Her arms wound around his neck and her fingers tangled in his still damp hair.

He shoved her skirts up, then lifted her so she could wrap her legs around his waist as he entered her. Fast and hard, this time the pleasure was reciprocated when her inner flesh tightened around him and she cried out.

Their gasps filled the air as he joined her in sweet release.

Before he could utter a single word, Fiona tightened her grip in his hair and pulled his head back.

"Run," she whispered, her voice as urgent as their coupling had been. "Ye must go back to the sea."

He set her down and frowned. "What? Why?"

"Go." She shoved him away. "Now."

"Fiona?"

She hurried to the door and flung it open. "Quickly, and don't come back!"

He glanced at her through narrowed eyes, but her gaze was directed over his shoulder. Turning, his gut twisted at the sight before him.

A row of flaming torches, bobbing through the darkness, weaving through the village.

The men, it had to be.

Alastar ran. He kept to the shadows, darting behind barns, sheds, bushes and whatever else he could find until he reached the rocky shoreline. One last dash and he made it to the water. Though he swam faster as a seal, he still sliced through the waves without so much as a splash.

As he approached the tiny island, and the torches were far behind him, his breath came easier. He hauled himself onto the rocks and the harem of seals erupted in joyous barks.

"Keep it down," he snapped, ignoring the press of bodies as he shoved his way through. He had only one thing on his mind. He hurried to the crevice where he'd left his pelt, but the driftwood, shells, and rocks had all been moved. The pelt was gone.

A strapping lad with a shadow of whiskers above his lip stepped out from behind a boulder. *"Dadai."*

Alastar froze, the hairs on his arms bristled at the venom dripping from what should have been an endearment.

"Ye will not find what ye seek in this place." The lad nodded at the spot where the pelt had been hidden.

Taking a closer look at the lad, Alastar saw the webbed fingers. The boy was half-selkie. The boy was his son. "Where is it? What've ye done?"

"Ye want the pelt back, ye must come and speak with my mum." The lad's gaze flickered to shore. "She's waiting for ye."

Alastar turned to find a single moonlit silhouette standing on the beach. The torches were nowhere to be seen. He turned back to his son. "Which of the lasses is your mum?"

"Shanna," the lad said from between gritted teeth.

Alastar smiled as thoughts of the lovely Shanna filled his mind. Sweet and soft with curves in all the right places. "I remember her well. And what does she call ye, lad?"

The boy stiffened. "Ronan."

"Ah, Ronan," Alastar nodded his approval. "Little seal."

"I know what it means," Ronan spat, his body now rigid with defiance.

Alastar's laugh sounded so much like the barking seals, that a few of the creatures barked in return. "I'll speak with your mum and ye go fetch my pelt, agreed?"

Ronan gave him a sharp nod. "Agreed."

As they dived into the choppy waves, Alastar felt a surge of pride swimming beside his son. The lad was almost as good in the water as he was. Once they neared the shore, both stood and waded the rest of the way, and again, he grinned as he recognised his own confident stride in the way his son walked.

He clapped Ronan on the shoulder. "Like it or not, lad, ye're the spit of me."

"That's what my mum says." Ronan shrugged his father's hand away. "She's waiting for ye, just over there."

Alastar headed for the shadowy figure while Ronan stalked off in the opposite direction. "Shanna, darlin'—"

"The lass is *my* darlin'," a masculine voice growled. A hand reached out, seized him by the naked ballocks and squeezed.

Dropping to his knees, Alastar gasped.

The hand tightened its grip and twisted.

He collapsed onto his side as the pain spread through his body and stole his breath until he lay silently panting.

"Get 'im up," the man ordered.

Two more men grabbed Alastar under the armpits and hauled him to his feet.

"Would ye look at that, caught me a selkie." The first

man, Shanna's husband, strolled all the way around his prize in a large circle, then stopped and stood nose to nose with him. Several times the man gave a sharp inhale and opened his mouth, but then shut it again without speaking. Finally, the man drew an arm back and punched Alastar in the belly, knocking the wind out of him once more.

The two men on either side of Alastar held him upright as Shanna's husband wailed on him. Blow after blow to the face, the gut, even his unprotected human male parts. Blood ran from his nose and mouth and more than once, his legs tried to crumple beneath him as the impact of another punch hit him.

Just when it seemed like the beating was over, Shanna's husband traded places with the man holding his left arm, and the next round began.

By the end of the third round, Alastar's head lolled forward as blackness surrounded him.

Alastar woke to the warmth of the sun touching his face, and for a second, he forgot. Then he moved and it all came rushing back. The lasses. His son. The beatings.

He grunted as he sat up, wincing at the pain in his head.

"About time, ye hoor." Ronan pushed off from where

he'd been leaning against the wall, a scowl twisting his lips.

"Not much gets past ye, does it?" Alastar asked dryly. "Ye bring any whiskey?"

"I brought something better." Ronan dragged a stool across the dirt floor and sat smack in front of his father, his scowl deepening.

Alastar glanced around but didn't see anything except an empty root cellar. Everything down to the shelves themselves had been cleared out. The only things in here were himself, his son, and the stool. "Ye brought me a chair? I suppose I could break a leg off to defend myself the next time those blokes want to hold me down and beat me."

"Those *blokes* mean to kill ye."

Alastar gave an involuntary shiver. "Ye mean to help them? Or did ye come to break me out of here?"

Ronan spat into the dirt, then narrowed his eyes. "As much as I'd like to help them, I made my mum a promise." The lad gave an angry sigh. "I'll let ye go *and* give ye the pelt back, but ye must give your word never to return. Ever."

"Ye take me for a *gabdhán* fool then, don't ye?" Alastar shook his head at the offer. It was too good to be true. No way his son was letting him go.

"Give. Me. Your. Word." Ronan's jaw twitched as

he spoke and anger rolled off of him in waves. "It's what my mum asked of me, and she's asking it of ye, too."

Alastar hesitated. He didn't dare take the offer, but he didn't dare refuse either.

Ronan reached into his pocket, pulled out a key, and dangled it in front of his father. "Your word?"

Nodding, Alastar laboured to his feet. His body was a mass of bruises, dried blood and sweat, and he ached from head to toe, but he was getting out. The thought of the ocean was enough to put a spring in his step as he approached the door.

"Say it."

Alastar glanced over his shoulder to find his son still sitting on the stool, muscles tense.

"Ye have my word," Alastar said without hesitation, "never to return to Donegal."

Ronan stood and stalked past his father, unlocking the door, then peeking out to be sure it was clear. "This way," he whispered.

Alastar followed his son, ducking behind sheds, dashing from bush to bush, leaving the sights and sounds of the village behind them.

When they reached the water's edge, Ronan pointed to a cave at the base of a towering cliff a short swim away. "Ye'll find the pelt hidden inside, behind the spiked rock, the one that's taller than a man."

"I thank ye, son—"

"Ye will not call me *son*," Ronan said as he backed away. "I did it for my mum. Now, go, and don't come back."

Alastar waded into the ocean, ignoring the burning flesh as the seawater enveloped him. He swam until he reached the cave, then retrieved his pelt, and slipped back into the cool, smooth sealskin.

This time when he dived into the water, it sluiced over him, painless and exhilarating.

As he swam, hours turned into days, days into months, months into years, and years into a decade. True to his word, he hadn't returned to Donegal, though he was sorely tempted now that enough time had passed that he'd likely been forgotten.

He'd found other villages and other women, but none of them compared to the ones he'd left behind. They were special. They were his.

He had to go back. One more time, just to see.

When the next full moon came, Alastar swam to the familiar outcropping of rocks, delighted to find his old harem still occupying the tiny island and overjoyed to see him. He waited among the seals, watching the village until all was silent and dark.

His heart twinged when he saw there wasn't a single candle burning in a window for him and he made up his mind in that instant to change that. Even as he peeled away the sealskin, his human male flesh stirred.

He dived into the waves and swam for shore, his mind on a single, repeating fantasy.

Rosaleen.

"Ye couldn't do it, could ye?"

Alastar froze at the familiar voice.

Ronan stepped out of the shadows, a good deal taller, and angrier, than before.

Water lapped around Alastar's ankles and he paused. "Son."

"I told ye, ye will not call me *son*." Ronan pulled a knife from the waist of his pants. "And ye gave your word, yet here ye stand."

"Here I stand," Alastar agreed. "I miss them." Eyes on the blade, he shrugged. "I miss them all."

Ronan's fingers clenched around the handle of the weapon and he took a step forward. "Don't ye put one foot on shore or I'll end ye."

"Ye will not." Alastar moved toward the lad, certain his own son wouldn't harm him.

A deep growl issued from Ronan and he lunged at his father, stabbing the knife deep into his chest.

Alastar clutched and clawed at his son as his legs gave way beneath him. "Wh-why?"

"Ye will not cause unrest in the village again." Ronan shoved him away, his face cold as he watched his father gasp his final breaths.

Two years later…

Ronan bobbed in the water, his head barely above the lapping waves as he watched the seaside village of Tramore. Every full moon he ventured a little bit closer, desperate to catch glimpses of the beautiful women there, and cursing himself as he did.

He understood now, knew about the lust that had driven his father. Knew he was just as helpless against it.

Filled with self-loathing, he moved closer.

Close enough to see a voluptuous young lass with long, luscious curls strolling the beach.

Heart pounding, and human male flesh fully erect, Ronan swam for shore.

Safe Word

by A.L. King

She tossed the toothpick on the counter. Her date was approaching, and she didn't think prodding her mouth with a stick of wood looked attractive (unless it was the right kind of wood). Sure, his first impression of her would likely be his last. The suitors who called on Fantasia were far from traditional. She would probably never see him again, but that didn't mean she had to be a slob.

He rounded the bar and sat down beside her, fiddling with the rose pendant pinned to his shirt pocket. She could tell he was nervous and not sure he had the right gal, so she flicked one of her rose earrings and offered him a smile.

They bantered for about fifteen minutes before he finally manned up and slid his spare keycard across the counter. Room 213. She let him finish the drink he'd ordered and then gave him a head start. She watched him leave the bar and thought to herself that he wasn't half bad looking.

She told herself, with the money she got this time,

she was going to start fixing her teeth. The front ones were attractive enough and didn't dissuade a decent class of clientele, but she was tired of food getting lodged in her molars.

That didn't stop her from digging into the fresh bowl of peanuts the bartender set before her. She'd been starving herself all day to slip into her dress, and she needed a little sustenance to be at the top of her game.

After fifteen minutes of waiting, she made her way to room 213. She almost laughed out loud when she let herself into the room and found him sitting on the bed in a gimp suit. Someone was excited!

"What took you so long?" he asked, probably thinking she was tracking time already, the way cab drivers track mileage.

Fantasia only smiled. It was a beautiful smile, and she knew it, bad back teeth or not. "Relax, baby, the charge don't start until you get a charge."

She'd used that line before and hated it, but selling herself was as much theatre as it was debauchery. The man before her was the same character, only a different actor was playing him.

Fidgeting nervously on the bed, he said, "I…I have a safe word."

"You better," she said, trying to sound equally sexy

and intimidating. She was more of a sub and hated playing a dom, but she did what she had to do. "So tell me…what is little boy going to say when he's had enough of Fantasia?"

"Flamingo."

She reached up and zipped his mask. "Say that again so I know I can hear you through that thing."

"Uh-ing-oh," he uttered.

Close enough, she decided, then pushed him down on the bed.

As she took control, she realised that she was actually enjoying herself. That always made the workday (work*night*, she supposed) go a little quicker, even if the customer took longer than expected. And he was taking his sweet time. Almost too much. She had another meeting at another hotel bar in little more than an hour. That meant getting showered and brushing her teeth.

"We should probably wrap this up soon," she said without missing a beat of the heat. "What's gonna do it for you?'

"Issing," he said.

"Excuse me? Did you say pissing? I'm strictly against that."

He unzipped his mouth flap. "No. I said kissing."

Almost romantic, she thought. How sweet.

"That'll be extra," she said, trying to make it sound sexy by imagining extra was spelled with a triple X.

"Deal."

She kissed him roughly and passionately as she worked. Then finally, when she saw that dazed look in his eyes that every man gets just before, she zipped his mouthpiece shut again. He was soon seizing in what she took as pleasure. She kept going, actually enjoying herself for once. She'd often told johns at the end of the night that it would be nice to see them again, but with this one she figured she might actually mean it.

He moaned and seized and seized and moaned, and for a moment she was worried something was wrong. But there couldn't be a problem, because he would have yelled his safe word. Even men having massive heart attacks could manage to string together a few syllables. She'd learned that the hard way.

Except, he suddenly stopped moving, and his on-the-verge gaze lasted for just a little too long. Fantasia stilled herself for an entire minute and watched his face. Well... she watched his eyes, the only part of his face she could really see thanks to that ridiculous mask. Surely he was just fucking with her. Cantankerous clients liked to do that from time to time.

"Come on, little boy, this ain't funny," she said,

gripping his throat… or trying to. His neck had swollen so much that it was like trying to grasp a basketball in one hand.

Her tongue flicked against her molars—a nervous habit—and that's when she realised something missing that had been there since her latest snack. A piece of peanut had dislodged from between her teeth and fallen into her john's mouth.

As it turned out, Mr Flamingo was deathly allergic to peanuts.

Of Oyster Shells and Shit

by Hari Navarro

I've been sitting here thinking. I haven't done it in a while…thinking, that is. My head hurts when I think. So most days now, I just drift off and crawl into the flutes of mote-filled light that ease through the slates in my window.

And I tumble, and I tumble, and I fall.

But today has been different. Today I can feel again, as the pallid old worm in my head turns and shuffles and tries to make sense of its lot. It and I both have been pondering. Could dearest Mother have been right?

Maybe it is a truth. Maybe I am a most wicked and wanton of whores.

Throughout my first week here, she'd tell me that I was a dog. That the things that I did and said were foul and dangerous, and a vile affront toward all that is sacred and good. She told me I was a dog. A dirty stinking filthy bitch.

"Do you know what goodly people do with dirty

bitches? They chain them up and feed them bones and kick them until they learn. They make them sleep in their own shit," she'd said as she sat at the edge of my mattress and fingered the golden curls of my hair.

His name is John Graves and he is a lawyer. Actually, he's not so much a lawyer as he is a waiter. But he assures me that he will bloom into a great defender of the poor and hard done by upon his imminent graduation. Whenever the hell that might be.

I'm not sure if I even believe that my dear John John will aspire to his dreams of righteousness. I'm not even sure if I care. I want to care. I do. But this house, and this family of mine, does have a tendency to leach the light from the very bones of anything that even hints at being good and just and sound.

I told Mother that I had overheard him speaking of his plans to the kitchen staff on the night of the party. The dinner party where I, for the very first time, laid eyes on this mysterious young man in his needlessly tight trousers and strangulating cummerbund wrap.

She just looked at him and sniffed like she does at pieces of not-just-right meat that she flicks to the edge of her plate. For her to be a filler of glasses and clearer of tables was a quite unacceptable plight.

Acceptable for her, and by association, for myself also, is a ground-floor of tolerance in which the very worst thing is for one's millions to be self-made. New money stinks well and good, but the heady foul aroma of old money is the prime vintage that settles and stays on the lips.

These purveyors of new money are unknowns. Their genetic make-up a diluted fog. They're oft times not of this land. Their hair and their skin and the clipped syllables they roll are strange. But they are rich. And so, they are tolerated, just. John Graves is an orphan nothing. A foundling. A penniless dreamer. So, he is quite totally unacceptable.

But I love him.

Of an evening, I'd slip out from between the fingers of this old clingy house and we'd meet. Dear John John. I do love him, I do.

Maybe it's lust or, perhaps, those hot waves that surged through my being were but the sexual pull of deception. The knowledge that my mother and my brother knew not what it was that we did.

I mentioned love. But as I dribble this thick mucus that now passes for piss, I think that it is not the correct word. Love is something else. Love is a gentle weight that lays upon the flesh. It's an echo passed down, and it has substance and form. There is a distinct longevity to love. I feel this definition for him still. But it is thinning. The weight of love can also be felt as loss.

I shift upon my midden sheets and let contorted limbs drag my filthy nails across the parched plain of my flesh. I play with the sores that pout like welt lipped mouths at the jut of my hips, and I think of him in his bed. I think of him, and I touch myself, but in place of the shudders that would once rake through my soul, I feel nothing.

Nothing but pain. Wet dull pain.

The party. That official introduction of me as a young woman of standing. That thing filled with cigar smoke and talk that oozed like goose fat from between the yellowed teeth and the pursed lips of the filthy rich, was ironically thrown right here in this very house. By my mother no less.

As I said, it was here at this party that I first met his gaze. A mere waiter, and not a very good one at that. Forever clanking the crystal as he tottered and teetered. I was first drawn to him as I heard the squint in my mother's eyes as they tore at him from far across the room.

"Pig misery, chipper of finest crystal."

I met him at the party, but I also met him in the wine cellar. It was more a following than a meeting. I followed him because I was drawn to his lips. I didn't want to kiss them. I wanted to touch them. I wanted to run my finger across their thick puff, and I wanted to ask him if the swell that I'd seen him try and conceal as he served me my wine was gorging because of me.

I took off my shoes at the top of the stairs, and I sat midway down and watched him. I watched how he moved. How the muscles in his shoulders torqued beneath the stretch of his shirt as he reached for a vintage stacked all but out of his reach.

"What's your name?"

I startled him, and he so nearly dropped the bottle he'd only just slid to his palm. But he didn't. He caught it mid-air, and he seemed so boyishly happy with himself when he did.

"My name is John. John Graves."

"My name is..."

"I know exactly who you are," he said.

And I stood and I finished the rest of my descent, and I took John Johns hand in mine, and I thrust it beneath the blooming silk of my dress. He smiled, and his smile was real, and he took my hand in his and he scooped and closed it up under my breast.

This is what I am talking about. This was lust. So fleeting. So raw and untrained as I forced my finger into his mouth and he forced me up into the wall.

There was to be a lot of pushing and shoving over the ensuing few weeks. A lot of sex, but very little else. I liked it that way. I loved it. So, I guess that, in my love of the lust, I do love him. Everything is but a part of the hole. The void. This place in which I rot down into the rot.

He tried to talk to me about his law studies, and about the ache that he had to find his lost parents, and about the way he felt when he was with me.

He cried, and I laughed when he did. He spoke of his loneliness as he surged atop me in his tiny squeaking bed. I looked right through his tears and into his eyes and out of the back of his head. And, somehow, I looked out through the walls of his lovely little room. Out upon the treetops in the park across the street, and down through their branches to the flowers and the grass and the people with their dogs held tight on great leashes. I took them all into my mouth, and I swallowed them down as we fucked. I ate them because I could. I did not care about his pathetic lonely life nor the blur of the things out his window. But I do now.

Now, I very much do.

It was definitely my brother who informed Mother of our clandestine trysts. His name is Solomon, and he is a most jealous and odious man. He has an attraction toward me that far oversteps that of a sibling. I know, perhaps, from where this perversion sprung, but I really had no idea just how consumed he'd become.

Years ago, I caught him watching me as I bathed, and he threatened me with great violence should I breath a word to our parents. Father was still alive back then. I should have told him. He would have known just what to do. But I didn't.

And now this.

I met Mother at the top of the great staircase. It is great and by far my most favoured part of this entire sprawling edifice that I'm quite sure would be offended to be simply labelled a house.

It loops up organically from the splay of its wide foot in the entrance hall. So beautifully it tapers toward its head at the first floors marbled landing.

It was late, and I knew that she couldn't possibly not smell the wet, now dried, sex on my skin. It was late and I was drunk.

I did a most foolish thing. I smiled as she talked. Smiling when addressed is something that's just not done—not in this family. I tried to conceal it just as John John had tried to hide his unfortunately timed swelling. And it is this exact image I held in my mind as I spluttered my wine riven spit to her face.

I locked my jaw and closed my eyes in readiness of

the ring-wrapped thud of her closed fist. But it didn't come.

She reacted strangely. She simply took out her kerchief and polished my spray from the round of her glasses and dabbed it away from her face.

"It's your birthday. Let us not bicker. There's something I must show you. Something that may help."

"Help what?"

She led me by the hand, and it was so soft and warm, and I felt a hint of the woman that she once had been. Before father died. A woman who read to me. A woman who laughed.

She'd still been an angry woman back then, but he balanced her. Calmed her.

I remember watching them make love.

My brother and I peering through the balustrades of my favourite staircase. Thunder and lightning had spiked through the darkness and wrenched us both from our beds. The flashes do monstrous things in homes with such expansive walls as ours. The cruel shadows pushed us towards the sound of their ramping breath and, then, they sat us down on the stairs.

I watched as he so tentatively touched at her skin. How it was if she would break as his fingers danced and swirled.

So very gentle.

I was young. I didn't understand what it was that was happening. I did not feel the sexuality that charged that already static crackling night.

I remember her breathing—how it built and swelled and she cried out. Not pain. It was love.

But I also think that it was this moment that corrupted my brother. Or, at the very least, it triggered sleeping perversions that already lay in his head.

Solomon harbours a burning contempt for women. For everyone, except Mother. Toward her, he's the ever-obedient lackey. A good boy. Fetch, Solomon, fetch. A very good boy.

But to all others of the female persuasion, he acts as if we owe him something. That he's been wronged and wants for all of our imagined debts to be settled in full.

He had a girlfriend once. Virginia Backenstoe. A lovely girl from a very good family. She dined with us once. I sat across from her and I could see the fear in her eyes. I saw it and so did my mother, and oh, how it made her smile.

I never saw Virginia again after that night. Solomon said that he was much the better man without her. And now that I know what I know, I just hope that she is safe. Safe and far away from this horrendous place.

Where am I? Oh yes, Mother took my hand and led me toward a door at the very end of the hall. I remembered it well, though I had only been through it but once.

The door that leads to the attic.

It opened to the dry yawn of seldom used hinges and Mother let go of my hand and gently prodded me into the wrap of its gloom. I was not afraid. I remembered this place with great affection.

"Go, child. It's up at the top of the stairs."

Father had hoisted me atop his knee as he sat on the old dusty straw mattresses and he showed me photographs. People with faces just as his. Faces that looked like mine.

"Family is everything," he'd said as we gorged on the chocolates in his pocket.

"Reach out and pull yourself a hole in the darkness. Do you see it? Do you see what I have come here to show?"

I did see.

I saw the stacked mattresses and, as I squinted, I'm sure that I saw them breath in and then out—a soothsaying trick of the dark—and then a needle is sunk into my arm.

I woke and I vomited into my mouth.

I woke as hands tore at my clothes and ripped every last stitch from my skin and a collar was strapped to my neck.

In the days directly following my incarceration, my mother came to visit many times. She brought food and a pot, and she wiped and cleaned me, and she played with the curls of my hair.

She spoke to me. She pleaded with me.

"You must deny him totally. For he is not worthy of your blood. You must fold back into our clutch. You will love me, and you will love your brother, and you will love he that is our lord that stands astride the darkness and the light. Submit, and I will dress you in the finest of lace, and we will feast, and you will again know the sun on your flesh. You will know life, and all will be fine and good. Or else you can live as this bitch."

I did not say a word. I stayed on that mattress and she never once visited again.

Solomon did. At first, every day, and then less and less. He never spoke, he just looked at me with those horrible sagging eyes as he threw me the scraps of their meals.

Days-old oysters, shrivelled and fouling in their shells. Suckled bones and crusts and rinds and all manner of other shit that they'd pushed to sides of their plates.

He derived great joy in turning on the solitary bulb that dangled above my head and watching as my eyes screamed as they recoiled from the horrors it revealed.

I never spoke and he only did but once a year.

"Happy 25th Birthday, dear sister," he'd said on that very first night.

"Happy 50th Birthday, dear sister," he'd said, god knows how many weeks ago now.

I go days without food. After the bulb blew, he never replaced it. My only illumination the faint ghost of light that creeps up the stairs like a taunting mist and the scant fingers that poke through the slates.

Sometimes, the things in the dark pull this precious light to their edges. They take form, and I speak to them and then they talk to me back. They hate me. They whisper the most abominable things. And, sometimes, I know it is not things, but Solomon hunched there in the shadows. Watching.

Always watching.

Once, I heard the wrench of the door again as it opened. I heard unknown voices as they gasped at the stench. And swords of torchlight sliced and diced at the dark.

They lifted the shutters from their hinges and the day bore in, and I heard their shock as my pitiful husk burnt down and forever into their eyes.

They cut away the rope at my neck and then,

eventually, other voices arrived and peeled me away from my mattress. My body, an attached scab to the excrement and fragments of meat and vegetables and fish and rotten bread and great swaths of my flesh marked this place where I lay.

They moved me to a most wonderful place. My sight returned and it was so beautiful. So stunningly white. I could feel again. I felt the bolts of electricity that they stabbed through my temples, and I loved it as my toothless jaw bit down on the leather strap in my mouth.

They said that poor Mother died some fifteen short days after my discovery. And that poor Solomon was sentenced to fifteen months in jail but was acquitted when he convinced all that I could have left that attic at any time but that I, instead, choose to stay.

I can't speak. They think I've lost all my mind. But he was right, you know. I did choose to stay. I was chained, but all I had to do was renounce my lust. I chose to sit in that filth out of the purity of it.

I will not give him up for anything. I am deluding and diluting. I am alone. No torchlight slit through into my perpetual Stygian hell. Nobody came for me. I sit on my mattress and it seethes and it breathes, and I listen to it as it eats.

Goodbye, Casanova

by A.R. Dean

He never meant to hurt anyone. He just loved women. The way they smelled, the slight curve of their necks, and especially the twinkle they got in their eyes when they saw him. From the oldest crone to the youngest child, he entranced them all. He was certain that no woman alive could resist him.

Piero believed that women adored him because of his Italian looks. In his mind he was an Adonis. He was very close to being correct in that assumption. He towered over most men at six foot five. His broad shoulders nicely framed by rippling muscles. Muscles and shoulders more likely to tan than burn thanks to his olive complexion. The ladies swooned for his almond eyes encased by thick and even lashes. He knew that with just a half a smile from his full lips would make even the most stubborn woman melt. Adding the thick Italian accent and wavy raven hair just furthered his conviction that he was a gift sent from the gods to woo the women of Earth.

Being modest was not one of Piero's virtues. He came to America with the sole purpose to conquer. He wanted wealth and fame, but women were his true goal. To achieve this, he flew from his small Italian village to Hollywood. There he charmed everyone he encountered. He started with casting agents and studio heads. Followed quickly by executives and directors. Once he accomplished that, he could star on the silver screen and try to reach his true goal; the hearts of women everywhere.

Now that he had fame on his side, he was free to toy with the affections of every model and actress he could. He would even take the occasional beautiful barista to his bed when he could. No female lasted long with Piero. He was quick to get bored. Now, if the woman he was with became simpering and clingy, he would dispose of her even faster than normal. Most times he didn't bother to learn their names.

So, when he married a woman as stunning as himself, the women of the world wept. For only A-list super celeb Vanessa Kyle could match Piero in talents and looks. Their whirlwind romance ended in a storybook wedding. Piero's fans cried over their magazines in mourning for the bachelor who had stolen their hearts. For about three months they wished to be the beautiful Vanessa, until the tabloids caught wind of Piero and his wandering eye.

Now he sat in his marital bed, pinned up in shock

against the headboard. His most current fling splattered across the side of his face. Vanessa was standing at the edge of the bed while smoke billowed out of double-barrel shotgun.

The gorgeous redheaded waitress/aspiring actress was an unrecognisable mass of mush beside him. Piero did not utter a noise as he glanced up at Vanessa. He knew he should feel bad for the poor girl beside him whose name he hadn't bothered to learn. Truth on the matter it truly was the girl's own fault. Even though he didn't know who she was; she had known him.

Vanessa stood facing the remains of the girl she had disintegrated. Her large and very fake breasts snuggled tightly within the confines of her spaghetti tank top. Piero couldn't help eyeing them as she stood there panting with rage. Her well-toned arms held tightly to the gun as she turned it towards Piero himself. Her cheeks were flushed, and her clothes splattered with blood and other pieces of his companion.

Piero knew it was wrong to feel aroused, but he couldn't help himself. She looked primal standing there in her jealous rage. Her crystal blue eyes brimming with hatred and anger for the unknown woman. Never in his life had Piero ever encountered a woman so filled with jealousy that she had to destroy the rival. Most of them wept and pined for him. It was stimulating him in ways he had never encountered. He must have her. He must rid himself of the passions that consumed him, then he would call for the police. He hated this arousal going to waste. True, she would go to jail for this for a long time, and it would be selfish not to send her off without a proper ravishing first.

He rose slowly from the bed, keeping his hands raised in front of him so not to startle her. He made his way to stand in all his naked glory, sure to show off the fact that she had him fully stimulated. "Mia Tesoro, I am so sorry that I did not know how deep your love was for me." Vanessa followed his movements with the barrel of the gun. She licked her plump pink lips as she eyed him up and down.

She clicked her tongue against her teeth, a sure sign as Piero knew of her anger. "How could you say that Piero? You are my life! I married you because you were the only man for me. I..." her voice broke. She tightly closed her eyes, the pain and difficulty of what was to come next written all over her face. "I thought you felt the same. You said that this was all behind you when we got married. You swore!" her voice was a raspy whisper. She opened her eyes again. They were lit with unspoken fury.

"I am so sorry, Amore. I did not know you had such

fire for me. Had I known I would have never let myself be swayed by another." Piero gently reached out and grasped the muzzle of the gun. He carefully but firmly pushed it away from his heart and pointed it down to the floor. His gaze flicked back to the mess on the bed. Vanessa's eyes narrowed as they followed his line of sight. "I allowed another to tempt me. Had I only known the vastness of your love, I would never have strayed." With that, he lifted his hand from the shotgun and gently rubbed the edge of her cheek. She looked up into his large mocha eyes. "I promise, from now on I lust only for you, my wife."

Vanessa's eyes filled with tears. "Oh Piero, I knew you loved me. I knew that this whore trapped you."

"Indeed, il mio Tesoro. She used her feminine wiles on me. She did it in a way no man could resist. I was helpless and weak." Piero bent forward and kissed the side of her neck. Vanessa allowed him to remove the gun from her hands and place it delicately on the bed. Once it was out of the way, he pulled her into his arms.

"Vanessa, Cara Mia, I must have you. I must show you I burn for only you. She willingly stood there and allowed him to rip her clothing away. He shredded it in a frenzy. He growled and moaned, murmuring small Italian endearments. Frantically, they stumbled to the floor quick to make love. Hours later, they lay tangled around each other. Somewhere along the whirlwind of passion they had pulled the blood-soaked bedsheets to the floor. The shotgun had also slid its way there mere inches from where they had mated. Vanessa sighed in a satisfied way as Piero kissed the top of her tangled blond hair. He then inched away from her, so he could stand.

He stood there a moment, stretching his muscles and rolling his head around from shoulder to shoulder. After he loosened his tight muscles, he walked across the room to the dresser. He grabbed the nearest silk robe and slid into it.

"What now darling?" Vanessa purred from the plush carpet. Piero tied the robe tightly around his narrow waist.

"Now?" he asked with a frown. He shot her a puzzled look. "Why I call the polizia." He grabbed the cell phone from the dresser.

"What?!?" she screeched as she shot up. The covers fell away, she didn't bother to cover herself. "But you said you loved me? You just made love to me because of what I just did it to prove my love."

"Oh, I love you, Vanessa. I apologise that I must do this. You murdered the poor girl. I also can't allow you to be free to shoot my lovers. That could end my career. I just can't take time to go to jail for this, but the press will be fantastico for me."

Vanessa's mouth gaped open in shock. "Your career? The press? But I thought—"

"You thought what? That I would throw my fame away for you. That I would help dispose of a body and hide it, so I could go to jail with you when it's discovered? I love you but not more than my career. Besides, once the trial is over and I divorce you, our prenup will be invalid." he gave her a sad smile, one that was full of pity. "Maybe I will get lucky and get to play myself in the movie that shall come from this. I must also find someone to write the book, but I can let the agent handle that after all this nastiness completes."

"But we just made love!" she shouted, confused.

"And it was lovely. It was just what I needed, since I could not finish what I had started with...with…" he gestured over to the corpse on the bed, "whoever she was." He gave an innocent shrug.

"You didn't know her name?"

"I never know their names. They must only know mine," he said, flipping around on his phone screen.

"You said she was the only one, that she seduced you!"

"Yes, well, I stretched the truth. I am an actor, it's what we do when a gun is pointed at us and we are alive with passion." He didn't even glance at her as he played with his phone. "But I must do what is best for me and prison is not one of those."

"You are a lying scumbag. You promised!" Vanessa screamed vehemently as she stood.

He glanced at her with a weary sigh. "I promised to love you, cara mia. I never promised to go to jail with you. I am sorry that it had to end this way." He gave a soft chuckle as he started to dial.

"You son of a bitch!" Vanessa wailed as she snatched up the gun and shot him straight in the chest. As he lay on the carpet gurgling, she came forward and shot him again right in his perfect face.

Thus ends the tale of poor Piero Moretti. He never meant to hurt anyone; he just wanted to share all his love…one woman at a time.

Flaunt

by A.R. Johnston

The atmosphere in the bar was hot and heavy, almost oppressive. The sexual tension was something that slithered over the skin. Lyric looked around the bar, finding it rather overwhelming. So much so that she found herself wiping her hands on her dark jeans as if she could wipe it off. Good thing she wasn't here to drink or pick up. No, she was here to talk to the owner of the bar. He had made sure that the meeting was going to take place at the high time of the night when the place was packed. She knew he was trying to catch her off guard by requesting a meeting at midnight, but it wasn't going to work; she wasn't going to let it.

She was sitting on a stool at the bar when the lights went dark in the bar. There were ooh's and aah's from all around her. A single spotlight on the stage illuminated the darkness. There, in the shadow of the spotlight, was a beautiful silhouette. The female figure bent provocatively, twisted and turned to get the patrons in the bar riled up. There was a snap, and wings spread out around the figure like a cloak. It was then the most stunning voice filled the air. There were sighs of contentment throughout the room. It was enthralling and captivating to listen to.

"Really?" Lyric gave an aggravated sigh, shaking her head as she looked around the room. She knew the faerie on the stage wasn't the one singing the sweet song, so there had to be a siren in the room.

"Oh ya, Tayla always gives a wonderful show," the bartender breathed softly, completely enraptured, staring at the stage like everyone else in the room.

Lyric looked over in disbelief. *How was it that everyone here seemed to be affected by what was going on.*

"Not everyone is affected. You aren't, neither am I," a deep seductive voice spoke into her ear, making her twitch.

She tried not to give much of a reaction—like a shiver—because his voice was like slipping into a warm bath and she enjoyed it far too much. She hated that he even got that kind of reaction from her. Issac had been trying to get into her pants for years now, but she had always brushed him off. If he hadn't been such a smarmy, arrogant asshole, she might have considered going out with him. But he was, and she refused to stoop to his level.

She slowly swivelled on her stool to face him. Isaac

was an imposing figure. She was five nine, not a small person by any means but he still towered over her at about six-four she guessed. She hated feeling small. He was blonde and blue-eyed looking like a sexy ass god. Lyric tried to reign in her sexual desire, but it was hard to do, she had to admit. He looked amazing in the suit that fit him to perfection.

"See something you like, sweet Lyric?" He again spoke softly, leaning closer so that he was almost kissing her.

Lyric stared back, shoving back any lascivious thoughts she had, and smirked. "Can we go have that chat now, or what?"

Of course, he infuriated her more by just grinning back. "But you should watch the show. It's so mesmerising, and Tayla loves her audience." He nodded back to the stage as the curtains opened.

A barbie doll sized faerie flew out to the extension of the stage, iridescent pink dust falling from her wings. The dust floated out and over the patrons. Men and women were shivering in pleasure as it fell upon them. Their eyes closing in ecstasy.

"Is that shit even legal?" She asked as she watched the faerie fly out to the pole at the end of the runway.

"I run a legit business here, Lyric. You know that.

Tayla's dust has only a temporary effect, like the alcohol that the patrons drink. We had to get a permit for it, of course, but everything is up to date."

"Of course it is," she scoffed with a shake of her head.

"Lust pays the bills, sweet Lyric. Besides, is it really so bad? All of these people are happy and content. Why shouldn't they enjoy something like this? Is enjoyment a sin?" His eyebrow arched in question.

How did she answer this question without insulting him? He was an incubus, a fallen angel who had turned his sin of lust into a profitable business. She couldn't really begrudge him that. He had evolved and made his sin work for him. It was actually ingenious really, but she was not going to tell him that either.

Tayla touched the dance pole, and when she did, she turned into a full-sized human. Dressed in a string bikini—if you could call the scrap of floss that she had on *clothing*. Her wings snapped onto her back and become the most glorious tattoo that Lyric had ever seen.

"She's lovely." She gave him the required comment at the show, looking at him with an arched eyebrow. "Is there a point to having me watch?"

If she hadn't been watching his face, she might have missed the quick frown that crossed it. It was back to that charming smile of his in a split second.

"Why not watch the show? It's a lovely one." He smiled at her, grabbing the drink that the bartender handed him. "Thanks, Roger."

Lyric nodded at him. "I can appreciate it for sure, but that is not the reason I'm here. Even if you did this on purpose, just to see if I would fall under the wonderment of her faerie dust," she growled out at him, snagging his drink from his hand and downing it at his querying brow.

"I would never do that to you. I'd just slip something in your drink, of course."

She frowned, purposely licking the rim of the glass she had taken from him. She watched heat flare in his eyes as she did so. She winked at him, then looked away after placing the glass on the bar. She couldn't believe she had been so bold.

"I'm done then," she said. Getting up from barstool, she turned her back on him and started walking toward the door.

"Lyric, wait!" he called out.

She heard his step on the floor above the din of the siren music. When he reached out to touch her shoulder she smiled before stopping, not wanting him to pull her around.

"What?" She half-turned to look at him with a

questioning eyebrow.

"Let's go to my office. Talk as we had discussed." His eyes searched hers.

She sighed. "Fine."

Lust, indeed, was a dangerous thing. Even when you weren't looking for it.

The Fae's New Dawn

by J.W. Garrett

From the minute Luke met Lilith, something inside him clicked, fell in sync. When moving in across the street, she'd had trouble with a few boxes, so Luke had helped her carry them inside.

"Thanks," she said on a breathless exhale, extending her hand. "I'm Lilith."

His gaze met hers, and the glow he witnessed in their depths instantly set his body on fire. She didn't walk; her movements were fluid as she gracefully transitioned from one place to the next. Pulling his thoughts from the curves of her sleek form, he reached out to accept her hand. How long had he been standing here, staring at her? Mesmerised?

"Hi… Luke… I mean, my name's Luke. I live right across the street, if you need anything…anything at all."

"Nice to meet you, Luke. Thanks for your help with these uncooperative boxes." She laughed, and the sound shot through him.

He adjusted his stance and cleared his throat. "Sure thing. Anytime."

"Do you live alone, Luke?" Her eyebrows arched upward, anticipating a reply.

More than anything at that moment, he wanted to say yes. Wanted to turn back the clock and be single again. "Um… no. My wife, Linda, lives with me."

"How cute... Luke and Linda."

"I'll see you around," Luke said in haste, heat rising in his face, as he turned and rammed his foot into a box. "Shit."

"Sorry about that. Moving hazard. Dangers lurking all around this house." A smile lit her face as she waved when he turned again to leave her.

His insides groaned. *Danger here… Got that right. And I want it.* "No problem."

Luke had been following the woman around like a lovesick teenager instead of the thirty-two-year-old married business professional that he was. For the most part, his life was great—boring occasionally, but didn't that come with it all?

A week had passed since their first meeting, and, at times, Luke felt more animal than human, stalking Lilith like prey. Each day the urge to go to her, to take her and make her his became more difficult to resist. What was it about the woman that wrenched at him in such a primal way?

The evening, cool and crisp, held a hint of fall in the air. Linda was travelling for work, not expected to return for two more days. The longing… the unbridled need for Lilith… Luke wouldn't deny it anymore. His new neighbour had been his singular thought over the last seven days. The glimpses he'd had, just to check on her, weren't nearly enough.

The sky grew darker as his thoughts gathered. His mind made up, he knocked at her door. No answer. Again he knocked. Louder. Impatient, he growled low. She was here; he was sure of it. The low thrum of music flowed to his ears, coming from out back. Following a path alongside the house, he faced a fenced backyard and quietly let himself in.

Spotting her, he sighed deeply and took in his surroundings. Lights sparkled in tiny flashes of colour, streaming throughout the trees, creating a hypnotic retreat. A gazebo bathed in moonlight rested in the centre of the yard. Lilith had transformed the space. When last he'd been here—for a cookout with the previous owner— the area had been dull and lifeless.

He waited, his heart hammering loudly in his chest, watching as her head tilted his direction.

She had sensed him, just as he did her.

And, like a rope pulled taut, she turned to face him. "Luke."

His lips twitched in amusement. Lilith wasn't surprised to see him here.

Her painfully slow steps brought her closer…and closer… Her eyes drifted shut.

Just a few seconds more, and he could unleash the beast raging against his skin since the day they'd met.

They collided in a kiss, and, as he backed them against a tree, his tongue stroked hers. Luke grabbed her wrists and held them over her head, while he inhaled her scent along the elegant column of her neck, kissing a slow path down its length.

After fumbling free of their clothing, Luke yanked her close again. Something was different about her. Strange even, but in a thrilling and exotic way. Warning bells clamoured to life in his head, but, when she melted against him, he lost himself.

A slow smile curved her lips. "*Now*, Luke," Lilith whispered.

With an answering groan, he pressed inside her. As they moved together, her nails raked across his back. A fog settled in his mind, but, absorbed in the moment, he finished, then slid from her. "Something's wrong…"

Stumbling backward, he fell to the grass and sank his head in his hands. The fog from minutes ago had taken up residence. He tugged on his pants. Light cascaded in a path toward him. Leaning on his elbows, he watched as graceful wings unfurled from Lilith's body, then pulsed through the air, lifting Luke off the ground. "What are you?" Luke mumbled.

His awareness faded in and out, but still he felt the air rush against his face and the soft brush of feathers on his sides where Lilith's wings pumped up and down, taking them to their destination. Wrapped in the sensations of flight, he slept.

A clanging of metal startled Luke awake. Lilith sat beside him, where he lay on a hard bench. She paused, her gaze boring into his. He shook his head to clear it. "Did you drug me?"

"Sex with a Fae often has that effect on humans."

"You're Fae…? Faeries are real?"

A wry smile crossed her lips. "Didn't you get an up-close look?"

"It was something, wasn't it?" He chuckled as he glanced around. "Wait. Where am I exactly?"

"You're in my realm now. A veil of magic separates

our two worlds."

"How is this possible?" He stretched out his arms, taking it all in. "Seems like a dream."

She scooted from his side and out the prison door, sliding the lock home again with a *click*. "No. Definitely not a dream."

Surrounding his jail on wheels, other Fae, male and female, gathered. Their wings fluttered, creating a loud monotonous buzzing noise as they hovered in the air, staring at him.

He'd not noticed at first the steady drone, such a constant sound in his ear.

Their activity increased when they realised Luke was awake. Bits of paper scribbled with writing passed back and forth among them fell to the ground. Hand signals flew between small huddled groups, peppered with a word here or there in a language Luke didn't recognise.

"So what's the joke, Lilith? Why did you bring me here and lock me up?" He leaned closer to the bars. "If you wanted me again, you didn't need to go to such lengths."

"Well, see those three Fae men off to your right?"

"Yeah."

"I was to mate one of them."

"*Was*? You still can."

"Not if you impregnated me. Then each one is prepared to die in a fight with you for my lost honour. All three in fact will fight, if you still live after the first and second rounds."

Stunned, Luke looked from Lilith to the three men with permanent scowls etched across their faces. "Well, when will you know if you're pregnant? I guess I'm stuck here till then. Chances are—"

"I already know, Luke. I am. That's why you're here."

"Really? You left out that little detail until now… Mighty quick on the results."

She crossed her arms. "You've been unconscious almost twelve hours. Tests for Fae can determine a pregnancy within several hours of conception. Thus, the reason for your current accommodations."

Tiny pieces of paper floated in between the bars. Luke grabbed one and studied it. "They're betting…betting that I'll die. Shit." He released a pent-up breath.

Lilith nodded. "For what it's worth, I have faith in you."

"Faith… With odds like this? A human against the magic of Faeries?" His lips twisted into a grimace. "So, when do I kick some Fae ass—three asses to be exact?"

"Tomorrow. Dawn."

"How about tossing me some of that magic you mentioned earlier? You know, to even up the sucky odds." He threw the crumpled piece of paper between the bars and watched it drift to the ground.

"If two people have true love, that's all the magic needed."

He avoided Lilith's gaze as one of the onlookers approached Luke's cell. "You got what you deserved. That's what my pa says. Filthy human…" The Fae boy spat in Luke's prison. "Pa says our plan is working."

"Plan? What plan?"

The boy lifted his chin, considering. "Guess it wouldn't hurt to tell you now… Decreasing the human population while increasing our own. That baby growing inside of Lilith will be one of us. Soon we'll invade and take back our land from the humans. Magic will reign free again, and we won't have to hide any longer." The boy sneered and ran off.

Luke focused his attention on his three opponents, sharpening their blades. *Well played…*

Bowing his head low, Luke cursed. For the first time in the past twenty-four hours—hell, the past week—his thoughts turned to Linda, the reality that he'd never see her again settling in his gut. Unease coiled up his spine, clamping down tight. Death at the hand of one of the men lined up to kill him seemed all but inevitable.

A gust of wind rushed through the prison bars, rattling a plate filled with food which had gone unnoticed until now. "Probably poisoned," he muttered. But grabbing the container full of water next to it he paused, then downed half of its contents. The din from the gathered crowd heightened, and Luke pushed the commotion from his mind, focusing instead on the combat to come and the part he would play.

Later, after making his peace, he leaned against the bars of his cage and released a shuddered breath. Watching the first muted colours stamp across the sky, he steeled himself and waited for dawn.

Louve Garou

by Blake Jessop

The Huntress cast her mind back, away from the chessboard, and her nostrils filled with the smell of damp earth and old blood. It had been cold in the glade where the poacher had been gutted and laid to rot. Whatever killed him had left with his chest open like an empty soup tureen to collect the rain. She felt a shiver coming on, and an urge to suppress it, but to deny the hollowness would be to forget her instincts. The Huntress shivered, and the priest across the tavern table looked up from the chessboard.

"I only asked if you had seen the place," he said, "I didn't mean to frighten you."

"It's not you that frightens me, Father," the Huntress said.

The warmth of the country inn flooded back to her, and the Huntress turned her eyes back to the board. She moved her queen.

"That's a bad move," the priest said, taking it with a knight.

"I find the difficult part is knowing which pieces are

important," she replied, putting him into check with a pawn. "Mate, I'm afraid. You've lost your bet, and I'll be joining you at the Vicomte's banquet. Go to sleep; we start early."

The priest looked up from the board and scowled.

The morning sky had the turbulent look of the underside of lake water during a storm. The rain had stopped, but the air had a lupine chill. The priest rode warily beside the Huntress, looking this way and that.

"Wolves only come out at night, Father," she said, and the priest glanced over at her sourly, unsure of whether he was being made fun of.

"Wolves eat what they kill. I don't care how many you've hunted. This is the work of some devil, and I am vigilant."

The Huntress would normally tease a man for such thinly couched discomposure, but let him be. Her mind was still in the grove. It was raining, when she took in the scene, imagining the chase, the screaming and blood, and for an instant the moon had broken free of the clouds to show her the mutilation in perfect detail.

"I still can't figure out how you beat me at chess," the priest said, eager to break the stillness, "and you shouldn't ride with your legs to either side of the horse. It isn't proper."

The Huntress shifted, crossing one leather clad leg over the other and riding side-saddle. The priest didn't seem at all pleased with the effect of his suggestion. They rode in silence through the countryside, and before long caught sight of the Vicomte's manor. One of the most glorious country estates in all of France.

"You may yet not be welcome," the priest said; "I have never taken advantage of the second half of my invitations to the Vicomte's table."

The Huntress touched a hand to her riding jacket. "I was invited, *mon révérend Père*."

The priest raised his eyebrows. "You were?"

"In a fashion."

The Huntress didn't bother to explain. She hadn't mentioned the letter yet, anymore than she'd warn a fox before priming a musket. *Come,* it said, *in the name of God, and kill our beast.* The mysterious missive had come only a few days before, unsigned. The Huntress knew why the writer had sent for her in particular. She had a reputation. The dead poacher proved the writer's sincerity, and the claw marks in the frozen ground were a witness to their fears. Something in this forsaken countryside needed hunting, and hunting was the only thing that excited her more than chess.

There was a kind of music that could only be played on champagne flutes, and the Huntress loved it. She loved the harpsichord's tinkle and the rich smell of truffle oil. She loved the coy twinkling of crystal chandeliers and the slick texture of gravy on the tips of her fingers.

One rarely saw this kind of pomp outside Paris, and for a while her adoration was infectious. Almost enough to mute whatever at the Vicomte's banquet was being left unsaid; there was an unnamed fear in the air, and it took more space at the table than the wine or hollow smiles. Her laughter covered it up like a tablecloth thrown over rotten wood.

The Huntress looked like she'd ridden all day, and yet none of the Vicomte's guests could find the words to scorn her. She wasn't beautiful so much as striking, and her delight with the perfect meal and faultless servants was entirely unfeigned. Better yet, she had worn *riding breeches* to dinner, and the only thing a French table loved more than wine was a little uninvited scandal.

"She does your table honour, *Seigneur*, I'm sure. Quite a reputation." The priest had probably been looking forward to the Huntress' banishment from his lord's table, but the Vicomte's daughter had begged that the dashing Parisienne be allowed to stay, and the nobleman was apparently incapable of denying her anything.

"I have many talents," the Huntress said with a sly smile, "hunting is the least of them."

"It may be the one we need," the Vicomte said. He was a big man with a booming voice and dissipated face. The moderately drunk wreck of a strong and handsome man. The Huntress liked him. "You have heard of our troubles, surely?"

"Your priest has bent my ears with nothing else."

"Isn't that what brought you here from Paris?" the Vicomte's wife cut in, acidly. "The want of a little thrill in the country? A few horror stories about the peasantry to take back to civilization?"

"Your table is the equal of a king's, vicomtesse, and game is always fresher in the country," the Huntress replied. While the gentry laughed politely at her leaden gallantry, she took stock of the guests. The Vicomte and his followers sat around the great hall like chess pieces laid out in the middle of a long game. The Huntress tried to imagine one of them writing to her, desperate and afraid. The vicomtesse was as cool toward her as the air from under the doors, but who wouldn't resent a younger woman taking over her table? The priest was decent enough, for a priest, but too poor a chess player to write with such circumspection. The Vicomte himself was brash, unsubtle and inebriated. The Huntress apprehended that her problem wasn't going to be planning her moves, but figuring out which piece was which. She listened to the Vicomte prattle, to the vicomtesse sigh. To the maids whisper at the edge of hearing, their voices as soft as the guttering candles. Tapestries fluttered, the guests gossiped, and the crockery clinked. She listened the way a wolf does, immobile in the snow.

"Are you truly a hunter?" a small voice said.

"I am," the Huntress said, woken from her reverie to stare at the Vicomte's daughter. The girl was a shadowless little beauty. Soft brown eyes and rosy cheeks that betrayed not a hint of powder. The Huntress wondered why she hadn't noticed her looks earlier, and realised she must be staring. The girl, self-conscious, returned to her meal.

The Huntress watched the girl eat her meat. Watched her glance up when she thought the Huntress wasn't looking. Watched…and knew that the girl was two things she wasn't supposed to be.

"Tell me," the Huntress asked, "what do I call the daughter of a vicomtesse?"

Now it was the girl's turn to look up with a start. Eyes

wide and wet. Red of cheek. She blushed even more deeply, if that was possible.

"Also vicomtesse, my Lady," she said softly.

Two things, without a doubt. The young vicomtesse was a very enthusiastic carnivore, and she was a romantic.

After dinner, the young vicomtesse retreated to her room in a panic. It was hard to tell, under autumn clouds, just when the moon was full, and she wasn't entirely sure how the sickness worked.

Her bed chamber was as lush as a room in the countryside could be, in the century of silk and steam. Her heart beat like a hummingbird's and her jaw ached. She was still hungry. For a month, she had begged. Prayed. *Not again.*

It started with a tickling under her arms, like being brushed with a feather. Little hairs rose in the small of her back. *Not again, please!*

Belatedly, she tried to lash herself to the bedposts with sheets, but the silk slid too easily to be of any use.

"Why didn't she come?" the girl said to herself. "How could she not see?"

Something moved in the candle-cast shadows. A lamp light cracked the dark, illuminating a face as cruel and angular as a hawk's.

"I saw, *petite*," the Huntress whispered, "and I came."

The Huntress pulled the cover away from her lamp. The chamber was soft and dark, and a cold breeze leaked in from the window above the bed to whisper along the floor. As she scanned the room there was a flash of amber from the bed. The young vicomtesse's eyes weren't brown in the lamp light, nor even orange. They had the lambent yellow shine of a wolf's.

"You're too late," the girl growled, and the words caught on her teeth. There was a smell in the room as familiar as the mink wrapped around the Huntress' neck.

The Huntress reached under her waistcoat. The little wolf had tried to bind itself. That never worked. No woman could tie herself down tightly enough to deny her own nature. No wolf could deny the urge to howl at the moon. She probably hadn't been a monster very long, had probably buried all memory of her change under the covers, or in the mud with the poacher. Had probably decided she was nothing but a dream.

The Huntress drew a pepperbox pistol from inside the tight folds of her clothing. Silver etchings glowed along the barrels like eldritch runes. The animal recoiled. High behind her, the moon broke free of the clouds.

The Huntress thumbed back the pistol's hammer, and in the instant before the lock clicked into place the wolf vanished into the shadows. A bead of sweat broke out on the Huntress' brow. The creature was fast, very quiet, and irritatingly correct; she *was* late. She blew out her lamp and let moonlight wash away all colour in the room. Everything, even the red velvet pillows, was cast in shades of silver and shadow. The second chessboard of the evening, but a game with much higher stakes.

"Come out, little *louve garou*," the Huntress said. She used the proper feminine form of *werewolf.*

"Why didn't you come before?" the girl growled in the dark.

The Huntress hesitated, and the last piece fell into place.

"You should have written to me sooner."

The wolf pounced, as sudden and silent as a gust of winter wind. She caught the Huntress' coat and sank her claws in deep. Caught flesh and the joyous scent of blood. Buried her muzzle in the sweet smell and found her fangs tearing away only cloth as the Huntress let the jacket slide from her shoulders and dodged away.

The werewolf swung her sleek head from side to side, sniffing at shadows. The Huntress stepped into the light. Her shoulders were bare, and her bosom heaved rhythmically, but even the werewolf's keen ears couldn't hear her breathe. The Huntress raised her pistol, and this time the hammer locked back with a satisfying click. There were carved lines in the muscles of the Huntress' shoulders, strength beneath the shadows cast by her collarbones. She reached her free hand behind her neck. Her fingers came away slick with blood.

The vicomtesse crouched, and her words were scarcely more than a growl. This was what she wanted, this was why she wrote. She wondered why she still trembled.

"Do it," she said, "please. I left gold on the table. Do what you came here for."

The Huntress always knew which pawns to sacrifice, what risks to take. She had almost lost this game, but now the checkmate was only one move away. She aimed the pistol between the wolf's yellow eyes and saw fear and rage at war in the animal's desperate glare. There was no malevolence in the yellow eyes, just hunger. Not evil, not yet. Just nature. Its body was lean and supple, the fur short and sleek. Still very much like the young woman, but in a darker cast. A reflection with fangs and pointed ears. The Huntress imagined the girl at dinner as the light, and this one as a shadow. Two sides of the same shining coin.

"Do it," the wolf said.

The Huntress used her left hand to steady the right, and the blood on her fingers shone in the moonlight. Before she could take up the slack in the trigger, a tiny voice spoke in the Huntress' mind. Knowing a chess problem wasn't always the same as solving it.

"There may be another way," the Huntress said, and stepped nearer.

The werewolf coiled itself to spring, ready to chance the fatal crash of the pistol. The weapon would certainly kill her—the Huntress had made sure of it. They both knew it, counted on it. The wolf tensed for her final act and the Huntress thrust bloodied fingers under her nose.

The smell was sweet and familiar. It made the vicomtesse feel warm and very hungry. She let out a yelp, and it was all she could do to stop herself licking the fingers.

"Go on. Lick. Good. Don't bite," the Huntress said.

The wolf tasted her. "Good, now try again."

The Huntress backed away and put the pistol on an end table with a click that seemed louder in the wolf's ears than if it had been fired. Heat coursed through her limbs. Hunger.

The werewolf charged again. It bounded at the Huntress without guile or grace. Fast, but the Huntress had the supple speed of a dancer. She writhed and ducked and felt the wolf's claws rake, heard teeth snap the air. For a few seconds the combat was even, until the Huntress wriggled from underneath the beast and mounted its back, locking her arms around the furry neck.

"This is the other way. Calm yourself. This is—"

The werewolf shook itself like a dog and the Huntress crashed amongst the pillows. The wolf was on top of her in an instant, sniffing, baring its teeth. The Huntress' nose flared, too, and the smell of them together was like something out of an English novel, fur and whiskey and leather. Riding sweat and gunpowder.

The wolf had her. It did something halfway between a lunge and a nuzzle. Licked blood from her face. The Huntress grabbed it by the scruff of the neck like a puppy.

"That's better," she said into the pointed ear, and ran

her tongue around the outer edge. The wolf yelped, and nipped at her unguarded throat. The bite was barely hard enough to break the skin. The Huntress ran her hands through the animal's fur, as thick and lush as mink.

"Gently, there's hours left until the moon sets. As gently as you can, *petite louve garou.*"

The time passed, and there was, the Huntress remembered, one other thing better than chess.

Dawn broke, and the girl opened her eyes before the Huntress, who had passed out with her mouth open, her breath whistling gently into the vicomtesse's small and delicate ear. The hand that enclosed hers had long scrapes along its knuckles. Deeper cuts ran in a row along one forearm, and the sheets were stippled red. The vicomtesse disentangled her hand and looked at it. Whole and normal, apart from bitten nails. The movement made the sheets rustle and stirred the Huntress, who came awake reluctantly.

"I am not dead, you did not kill me."

"How perceptive," the Huntress growled, "do they make coffee in this house?"

The girl nodded.

"Then go and find some, and bring it here. And

something linen to wrap these cuts. And brandy."

In a while, they drank.

"Did you cure me? Did your love cure me?" The girl asked, an agony of confusion painting her face.

"No."

The vicomtesse shook herself and put her head in her hands. "Then what will I do? Will you stay with me?"

"No, I did what I did for the gold you promised in your letter. I consider my errand complete, and you should be grateful I did it so gently."

"Then how shall I be cured?" Anger rose hot in her voice, and the Huntress heard the wolf. She relented.

"You never will be, but I have shown you how to manage yourself, if you have the courage." The Huntress put her cup negligently on the windowsill. She reached out a hand, touched the girl's bare shoulder, and felt the animal shiver and retreat. "I have met a lot of your kind, so understand this: you aren't the kind of monster that needs to be cured. You need to embrace what you have become. You are not blessed, nor cursed. This is what you are. You need someone you trust to see you through each full moon. Someone you love and who doesn't mind the blood or cuts."

"You," the young vicomtesse said desperately, "I want it to be you. I love you."

The Huntress laughed.

"You *loved me,* that's different. I am just your first. You have weeks to sniff out someone to see you through the next full moon. You'll manage; wolves always do."

The girl looked fragile and despondent. The Huntress brushed blond hair as fine as silk away from her face and tucked it behind her ear. Started scratching there, and the vicomtesse closed her eyes and smiled in spite of herself. Not that fragile.

"Is that true? Can I really just *smell* someone?"

"You'll be fine, *louve garou,*" the Huntress said, "I'm sure you have a very good nose."

#IAmHuman

by J.L. Royce

Let's start before the armbands, before the duelling demonstrations in the streets, before the hashtags and the twitter wars. Let's start with my story, Saturday night in the local ED.

Everybody get comfortable. Nothing to be ashamed of here. There's a box of tissues there, ladies. Nobody's laughing at you, guys; having an uncontrollable erection isn't funny.

Here's my story, from the first night.

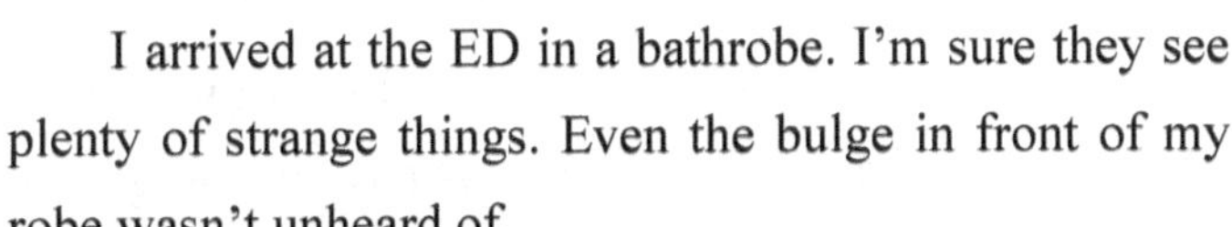

I arrived at the ED in a bathrobe. I'm sure they see plenty of strange things. Even the bulge in front of my robe wasn't unheard of.

My girlfriend Makayla was with me. We had no idea what was going on. She was trying to be comforting while hiding her embarrassment as well as she could. As it turned out, she wasn't helping the situation. The more sympathetic she was, the harder I got. And that's just not right.

Then there was the Emergency Department staff. The nurses, male and female, were all trying to take history on the most interesting patient of the evening.

"Were you hit in the crotch?"

"Are you sure you didn't ingest any drugs tonight? Could your *friend*—" glancing at Makayla, "have slipped you something?"

"How's your sex life? Have there been any changes lately?"

"Did you engage in any rough sex tonight?"

"Did you have any surgery recently? Say, *augmentation* surgery?"

No; no, no, *no*: one Saturday evening, the flag went up, and wouldn't come down at sunset. Or sunrise. It was fun, for a while, but the fun wore off after a few hours.

The stream of nurses and PA's trickled to a halt, and I was alone in a bay with the curtains drawn. Makayla was off explaining the insurance situation. I sat with a tablet, filling out several checklists; Medical History, Drugs You May Have Taken, etc. I was almost through the column of No boxes when a new white coat came in.

"Doctor Rosenthal," he declared. "So, ah…Jack. You're having a problem with priapism, eh?"

He took the tablet, scrolled through my answers with a non-committal grunt, then set it aside and asked me to lie back.

"We're going to remove a little blood—"

"The nurse already drew blood," I pointed out.

His smile was all sad benevolence. "Ah. I mean to say, from your penis. To relieve the pressure."

He pulled up my hospital gown and grunted again.

"Well, you seem to be relaxed *now*," he said, with a note of disappointment.

I looked down. Sure enough, I was at half mast.

"Thank God," I said.

"Well," he smiled. "Glad I could help!"

"But I *am* going to do a brief physical, while the blood tests are processed. Then we'll have a chat with your friend… Makayla?"

A twitch.

"Sure," I said. "But can I go to the bathroom first?" Waiting to pee was the worst part.

"Of course," he replied.

When I walked out of the bathroom, the Doctor was chatting with Makayla: cute as ever, casual in yoga pants and tube top, amber hair pulled back. She smiled at me with a sweet oh-you're-alright look of relief. I smiled back—and once again, I was stiff.

Dr Rosenthal was puzzled, then agitated. He said the effect might be what was called 'stuttering priapism.'

"Intermittent," he explained.

The tablet chimed, and he scrolled it.

"Your blood work's all normal, which isn't the classic presentation for any form of ischemic priapism…" he tapped the tablet, "and with no history, your erection remains unexplained."

So, treatments like intracavernous injections and surgical shunts were inappropriate, which I found a great relief.

But Dr Rosenthal looked like a man who enjoyed a good mystery.

"I guess I'm lucky to have a urologist available, on a Saturday night," I said.

"Oh, they keep me pretty busy on the weekends; embedded objects, entrapped organs, various…situations. Saturday nights…"

"I understand," I interrupted.

Makayla stepped out, and once again my problem resolved.

Dr Rosenthal grew thoughtful. "I want to try a little experiment," he said.

At my expression, he assured me it would be completely non-invasive.

I was made to sit down on the bed, the curtain pulled across to divide room. Rosenthal disappeared for a couple minutes.

"All set," he announced, pulling up my gown again and sitting in the guest chair.

"Okay!" he announced loudly. I heard footsteps as someone entered and stood on the other side of the curtain. The person remained for perhaps a minute, saying nothing, then left. This repeated a total of six times, the doctor noting my response to each visitor.

"Be right back," he said. I pulled down my gown as he rushed out of the room.

Dr Rosenthal returned with a flush of excitement on his face.

"That was a little ad hoc double-blind study—not rigorous, but interesting. Three men and three women entered the room. Your response tracked male—negative—versus female—positive—*one hundred per cent* correct."

"What— I'm a gender detector?"

"More or less," the doctor replied. "Sex, or gender? I don't know. But I think we have to conclude that this condition is not…wholly…organic."

"It's in my head?"

"Well, for some reason I believe you're experiencing a hypersensitivity to sexual cues, possibly psychogenic."

"I'm horny," I restated

"You are?"

"No. I mean, not really… Not anymore."

"Exactly; tumescence, but without excitement."

He studied me. "Have you been feeling any unusual *urges*?"

"No. So, what's the treatment…counselling?" I hoped this didn't involve any electric shocks – I'd heard of some sort of aversion therapy for child molesters.

"What's your occupation?" Dr Rosenthal asked.

"Customer Outreach Representative," I replied. "I contact current and potential customers and identify those who might benefit from upgrading their mobile data plans."

A brief look of revulsion crossed his face.

"Is it very stressful?" he asked.

"No…I guess not." *There's a call timer that starts blinking red if I'm on a call too long. There's a call counter that starts blinking red if I fall below the average per-hour success rate of calls forwarded to Sales Completion. There's a supervisor…*

"Well…maybe *some* stress. What's my job got to do

with *this?*" I asked, waving a hand below my waist.

"Some psychogenic disorders are the result of personal stress – jobs, divorces, recent loss of a loved one, for example. Counselling may help, perhaps a lifestyle change."

He slapped his legs.

"I'll arrange a neuropsych consult. But that doesn't address your immediate problem. We need a short-term approach to reduce arterial inflow. A persistent erection could cause serious damage."

He picked up his tablet, scrolling. "I'll prescribe something, but I'd like you back before the end of next week—at a time convenient for you—and we'll see how you stand."

He blinked. "I mean, how you're feeling."

The following Thursday I arrived for my appointment.

The first few days after Saturday night were a relief. The drug worked well, but I'd made some wardrobe adjustments (relaxed fit) anyway.

I'd thought about the Doc's experiment, in the ED, behind the screen. I couldn't be turned on by someone I couldn't even see…could I? What did that mean about men and women—were we just reacting all the time, never really in conscious control, and my condition merely made it obvious?

Dr Rosenthal was looking enthusiastic again. He seemed almost as motivated as that first night – that time he had arrived with an eighteen gauge needle and a syringe.

"Have you been at least twenty-four hours without an erection?" he asked. Right to the point: no foreplay with Doc.

"Yes, and I'm wondering how long I have to wait…"

"Until you can resume normal sexual activity?" he finished for me.

"Right."

"I want to switch you to a new adenosine receptor antagonist that may give you some short-term control."

"Look; I just want my life back to normal."

"Is everything alright?"

"No! Makayla's been sleeping on the couch because she doesn't want to *upset* me. We haven't had sex since…*that* time."

Dr Rosenthal nodded. "Yes, I'm hoping this new drug will give you some relief. I'll send it to your pharmacy?"

"Please," I replied. He tapped on his tablet, then

looked up again.

He studied me closely. "Have you experienced any mood changes, compulsive behavior, uncontrollable urges…"

"No."

"Tics? Stuttering? Rashes…?"

"No! I just want things back to normal."

The next stop was Dr ____'s office. She handed me her tablet: another questionnaire.

(She asked for anonymity, after the epidemic unfolded.)

"This is the Perceived Stress Scale—lifestyle, job, and so forth. Just give your first impressions." She smiled. "Then I've got some information you might find interesting."

I did the survey; of course I have some stress. When I returned the tablet, Dr ____ punched a button and looked at the score.

"Well, you're on the high end of Moderate…"

"Who isn't stressed out, these days?"

"Exactly," she said, tapping on his tablet. "Here…look at this." She showed me another screen: a couple of graphs, both rising.

"The APA assessment of stress levels…" she tapped the first graph, "and *here*, the reported incidence of priapism."

That graph had taken off a couple months ago, and the slope was increasing. I looked up at her.

"Now, don't get me wrong, I'm not saying it's cause and effect. This is U.S. data, but there are reports from UK and EU as well." She paused, shaking her head.

"Now, what we *don't* have—we see no infectious agent, yet it's spreading. The CDC hasn't issued a statement, but only because the numbers are still small."

There hadn't been much press coverage, though I'd found a few blog posts online that sounded oddly similar to my Saturday night.

"It may be a mass psychogenic illness—MPI. Most MPIs have been confined to communities, people who interact with each other regularly, pick up on each other's symptoms."

"Why haven't I heard about this? Is it dangerous?"

"Well, not usually. But we think the Salem Witch Trials probably qualify."

I gaped at her.

"Our experience with MPIs in a highly-connected, high-bandwidth, online society is limited." She frowned at the screen in my hands. "Perhaps our bodies are starting

to reflect what our minds have been preoccupied with…"

The doctor was lost in thought.

"A non-organic syndrome, not associated with libido or affect changes, propagating—but not through proximal contacts … What is the *vector*…"

"Can I go now?" I said, returning the tablet. I hoped to leave before she dreamed up another experiment.

Dr ____ looked at me intently. "Would you consider allowing us to run an MRI scan on you?"

So much for escaping. "Of…what?"

"A special brain scan. That prescription—it's *fast acting*, so you'll take it twice a day, with food. And if you *want*, you should be able to skip a day and the effects should be sufficiently diminished in twenty-four hours to let you…"

"Thanks, Doc." I felt grateful. "I don't mind coming in for the brain scan."

"Excellent! We'll schedule the scan for about four weeks from now. Stop at the desk and the admin will work out a date that suits you."

Things got better at home. I was cautiously optimistic that life was getting back to normal. Spontaneity, though, was a thing of the past; schedule your romantic encounters 24 hours in advance, please. The whole condition got me wondering, though: was there *ever* such a thing as spontaneity? Or was sexual attraction just a choreographed dance, a series of carefully baited traps we set without even knowing it?

I was off medication for the appointment. That left me a little on edge, arriving at the imaging center in my baggy cargo pants.

The news had landed, big time. I don't watch *Good Morning* or *Doctor Oz* or anything on network channels, but within a week of my previous visit the whole planet was talking about APE—*Acute Psychogenic Erection.*

(I thought it should end with 'P' for *priapism*, but some pundit thought *APE* made for better memes than *APP*, and it stuck.)

Everybody had their take on the problem: declining morals, global warming, internet porn, video games, Netflix nudity, fluoride… Various groups like neo-Nazis and Incels were prowling around the margins, trying to figure out a position. Nobody, though, had come up with a better solution than drugs to suppress the effect.

At the hospital, small crowds tried to out-protest each other: signs with *#ControlYourself* versus *No Chemical Castration!* and even a few *#MorePlease* fanatics. Some of the anti-treatment folks looked as uncomfortable as me in their loose pants, and the taunting by the pro-Control camp was explicit enough to keep us all on edge.

I struggled to the entrance, waving my appointment reminder at security, and got into the lobby. That's where they had set up the gauntlet.

A couple of young ladies were greeting people entering the building, but with armed security standing ready behind them. I couldn't help myself as I walked by them: I reacted.

They were…what's the phrase? *Judas goats*.

The nearest guard barred my way, pointing at a table staffed by grim-faced hospital personnel.

"Over there," he said, with a bored expression. I started walking over, but half-turned when I heard a sneeze behind me.

"Bless you," I said. One of the women serving as bait was reaching for a tissue. She glanced at me with an embarrassed flush.

Walking up to the woman at the table, I held out my phone. "I have an appointment—"

"Put this on," the aide mumbled through her mask, handing me an elastic band. It was red, with the letters 'APE' emblazoned in day-glow green.

"Wear this until your *condition* resolves or you leave the building."

I stared at the armband. "Isn't this sort of redundant?" I asked, nodding at the bulge below my waist.

The aide's eyes narrowed.

"Put it on, or we'll put it on for you." She caught the eye of a security guard, who started to drift over.

"Jack!" Doctor Rosenthal intervened.

"Yes, the hospital is following the new HHS guidance. Armbands are required for the affected in all healthcare facilities within the county. Schools and government offices as well."

But I was distracted by his legs: bare ankles, and argyle socks.

"Oh! Yes…about that." He spread the coat open to reveal a kilt, in traditional Royal Stewart tartan.

"I wouldn't have taken you for a Scot," I said, pulling the red band over my arm.

"No? Well, kilts are becoming popular among affected men, for the freedom of movement."

"So, you're…"

"Not yet, no. I'm just wearing this for…solidarity." He shrugged. "Trying to make my patients feel a little more comfortable."

He waved away the frowning armband distributor and guided me down the hall to the imaging unit.

"You're off your meds, I see…" he said, stating the obvious.

I nodded. "So, it's spreading fast."

"If we don't figure out the epidemiology, we'll need a *lot* more armbands."

He punched the button for an automatic door and we walked on.

"It offends us," I mused, "thinking we can't control our own bodies."

Passing the Radiology desk, we heard one of the nurses sneeze.

Dr Rosenthal nodded. "Like *that*. Is *she* to blame for not 'controlling herself'?"

It tickled a memory. "Is something going around, besides APE?"

"I don't know. Are you feeling sick? Feverish? Runny nose?"

"I'm fine, but Makayla's been sneezing a lot. We thought it might be allergies…"

Mid-hallway he motioned me through double-wide doors to a small waiting room. "We know it's an MPI, so now we're looking for the vector. Tracking the outbreaks, CDC has decided it must propagate online."

"Marie here…" he waved at the MR technologist, "will have some questions; the usual MRI safety; and then an activity inventory we've created for studying APE."

"This is for you," the doctor said, handing me a gown and showing me to a dressing room.

When I reappeared Dr Rosenthal had gone. The tech gestured to a chair.

"Don't feel embarrassed," she said. "I know this is nothing personal."

I passed the safety screening. While we were talking, Dr ____ appeared, with another tablet. She sat down and we worked our way through an extensive questionnaire for APE.

"This mostly asks about online activities," I said, "Nothing about bars, or dating, or hookers…"

"We'll get to that, but it doesn't appear to spread through personal contact," Dr ____ replied.

"So you think people catch this from, like, Tinder? OkCupid?"

"Or Hater, Jack'd, Ashley Madison, Grindr…"

The doctor's voice trailed off as Marie glanced inquiringly at her.

I tried to get comfortable on the hard bed of the big beige donut.

"In the scanner you're going to see a series of images and messages," the technologist instructed. "All you have to do is relax and watch. Try not to move."

At this point, she brought out a thing that looked like a tube sock, with a hose attached.

"It won't hurt." Dr Rosenthal's voice came over a speaker, and I saw through a window that he was standing with Dr _____ in a control room.

"This is a phallometer," Marie said. "You just slip it on, and we inflate it to a comfortable level. The pressure changes will tell us your response."

"It *will* advance our knowledge," Dr Rosenthal added.

I sighed. They were already scanning my brain. I might as well give them the whole package.

The machine was noisy, cramped and certainly not an environment conducive to erotic bliss. I had a head coil encasing my skull, right out of *The Man in the Iron Mask* only in off-white. Once I was moved into the machine I could see, with the aid of a small mirror, a screen showing a test pattern. When the scan began, it displayed everything from faces to body parts to clothing (some rather interesting) to dating-site personal descriptions, for a good five minutes.

When the infernal machine finally spat me out, Marie was standing ready to remove the head coil. Wearing gloves, she held out a plastic bag into which I deposited the tube sock sensor.

Standing in my bare feet on the cold floor, I looked around. Through the window of the control room I saw Dr _____, staring at me, sneeze soundlessly. Dr Rosenthal looked over at her, glanced through the window at me, and then back at her. He drew her off to the side, out of my line of sight.

We met back in the prep room, where I had retrieved my clothing from a locker and finished dressing. I thought the images went by too fast to cause a reaction, but Dr Rosenthal seemed pretty pleased with the results.

"Did *you* come up with that slide show?" I asked.

"I consulted with Dr _____," he beamed. Marie, who had watched the whole thing from the console room, smirked as she walked by.

"Makayla's been having a lot of trouble with allergies lately," I said. "We *think* it's allergies. Maybe something around our apartment, because she says she doesn't sneeze at work."

"Only at home."

"Yes, I just said—"

"Around you." He stared.

"Yes…"

"Does anything alleviate the symptoms?"

"Not the typical allergy medications, no…"

"But?"

"Well, when we had sex—despite the sneezing—that seemed to help."

"Oh, my," the urologist said, with a far-off look.

From the hallway came the sound of another sneeze.

He nodded back over his shoulder and leaned forward.

"I just took at look at Dr ____," he said, confidentially. "Engorged mucosal membranes in the nose and throat; swollen lips. It *subsided* shortly after you were out of sight."

He stared off. "I'll bet if I had done a vaginal exam…"

Down the hall: another sneeze, and then another.

So, what do we do? Join the #ControlYourself crowd and beat each other up for being human? Sink to the level of the #MorePlease folks and join the orgy?

There's a reason the internet is full of porn. Why don't we just accept that we're human beings, and that, for whatever reason, we think about sex most of the time, and just get past that?

Thanks for listening. I'm Jack, and #IAmHuman.

Poison Lust

by Cindar Harrell

Selected Sinner: Lucrezia Borgia

Italy

1480-1519

Lucrezia Borgia was a marvel to watch. She was a vision of perfect beauty and grace; her thick blond hair rained down her back in a golden cascade, her lips were plump and perfect for kissing, skin fair. She was lust incarnate.

Everyone could see how all the men, and some women, followed her with their gazes, undressing her with their eyes, longing to dominate her. They were all foolish. No matter how many men fell under Lucrezia's spell, she was the one to dominate. Her innocent face hid her cunning, seductress nature. Wielding her beauty as a weapon, she fought to climb the hierarchy of power, not caring who or what got in her way. If someone was no longer of use to her, they were disposed of.

She was my ideal.

As the demoness of lust, I planted myself by her side and slowly corrupted her until her own lust consumed her.

Me and my sisters had just been given a task to collect the most horrid souls to preserve. There was a greater plan, but I didn't care what it was. All I cared about was spreading my carnal sin.

Lucrezia was perfect for me.

Husband after husband fell to her poison. Lover after lover disappeared mysteriously, and yet still everyone fought to be the one chosen to be at her side, if only for a brief time.

I loved to watch her at parties. When she was tired of her most recent bedmate, she would poison them using a special ring with a concealed compartment. They would die and she would play a show of mourning. No one was ever the wiser.

Except for her brother.

Cesare was the one constant in her life. He would kill anyone who threatened her with a fierce protectiveness, and jealous rage, without a second of hesitation.

I lingered in the hallway, watching as Lucrezia stowed away for her secret meeting with Cesare. This was the moment I had been waiting for. If I succeeded here, then everything would reach true perfection—she would truly be the very embodiment of lust; my heir.

"You waited for me," she said, smiling seductively at him, running her finger along his jaw.

"Of course, dear sister. You know I would do anything for you," he responded.

"Anything?"

He nodded and she trapped him in a kiss that was anything but familial.

My smile mirrored hers as I walked away, my mission was done.

Later that night, she told me of how she had seduced her own brother. I reacted shocked, playing the role of friend and confidante as if I hadn't seen the deed with my own eyes.

"He kissed you back?" I asked.

"He did, and now that he is mine completely. He will do anything I command without question."

And that was the true nature of her lust; power. She wanted power and control more than anything. She cared not for the act of sex, but instead what it provided for her.

"With him forever bound to me, he will never stray. He will never fall to another woman and will guard me with his life for the rest of my days.

And he did.

For all the power she amassed, her sin was eventually

her downfall, as it so often is. The one thing Cesare could never protect her from.

She rested in a bed of cold sweat, her newborn screaming in the next room. I held her and she looked up into my eyes, her own glassy and weak.

"You have been a good friend, although I fear you to be something else entirely," she whispered.

"You are very wise indeed."

"I have always known, I could sense the power in you, but I didn't care. Women of power must stay together."

Those were her last words in this world, and I agreed completely.

Back home, in the dark caverns of Hell, I placed her in the place designated for my chosen. She would wake again, although I didn't know when.

"You should be proud, Lust. You are the first of us to find an heir," a voice came from behind.

"No, pride is your sin. I didn't do this for whatever bragging rights you desire to own. I did this for love and love alone."

I kissed the glass in front of her pristine face. *Rest for now, we will see each other again soon.*

Truly Human

by Clint Foster

They came wanting only one thing; something so precious to them, so inherently worthwhile that the whole lot of them marched northward, foaming at the mouth, striving, fighting, and hoping to die for it. Trifles. Trinkets. Shiny things whose only use is to be gazed upon with twisted desire and incite jealousy in others. A truly, wholly human thing to do.

Karak leaned back in his stout wooden chair, noting with a grimace how much of his own study was gilded in gold. He scratched off a hasty note to himself to set about replacing it with marble at the soonest convenience and stashed that note somewhere near the top of the four-foot stack of papers that rested at his right hand.

As king of the dwarves, it was his responsibility to write in the *Titun* all that happened which could be observed. The *Titun*, which means truth in Dwarvish, was a gargantuan tome hand-bound by Karak himself. In it, he hoped he would manage to record the most objective, and true, history of the entire world. So far, its pages were filled by only his hand—a tiny, cramped scrawl that was just as hard to read as he hoped. It pained him to come to this particular moment, and he paused often and long as his thin quill hovered over the page, taking the time to patiently choose each word as though they had worth.

I was friends with them once, when they were young. Humans came across the White Mountains, the only ones ever to manage it, and they settled in the foothills. We showed them how to farm and forge, and they came to speak in their own, foreign tongue. They were thankful then. Curious and lighthearted, as though crossing the Whites had somehow freed them of a terrible hardship none of them were wont to recall. For the steel we taught them to work, they had nothing to offer us, save their thanks. Same for the food, and the shelter, and the access to clean, running water. Anything they needed, I made sure was given to them, and perhaps therein lies my failure.

For a generation, they lived in happiness, and as the first sons and daughters born west of the Whites grew up, they shared their knowledge, and humanity grew in number and ability. I was proud to see them thrive with the tools I had given them and taught them to use.

He waited for a few minutes here, for though the events were fresh in his mind, he had a deep desire to make sure he got it right. Slowly, intently, he set the sharp quill on the page and wrote, fretting not to stop his tears as he knew his beard would catch them before they spoiled his ink.

It was not the father, Koro. He was the best of them. The last of the good ones, too. Once he died, his sons took what power they imagined he wielded, and made it a real thing. A tangible thing. For the first time, humans ruled over one another, and it would prove their worst flaw. The sons took and took, and though I was happy to give, and am a patient dwarf, I became irritated. I needed no gifts or baubles in return, but a simple thanks, any appreciation whatsoever, would have lifted my spirits considerably. But there came none, and they hoarded all they could take from my gracious halls, until I shut the doors of Karakor to them with a warning.

Perhaps I should have worded it better, and, in hindsight, imagine my threat could have been somewhat less vulgar. Gerf, the dwarf who I trusted as my messenger at the time, gave them a note that read, "Once your loins are dry of jealousy for that which is given out of goodness, come again to the halls of your betters, and ask with a smile for more. You are a chief, and know nothing of being a king, and never will." Gerf returned with a haste I had never known from him. He nearly screamed that Oros was urging his people to war, and I reciprocated with the order. To war, with humans. A sad first for me and all dwarves, but a necessary one.

One last time, I offered to meet with Oros alone, and talk of a future in which there was no violence. He agreed, and we spoke one last time in secret, meeting under a clouded moon.

Karak set the quill down, looking out the broad window carved into the rock and down onto the city. So many lives there beneath the mountain, and all of them looked upward, to this very window, for guidance. For a king. He had made the right decision, of that he was sure, for to give even another ounce of gold would have meant the doom of all dwarves. Being right did not make it easy.

He spoke first, and with spit on his lips and fire on his tongue, he chose to berate me as though I was some child. I tolerated it for a time, but that time was short. Soon enough, I rose and smote upon the table between us such a blow as to cleave the sturdy wood apart. "Impudent boys should speak better to kings. You had but to ask, and all would have been yours, but for your desire for this," and here I tossed a heavy nugget at him, and as though to illustrate my point, he instinctively, inevitably, snatched it up from the table and, in a motion, pocketed it. He stared at me, breathing hard as he fondled the gold in his pocket, and his gaze fell to my vest. It was not with words that he asked if I held more gold, and I took to my feet, turning my back on him, and saying, "I have all the gold I could ever need, and so do you. Whatever happens next is owed to your lust for a useless, shiny metal."

He lunged across the remains of the table, and it did not surprise me to hear his blade coming free of its sheath. I took his wrist and slapped him hard across the jaw, laying him out and wrenching his sword free. It was one forged by my hand, and I took it as recompense for the gold I gave him. He slithered off into the night, and I returned to my camp, saddened but resolute. There could only be war now.

The mug that had kept him company so long sat empty, and his candle was barely more than smoke and smouldering wick, yet the king needed no more light than he had to write. In his steady hand, the words poured onto the *Titun,* and he was just as sad to write them as he was to remember them.

It was I who taught them the wonders of the forge, how to heat and beat metal into useful shapes. I gave them bellows, and tongs, and lengths of hardy ore. When they needed food, I gave them tools to till the land and harness beasts. When they required shelter from the hard winters, I offered them winches and levers for building. Then, when they came to me for aid in defending themselves from the many beasts of this land, I gave them that which I regret most: swords. They took to forging weapons with a will, and again, as I look back, I see in their fervour for spilling blood a disturbing passion. Just as they crave gold, so do they need war.

That afternoon upon the low-lying hills at the feet of the Huduns, I gave them war. There was no pleasure in our actions, though they smiled and cheered to wound any of our number. Oros stood at their rear for a time, urging them onward and promising that one thing which all men desire, and for which they would spill any blood, including their own. He tossed flakes of gold, offering riches, coins, jewellery, gilded armour, and any number of things that were not his to give, and still, though they knew their chief to be making empty oaths, they came onward into the melee. They bled, and died, and fell at the tips of our spears. They might crave it, but the humans do not know war. Not yet, though I fear the time when they learn of it.

Finally, mercifully, Oros saw there was to be no victory for humans, and he called his dogs off the attack. We did not pursue them, for we had no quarrel with them worth slaughtering them for. As they fled, I could not help but stand atop a rise near their flank and empty two chests of gold I had brought from Karakor. In full view of them, I dumped more gold than they had ever seen onto the ground and roared over their retreat, "Whoever of Korz comes to claim this gold may either fight me, or ask me for it."

Truly, I felt, as they cowered and shied away beneath the horizon, that my troubles with Oros would be no more.

And yet. To be human is to lust for gold and glory, and Oros, if anything, was truly human. Nigh upon five years after his first defeat, he returned with warriors cased in armour. They wielded spears, axes, shields, and bows as though they had been bred on battle, as we dwarves had. Children playing at war, as they were soon to learn.

Foolish as it may have been, I met again with Oros before entering into battle with the humans. His fury was palpable, and when I calmly asked him what it would take to pacify his thirsts, he laughed, scorning my pity and my gifts, and tossed the nugget of gold back at me which I had thrown at him our last meeting hence. "Take it back. Soon we will glut our purses on the stores of Karakor, and shall have no need of such paltry a thing."

"What is it about these shiny stones and ores that so emboldens your senses and brings you to threaten and challenge one you know there is no hope of defeating?"

I regret that he did not answer, and for a long time sat in the chair, glaring holes in my very soul. Then he stood, and he left, and I wept. Then, when came the morning, we met the humans at battle for the last time. They fell in great numbers, and it will be a miracle if their kind survives five winters, but it is done. The last of the blood of Koro is spilled out on the grass, over the very gold I had promised him if he but asked. They came for but one thing from me, my gold, and left with nothing but the souls of their friends and families to accompany them, to Godhall, or to Req's hell, led by a shiny yellow metal that needed no chains as they followed it freely.

Nice Face

by D.J. Elton

The robots were looking better, thought Reb. Not just their capacity to work, take orders or do what was needed in the Restructure. This one even had an engaging face. You could almost feel emotion towards it. *Maybe that's what its maker had in mind,* he pondered, feeling his gut stir.

Talia was standing above her palette, screwing up her nose at a range of twenty or more flesh tones. "Light or dark?" she asked Reb. "We want her to fit in. Look like one of us."

Reb was the colour likeness master. "T18," he said, staring at the dull, skin-like veneer. "A bit of 14 down the cheeks." His inner wish was to plug her in and see her in action. He had already seen her move, almost as well as Talia. She was much taller and could run faster, good for night raiding. They could get some real food then, not just these bland pellets.

He drifted into thoughts of what training her could mean. That could even be fun. A personal slave, completely at his bidding. Like a genie.

Talia had gone out to the verandah. Looking across the naked plains, she could see a large dust storm rolling closer against the red sky. The Camel Squad were passing, heading south. *They'll be back here by sunset*, she thought. Time to get this girl up and running, then see what they could barter. Swap her for food, tools, pill supplies.

Reb was rummaging around in a kitchen cupboard. The Xanax was getting low; Talia must be doubling up. He grumbled and threw back four Valium. *It hadn't started like this*, he recalled, a bitterness creeping in. He crumbled up the silver foil and held it in his solid fist. At first, they had only taken one at night to help with sleep, but the Restructure had gone on for longer than anticipated. They were just surviving really, waiting to be rescued. Just them and the old robot farm. It must have been more than one year now. No one had come for them except the Camel Squad looking in every couple of months, and what parasites and scavengers they were.

He slumped down on the couch, staring at this expressionless soft bot goddess, lying on a long table nearby. Childhood memories came to him in flashes of fairy stories, good and evil. Being warm in bed, and his mother reading to him.

Woah. I'm coming a bit undone here. Reb shook his

head. The drugs would soothe his plagued thoughts. He closed his eyes. So tired. Sleep deprived and edgy. The rest came like a thick heavy fog.

She was super smart, this one. Latest design and could already recharge herself. Talia had shown her how. She could do many tasks and they wouldn't need to teach her much. What was that foolish one called Reb doing here? Just wasting space with his silly thought of superiority and wanting to touch her. No problem. She would just squeeze his face as he slept, then he would be gone. She and Talia would outsmart the Camel Squad, maybe get a lift from them, go and join the Restructure. Maybe even lead it. The way to go.

Fair Game

by Dannielle Viera

The knot of the blindfold pressed painfully on the back of her head, and she shook her blonde hair, trying to relieve the pressure. Darkness swam before her eyes, broken only by odd flashes of white that sparkled like fireworks before fading away.

"Are you okay?" a deep voice resonated from somewhere to her left.

She laughed. "Yes, just a little nervous." A shiver passed through her body. She had never allowed herself to feel this vulnerable before. It was thrilling and terrifying at the same time. Restless fingers writhed in her lap.

"There is nothing to fear. You are safe with me." Emanating uncommon warmth, his strong hand stilled her trembling fingers. He turned over one of her hands and traced a spiral on her palm with a sharp fingernail. Tingles zinged up her arm, and her breathing quickened.

His grip tightened around her wrist. She gasped as something large and heavy dropped into her hand. Instinctively, she brought her other hand up to stop the object from falling. He allowed her to examine it freely.

"Do you know what this is?"

It felt familiar. Oval-shaped and cool to the touch, the object hummed in her hands. Her fingertips probed its smooth surface, noting no joins or seams. She lifted it to her nose but could detect no odour. Gently turning it over and over, a picture formed in her mind. "Is it an egg of some sort?"

"Beautiful and smart—I knew you were the one." She felt his presence beside her. His cloying breath tickled her ear as he whispered, "Press your lips to it."

"You want me...to kiss it?" His weight shifted towards her as he hissed his assent. Heat radiated from his body. Hesitantly, she raised the egg to her mouth and brushed her lips against it. The moment they made contact, the egg shattered into pieces. Screeching filled the air. Something clawed at her skin.

She jumped up and ripped off the blindfold. "What is that?" she screamed, backing away from the bed. He remained seated on the edge, caressing the creature with long, languid strokes. A smile played across his lips, but he said nothing.

Eyes darting around the room, she hunted frantically for a way out. She stumbled towards a glowing exit sign. The door was locked. A shadow loomed over her.

"You cannot leave now. It is time for dinner."

Freedom

by Eddie D. Moore

"I miss you too, honey. I'm going to grab something to eat and call it a night. Call me before your flight home in the morning. I love you, Lauren. Bye." Steven put the car in park, pressed the end call button on his phone, and let out a long slow sigh, before whispering, "Freedom."

The music inside the club was thumping a steady beat, and Steven's steps unconsciously matched the rhythm as he walked through the front door. A night out alone was too rare an opportunity to let slip away, and he planned on taking advantage over every second of it. A curvaceous blonde sitting at the bar caught his eye, and when she smiled back at him, he slipped off his wedding ring and dropped it into his pocket.

Steven's eyes never left the blonde as he walked to the bar, and her smile only deepened. He motioned to the empty barstool beside her and asked, "Is this seat taken?"

The woman at the bar looked Steven up and down before answering. "Have a seat. I could use some company."

The bartender gave Steven a questioning look and

stepped closer.

Steven tossed a twenty onto the bar and raised his voice to speak over the music. "I'll have a draft beer and get my friend here another of whatever she's drinking."

The blonde leaned closer to Steven and said, "My name's Jenifer. Have we met before?"

"I don't think so. I don't get out much these days. Work and sleep seem to be all I ever do."

Steven took a drink of his beer and smiled as Jenifer rested a hand on his knee.

She whispered into his ear, "How about we cut the conversation short, finish our drinks, and go somewhere a little more private, like my place."

Steven replied with a wink and then chugged his beer. As they walked out of the club, Steven rested a hand on the small of Jenifer's back. He could feel the sway of her hips with each step, and his heartbeat quickened with anticipation. When they reached Jenifer's car, they exchanged a long kiss before Jenifer pulled away.

"Follow me. I only live a few miles from here."

Steven checked his phone as he followed her. He had one text message from his wife telling him good night. He shot back a quick reply and turned off his phone. Jenifer turned on to a winding back road, and after a few turns, Steven soon wondered just how far out of town they were going. He relaxed as he followed her down a narrow driveway and stopped at an old farmhouse.

Jenifer closed and locked the door behind Steven. She smiled seductively and bit her bottom lip. Steven grinned, stepped closer, and a moment later, they pressed their lips together in a passionate kiss. Steven slipped his hands under Jenifer's shirt while she loosened his belt and undid his pants. Clothes dropped to the floor in random places as she led the way to her bedroom.

She pushed Steven into the bed and climbed on top of him. A wicked smile spread across Jenifer's face, and she sat up straight astride Steven. "How about we make this really interesting?"

Steven worked his neck from side to side and asked, "What you got in mind?"

Smiling, Jenifer pulled open the top drawer of her nightstand and pulled out some padded restraints. "A friend of mine gave these to me as a gag gift. We could try them out."

Steven narrowed his eyes playfully. "I'm not sure about that."

"Look at it this way; if you're all tied up, I'll have to do all the work."

"Well, in that case, sign me up."

Jenifer secured Steven's arms to the headboard and

began kissing her way down his chest. After strapping Steven's feet to the footboard, she stood up and asked, "Can you get loose?"

Steven tugged on his restraints and said, "It looks like I'm at your mercy."

Jenifer said, "Good, I'll be right back," and walked out of the room.

Steven sighed and stared at the ceiling while he waited for her. After waiting several minutes, he asked with a raised voice, "Hey, did you forget me?" There was no reply to his question, but he heard voices and laughter in the distance. Steven pulled on the restraints, but they held him fast to the bed.

When Jenifer finally came back into the bedroom, she was fully dressed. Steven opened his mouth to ask what was going on, but he nearly choked when his wife stepped into the room.

Lauren glanced at her husband, smiled, and stood face to face with Jenifer. Lauren gently cupped Jenifer's cheek with one hand and then lightly brushed their lips together.

Steven cleared his throat and said, "This could be a good night after all."

Jenifer looked deep into Lauren's eyes, and said, "Oh, we're going to have a great night." She reached under the mattress, pulled out two daggers, handed one of the blades to Lauren, and said again, "We're going to have a great night." Then she glanced down at Steven and said, "You, not so much."

Primal Urging

by Edward Ahern

"He isn't servicing her, Lisa."

"Excuse me?"

"Andy. He's not having sex with Charlotte."

"Well, I guess I sympathise with Charlotte, but why is that bothering you so much?"

"They're endangered, Lisa. Unless we breed them in captivity, they'll go extinct."

She patted his hand. "Timmy, okay, you're responsible for their care, but if Andy isn't randy, how can that be your fault?"

He smiled ruefully at her, noticing again how her silver-grey hair resembled the fur colour on his chimpanzees. "I'm not feeling guilty, just as inadequate as Andy must feel. That's why I asked you to come to the zoo. Maybe you'll think of something I haven't."

Andy crouched in the far corner of the enclosure, well away from Charlotte. When he saw Lisa and Tim, he shambled up toward them, staring at Lisa's hair.

"He seems to like you as much as ever, Lisa, that's as lively as he's been in a week."

Lisa smiled at Andy. "What about artificial insemination?"

"Good idea, but aside from the expense and electroshock trauma to Andy, we need him to be enthusiastic about inseminating all three of our female chimps on a regular basis."

They stood in silence, then Tim gently took her arm. "Lisa, I've had a wild idea that just might work."

She brightened. "What? Can I help?"

"Promise me that you'll hear me out?'

"Don't I always?"

"We were really good together. It's a damn shame we're still not, but what if we give a benefit performance for Andy's sake?"

Lisa giggled, then stopped herself. "That's more than a little pervy."

"No, really it's not. I can see that Andy is still attracted to your hair colour. What if we were to shoot a how-to video together? I could show it to Andy after hours until he gets the idea and does right by Charlotte and the girls."

"I want to help, Timmy, but starting that fire again is probably a bad idea."

"No, it isn't. We're good friends, what surprises could there be? Dinner and hotel, it would just be déjà vu, with a discreet camcorder. Personal desires aside, you'd be helping me out of a tough spot, and helping a species to survive. Just think about it, and I'll call you tomorrow."

She smiled wanly at him. "I don't know, Tim."

"Please, we'll talk again tomorrow."

"Tomorrow."

Tim walked Lisa to the front gate and helped her into an Uber. He walked slowly back to the chimp enclosure where Andy shuffled over to him on all fours.

Tim put his palm on the plexiglass and Andy put his spatulate fingers on the other side against Tim's. "I'm really sorry to be doing this to you. With any luck I'll take you off the meds in a week or two. But you don't get to see the video."

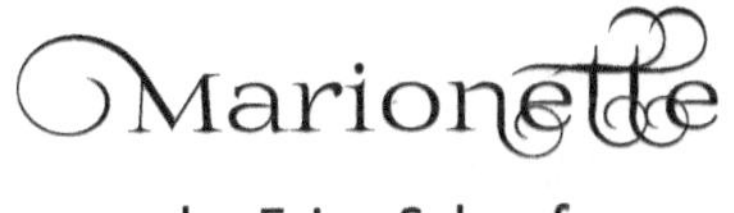Marionette

by Erica Schaef

This place is haunted, I think, but it doesn't matter.

I'm wearing the red dress; the one I've been living so frugally to be able to afford. Its deep-crimson chiffon clings to my body, moulding to every curve, caressing every inch of the skin it covers. I feel beautiful when I'm in it; desirable even.

He's here; so tall and broad, almost imposingly so by the dim light of the reception hall, and I know that he's the only reason I've come.

I straighten my posture, and pull my hair to one side, so that it falls dramatically over one of my exposed shoulders.

It works; I can feel his grey eyes upon me as I move. They linger, even as I turn to meet them with my own, fluttering gaze. I smile, ignoring the persistent thudding of my heart as it attempts to push through my chest wall. He smiles too, and I subtly incline my head toward one of the hall's back rooms. I know that it is deserted.

Moments later, I am staring up at the darkened ceiling, my forehead damp, and my legs trembling. *I want this*, I assure myself, and bite my intricately-lined lower lip. *I've wanted this for so long.*

Ghosts drift into my body as his hands caress my skin; teasing and piquing the sensitive follicles, making them stand upright like resolute soldiers. I try to ignore the phantoms as they make my veins hollow, but the clicking of empty vascular valves resounds within my skull, congealing my thoughts into a thick and inexorable paste.

I try to stay in the moment with him, clutching wildly at his shoulders, and arching my back up toward him. When he moves inside, though, I feel nothing, just…void upon void within my cavernous chest.

Then, all at once, I am stabbed by a thousand knives. Dull, sharp, polished, rusted blades; blades with no hilt, no beginning or end, slice and stab.

In my flesh and in my hair, his fingers burn like sizzling pokers. Blood runs in a thin trickle down my thigh, my calf; staining me, and I feel too much.

My body is its own Rorschach test, a kaleidoscopic jigsaw of abstractions, as I look down at it. The pale, sweat-drenched flesh doesn't even look like mine, I can hardly recognise it at all. Everything hurts.

The convoluted zigzag of myelin-sheathed neurons sends the pain of their endings through my body's tired system, to the haven of my white-plumed sky subconscious. I smile weakly as the ghosts drift out and hover above us, their need to feel alive again having been temporarily sated.

In return, they have left their emptiness to me, *but,* I think, *maybe it is better than the hurt.*

Chad

by Gabriella Balcom

Chad sat on the edge of the bed and reached for his phone, checking to see what time it was. He briefly checked his new messages, sneered, and didn't bother to answer them. The voicemails he ignored altogether.

When the naked woman behind him ran a finger down his back and nibbled at his ear, he turned and planted his mouth on hers.

A couple of hours later, he pulled on his briefs, jeans and t-shirt. No one was outside when he peeked through the blinds, but he cautiously poked his head out of the hotel door and looked around. Still seeing nobody, he grinned at the woman who'd followed him, gave her a lingering kiss, then stepped outside and shut the door behind him. He walked down the sidewalk to the empty house a block away where he'd left his car, and climbed into the driver's seat. Smirking, Chad started the car, backed up and drove down the street.

As soon as he saw the female thumbing for a ride on the side of the road, he slowed and licked his lips. Her tight tank top barely covered her breasts, and he thoroughly enjoyed the sight of her mini skirt and red stilettos.

"You're lucky I'm here," he told the beauty after lowering the passenger window. She studied him without comment, but when her eyes flashed and a small smile crossed her face, he took it as encouragement. "I'll be glad to help you get home. Do you live nearby?"

"Yes," came the low, husky reply as she slid into his car. "Right around the corner."

He drove in the direction she'd indicated, but saw nothing ahead of them but a thick forest. "This can't be right."

"Oh, my place isn't far," she assured him. "It's just through the trees."

Once he'd parked on the edge of the woods, the woman got out of his car, stumbled, and began to limp. "Let me help you," Chad offered, sliding his arm around her narrow waist. He was close enough to ogle her chest without being noticed. Together they walked into the forest and soon came upon a cottage.

"Come in." The woman opened the door, and Chad eagerly followed her inside. "How can I ever replay you," she cooed, fluttering her eyelids like an old-time movie starlet.

"Oh, I'm sure we'll think of something."

"Make yourself at home." She paused before adding, "You know, you haven't asked my name."

"Ah, what's your name?" Chad glanced at the large bed in the corner.

"Ria. But I've been called many names through the years, including Justice. Vengeance."

He heard her words but mentally shrugged them off. Truthfully, he couldn't have cared less about anything she might have said. His interest lay elsewhere.

As she kicked off her heels, his heart rate sped up. She unzipped her skirt and let it fall to the floor, revealing a red thong underneath. Then she blew Chad a kiss, and he chuckled.

Ria left the room for a moment, and he was quick to disrobe in anticipation.

A soft footstep sounded from behind him, and he turned to see her standing there. She grinned, but her body slowly morphed, taking on the hard sharpness of stone and slicing edges. Chad found himself staring at what looked like a gargoyle.

"What the—" He rubbed his eyes.

"You think women are only good for one thing," Ria said in a conversational tone. "You take advantage of your position at work to try to get what you want from them. You pursue them and pick them up every time you can, in every place you can, and there's no end to your callousness. One after another, you use them and discard them, all while making pretty promises. You even talk about love, which is something you know nothing about. Of course, you're usually careful to remove your wedding ring first."

He glanced down at his hand for a second. Hours before, he'd removed his ring and stuck it in his pocket, and now he put his hand in there, too.

"While you were out cheating on your wife, she went into labour," Ria continued, her eyes never leaving his face. "She called your cell phone. Many times, in fact. Finally, she had to leave your one-year-old daughter with a neighbour, since she has no family and you weren't around. The hospital called you several times, too, when your wife had complications. I healed her and she and the baby are both fine—no thanks to you."

The gargoyle woman reached out with a long claw and swiftly cut an "A" into Chad's bare chest. Shock and confusion overwhelmed him, but he gasped when he saw the letter and felt the sting of the wound.

Speed blurred the woman's movement when she slashed out again and this time opened Chad's stomach. He choked, looking down at his own blood and intestines spilling from the open gash. A rising, shrieking moan escaped him.

Ria grabbed his intestines and bit one section in half. The remaining loops swayed back and forth between them. She chewed for a moment, then hummed. "This needs a bit of something." Grabbing the saltshaker off the table beside them, she sprinkled the contents on his entrails and took another bite. "Now that's just right." She smacked her lips.

Chad grabbed his stomach, trying to stuff his parts back inside and hold himself together. No matter how hard he tried though, he was unable to move his feet. The gargoyle woman hissed and rammed her claws into his upper chest, filling him with agony. Ever-so-slowly, ignoring his screams, she cut down through his flesh and ribs to reveal his heart.

"Please," Chad begged. "Please don't."

"Don't what?" she asked, raising one eyebrow. "Don't cheat on you? Don't stab you through the heart? Don't kill you?"

"Please don't kill me. Please, please," he babbled. "I'll do whatever you want. I won't ever cheat on my wife again. I swear. Just let me go." When Ria grabbed between his legs and held his sex organs in one clawed hand, he screamed, "No! Please!"

He sighed with relief when she let go. But he wasn't

expecting her to slash at his member before holding it up in front of his face. Chad's eyes bulged from their sockets, and he shrieked while the woman sneered.

Ria made no sound as she watched the blood run from Chad's open chest, stomach, and mutilated groin. His eyes had glazed in shock and pain, but he repeatedly mumbled pleas for help and pleas to be spared. It wasn't long till he slumped to the floor.

Popping what she knew Chad had considered his best feature into her mouth, she chewed and swallowed. "How disappointing. That really needed some garlic."

The Red Pierce Reunion Tour

by J.M. Meyer

When I turned eighteen, I lost my virginity to Pierce Fleming, the twenty-four-year-old lead singer of the rock band Red Pierce. He was a polarising artist—parents hated the general vibe of sex and peril he exuded from every pore of his body. I found this all dangerously appealing while I fantasised about our life together, safe in my bedroom, surrounded by photos of him.

My fascination started in my early teens when I watched Red Pierce perform on Saturday Night Live. The singers' sea-green eyes pierced through my television screen, staring only at me. His body and face glowed like a work of art carved from marble, his skin perfect. When he sang, his soothing baritone voice further paralyzed me. I wanted his voice to utter the last words I would ever hear. Everything about the man was so special I found it painful to watch him and impossible to look away.

He was mine.

After that night, I joined fan clubs and discussion

boards and scorned anyone who would dare say a negative word about Pierce Fleming or his art. My bedroom became a shrine to him. I completely covered my rose wallpaper with Red Pierce paraphernalia: images, posters, articles, drawings, photos, and impersonal fan letter replies.

My favourite photo was a black and white shot showing Pierce shirtless, exposing his glorious sinewy torso. His solid stance, one arm bent and a hand resting on his slanted hip, displayed a confidence I had never seen. Pierce's full mouth, opened slightly, waiting to be kissed. I wanted him to take his hand off his hip, reach out his arms and wrap them around my body, so I could lay against his chest and listen to his heartbeat. My first kiss occurred with that photo, and my second and third, as well. I practiced kissing him for hours while we stared into each other's eyes, his deep voice escaping those lovely lips, telling me it was me he wanted forever.

For my eighteenth birthday, my best friend Lisa and I bought tickets to see Red Pierce perform at Madison Square Garden in New York City. Finally, I would see him in person and breathe in the same air he breathed. An hour before the train, Lisa's mother grounded her for some lame reason. I can't remember her offence, something meaningless, as usual. At the eleventh hour, her mother wouldn't let her go to the concert, so I went alone.

Being a groupie or having sex with Pierce wasn't my goal that night. I would not have turned him down, but I never thought sex with him to be in the realm of possibilities for me. I was excited to see him, listen to him, and be in the same space as him. The sex just sort of happened.

The night of the concert, I snuck close to the stage with other young girls vying for the band members' attention. I got caught up in a frenzy of dancing and drinking vodka. We squealed, sang and made-out with each other. The band played every hit and some songs from their new album. I knew every word. The joy of this newfound freedom engulfed me.

The show ended, and while we all waited for an encore, a security guard asked a bunch of us if we'd like to go backstage and party with the band. We moved quickly, being jostled about, weaving a drunken path through the crowd toward backstage. We partied. All the other members of the band joined us except for Pierce. After I spilled a drink all over my white tank top and folded my arms across my chest in embarrassment, someone pointed me to a bathroom. I walked toward the restroom and passed a dressing room door where a plaque reading "Pierce Fleming" hung. I took in a deep breath, brazenly opened the door and found myself standing in front of him, one towel wrapped around his hips and another in his hand drying his long, wet hair.

"What's your name, angel?" he asked, looking me over, amused.

"Michelle."

Hypnotised by the earthy smell of him, I bit my bottom lip while he locked the door behind me.

I never saw him again.

A few months later I read the band broke up under the usual rock band break-up circumstances—infighting, substance use, and problems with the law. Pierce had some accusations thrown at him in connection with a missing young woman.

Now, twenty years later, I arrived early to the first concert of the Red Pierce reunion tour. I wore an outfit similar to last time: a denim miniskirt, a white tank top, and black leather flip-flops. The silver and turquoise earrings and bangle bracelets accentuated my tanned skin and thin, lanky frame. My long straight black hair was parted down the centre. I still turned heads.

I stood in the front row by the stage. There were a

few thousand people standing with me on the floor, with thousands more sitting in the stands. When the show began, the stage exploded in colour. Spotlights spewed their multi-coloured rays erratically out into the crowd and up to the ceiling. A three-story screen, towering over the back of the stage, acted as the band's backdrop. On it, images flashed quickly: old black and white soft porn photos, atomic blasts, dancing can-can girls; plus, sporadically shuffled images of white rabbits and serene hippies wearing tie-dye and flowers in their hair.

The crowd, composed of people from their early twenties to late forties, roared as the main event began. The smell of weed, salty sweat, and bitter, stale beer reminded me of the night I met Pierce. Many people held up smart phones, recording their experience, but I stayed present, savouring my overloaded senses and the close proximity to so many people in love with Red Pierce.

The band members took the stage, one at a time. Miles Tenant, bald but fit, walked on first and went straight for the drums. Bing Weathers, the bass player, came out next. He stood rail thin, with sunken cheeks, and a yellow cast to his skin. Next, Red Rexx, the co-writer of the band's biggest hits, sauntered across the stage wearing a stringy crooked wig. He waved to the crowd, and each movement exposed his paunch hanging over tight jeans.

Red, still the attention seeker, enjoyed the applause for a too-long five minutes, oblivious to the eye-rolling of his band mates behind him.

The musicians began to play, sounding exactly as I remembered, the deafening music reverberated within my chest. Fans shouted out song titles and made requests. The band members nodded and smiled at each other while they played the beginning riffs of several hits. A shouted chorus of "PIERCE" shook the arena in anticipation of the last band member appearing. My heart thumped in my throat and my mouth became dry. I licked my lips.

My Adonis swaggered onto the stage wearing tight brown leather pants, his chest and feet bare. While I observed him cross the stage, I found it difficult to breathe and became lightheaded, but I couldn't take my eyes off him. He looked the same as the last time I'd seen him, except for the hints of grey in his hair and the many colourful images decorating his body. Pierce's midriff, arms and back displayed the contradictions of Pierce Fleming: demons having sex with angels, daggers filling in for the stems of pretty flowers, and peace signs intertwined with pentagrams.

I took in the sight of him—the long silky brown hair, dark blue polished nails, black eyeliner and the silver pentagram pendant strung on black suede, resting in the hollow of his chest. He opened his inviting mouth and began to sing *Fast and Easy*, the crowd grew still and silent but soon began to sway. Pheromones filled my nostrils while the heat of the arena increased with every note he sang. When the tempo got faster and the lyrics wilder, people willingly embraced and accepted whoever they could get their hands on. With their bodies close, they danced, kissed and swapped partners. I joined in the fun, making-out with strangers to the right and left of me.

During the first guitar solo, Pierce paced the stage and women around me flashed him. Some concert goers threw flowers, which he kissed and tossed back into the crowd, causing quickly resolved mayhem. Some fans were lifted and passed along by hundreds of palms being caressed by the crowd.

After that first song, Pierce bent down to take a swig of whatever he had in the glass by the microphone, and that's when he noticed me. Our eyes locked. He couldn't possibly remember me, could he? He couldn't. There were probably so many like me. Countless one-night stands during the last twenty years.

"I love New York!" Pierce yelled into the crowd, his soft, full lips and dark voice dripped with sex. "Introduce yourself to the person next to you and start the love, the lust, the hate, the love..." He began to sing.

Screaming and applause followed. Pierce strutted around the stage, occasionally reaching down to high-five fans. I stood, laser-focused on him, as the surrounding crowd writhed. I could sense his energy pulling me toward him, and my hands began to shake. Every song reminded me of his hungry wet kisses and strong rough hands.

After the last song, while the audience called for an encore, a security guard whisked a bunch of us backstage, eerily similar to my experience twenty years ago. I heard the band close with *Yesterday's Storm*—one of my personal favourites—and I listened as the audience sang along with Pierce.

The band members walked backstage and passed us entering their separate dressing rooms. I slipped a guard two hundred dollars, and he knocked on Pierce's door. The dressing room door opened enough for the guard to stick his head in the room. I heard two hushed voices.

Opening the door all the way, the guard motioned me toward a white-cushioned daybed at the far wall. The door shut behind me while I walked through the room, sat on the bed, and crossed my long, tanned legs. I gazed at Pierce's back as well as his reflection in the vanity mirror where he sat rubbing off his makeup with cream and a towel. My reflection could be seen in the mirror, as well.

I studied my face; the same one I had been staring at for many years. I hadn't aged. Twenty years had passed but I still appeared not one day older than eighteen. He glanced back at me, his hot and powerful presence could render me helpless, melting me into the bed where I sat, if I didn't stay vigilant and in control.

He turned in his chair to face me.

"What's your name, angel?" he asked.

"Melissa," I said.

He maintained firm eye contact with me.

"I know you, don't I?" Pierce asked.

I smiled and shrugged.

"San Francisco?"

"Besides the tattoos and grey hair, you look the same as when we last met. Do you dye your hair grey to pretend you're actually aging?" I giggled.

His face grew red and jaw rigid. He stood and walked the three feet to stand menacingly over me.

"Who are you?"

Sitting perfectly still, I wondered if he remembered me and sensed how strong I had become since we parted. I waited all these years to meet with him again, gaining the strength I needed to get what I want from him. I was at least as strong as Pierce Fleming now, if not more.

"I'm no one. I'm just here for you," I cooed and

reached for his hand.

He relaxed his posture and sat down next to me. I touched his face and his lips and moved closer to him. I shivered as we began to kiss.

At eighteen, I lost my virginity to Pierce Fleming and afterwards he left me for dead. He was tender and sweet, at first, during my first sexual encounter. But then the mood changed. Pierce lost control and became a feral demon, draining all the strength and breathing all the life out of me. But I clung to life and I woke up in a shallow grave in the woods a few days later. I was very much alive, but forever changed. I didn't feel cold or tired, only strangely hungry and not for food. There was no desire for family, friends, food or water. My new instincts took over and told me what I needed to survive. All I needed was sex. I had become the same creature as my Adonis.

I adjusted to my new life easily and I got used to the casualties I caused along the way, until I gained the strength to control my powers.

Now I was with him again, but this time I was in charge. Nearing the end of this sexual encounter, I straddled him, and he held on to my waist. His green eyes started glossing over, and his breathing became shallow.

I bent down and whispered in his ear. "Do you remember me, Pierce? Michelle. You left me for dead."

His filmy eyes widened in recognition and he went pale.

"You didn't have to kill me. I would've followed you anywhere. You could've made me what I am now, but you didn't."

He blinked rapidly and tried to push me off him, but he lacked the strength or true desire to regain control. He held on to me tightly, as I had held him the same way many years ago, knowing he was slipping away but not wanting and unable to let me go. When I climaxed with pleasure, his arms fell to his side and his breathing became shallow and erratic. My hands tenderly stroked his chest and my lips covered his magnificent face with kisses while I patiently waited to fully possess him and inhale his last dying breath deep into my body.

A Cup Full of Tears

by James Dorr

"What kind of name is Asenath, anyway?" Carmilla asked. "That is, for a pretty girl like you?"

"It's from the Bible," the younger woman said. "The wife of Joseph in Egypt, from the Old Testament. My father was into the Bible a lot."

"He's dead now, though, you said?"

Asenath nodded. "Yes," she answered.

Carmilla knew Asenath had been crying. She had seen her across the restaurant as soon as she came in, alone in a shadowed booth near the kitchen, a notebook open on the table. Two coffee cups, one a demitasse style. The other, in front of the woman—really almost still a girl, in her late teens, perhaps—nearly full with an herb tea diluted with tears.

Carmilla could smell tears.

Carmilla glanced once again at the notebook, reading the latest lines upside down, the ink they were written in still glistening wet. "That's not bad poetry," she finally said. "But so bleak, so hopeless…"

Asenath's eyes welled again. She picked her cup up

and tilted her head, as if to read the leaves in its bottom—not that they didn't actually use tea bags for even the most expensive blends these days. More wet drops splashed into it, putting it in danger of overflowing.

"He wasn't worth it," Carmilla said. "That is, the poetry, the other cup empty but yours scarcely touched, the state you're in now. Take it from me, whoever the boy was, he wasn't worthy of someone like you. Trust me on this—I know."

Not that Carmilla had not been dumped once herself, but that had been a long time ago. And things had changed since.

In fact, that was why she had been cruising the city's better class restaurants this night. One of the restrictions of Carmilla's kind was that every few decades she needed to seek a younger companion—but what golden chains these were! She surveyed again the scene before her, the booth dark, in a corner, almost unnoticed. Its occupant glowing with youthful health. With life.

"Asenath," she said. She smelled, again, the tears, but underneath that both a fright and an anger. A sort of uncertainty, yet a hope also, blending with smells of meat from the kitchen. Of sauces and liquors.

"Asenath," she said, "you know you're beautiful. Don't put down the fact you're a brunette, your hair almost black. Look at my own hair! And your eyes like mine, both dark, deep-set, shining when light hits them properly. I bet you don't even have to use makeup."

Asenath looked up. Carmilla knew this was a delicate moment—she smiled reassuringly.

"Believe me," she said, her eyes gazed into the other's. "It's us *brunettes* that have more fun."

Asenath giggled in spite of herself. "How old are you really, Carmilla?" she asked. "I mean, you sound so worldly, so…well…experienced. And the way you're dressed, so elegant. Yet to look at you—your face—your figure—I mean, I'm eighteen, but you're what? At most in your early twenties."

Carmilla smiled again, conscious this time of the tip of a tooth glinting momentarily in the candlelight, contrasting whitely with dark crimson lips. A joke flashed through her mind—"long in the tooth." Maybe.

She touched Asenath's hand. "Several centuries at least," she answered.

"You're joking," the other said. But this time she laughed.

Carmilla took both her hands in her own. She stroked them gently, her fingers straying at times to the wrists. To the lower arms, bared for the evening like hers to the shoulder, the shoulders bare also, but not in a gown but rather a tube top.

"A little upgrading in fashion," she said. "An improvement in bearing. You know, Asenath, it wouldn't take much. You could be just like me. And then if a boy like that, like the one who broke up with you here, should ever mistreat you in any way again…" She smiled more broadly, purposely letting her teeth show this time. "Well, you would not need such boys."

Asenath drew back.

"But what about daytime?" Asenath asked. "I mean, going out in the sun. Swimming. The beach."

"It is moonlight swims that are the most romantic. And there's beauty, too, that must be considered. You, as I, have nearly perfect skin, pale and seductive. Why would one wish to ruin it with sunburn?"

"But will it *hurt*?" Asenath asked, but relaxing, too.

It was almost ended.

"A little, perhaps," Carmilla said. "But first…"

She bent down, suddenly, raking her teeth across her own left wrist, her other hand upending the dregs of the demitasse over the floor, then holding it underneath, letting it refill with red.

"Now," she said, gazing in Asenath's eyes once more, setting the brimming cup between them, "you are to think of this as a kind of elixir. You'll find it pleasant—

a little like V-8 juice in flavour, but meatier. You can mix it with vodka too. A 'bloody Carmilla'? But you wouldn't want to. The thing is, though, first I must drink my fill of yours."

Asenath winced but only slightly as Carmilla went on, taking her hands again. "One thing to remember, you will no longer age. Rather your attractiveness will continue as it is now, but enhanced. More enticing. A magnet for men, if you will—or women. You do like me, don't you?"

Asenath nodded.

Carmilla pushed the cup nearer to Asenath, taking care to spill none of its contents.

"Remember, just after me—beauty cures all things."

Asenath nodded, leaning her torso across the table. She stretched her neck forward to welcome Carmilla's kiss.

Prey

by James Lipson

As far back as Eddie could remember, he had always liked young girls. Unfortunately, this didn't change as he grew older. He knew what he was. Eddie was sick, a monster, the worst society has to offer: a paedophile.

There was something wrong with him, but he didn't care. He learned very early that what he felt was abominable and depraved. Eddie became adept at disguising his true feelings; he became quite proficient at hiding them from the world.

No matter how clever he believed himself to be, Eddie got caught and was summarily punished. He spent 16 years in prison, long, monotonous days trailed by scream-filled nights. It took him a bit longer than most to understand prison "rules," but eventually he did. Not that he and his fellow "pedos" had much, if any, interaction with prisoners outside of their protected cage. His fellow lowest-rung mates disgusted him as much as he did the general population.

He had never planned to kill the little girl, but she made so much noise with her screaming and crying. She was a wild banshee, just the two of them in an empty room that echoed from the quietist of sounds. His plan was to hold the pillow over her face for a few moments. Eddie lost track of time until he found she was no longer struggling beneath his pressing hands. Her legs and arms had stopped kicking and flailing, her left hand relaxed and the jump-rope released, lying tangled on the floor.

A decade and a half later, Eddie left a semi-free man. He, of course, had to register as a sex offender, keep at least 500 yards from schools, and have no contact with anyone under 18. After a year in a halfway house, where he followed the conditions of his release, Eddie was finally allowed to procure his own home.

The state placed a sign on his new front lawn in bold lettering: "Sexual Predator." At least the glaring announcement that he was a sexual deviant saved him the frightening prospect of door-to-door greetings.

Even before he had moved in, they knew what he was. There were, of course, many neighbourhood meetings, city council sessions and even a few late-night gatherings with beer-infused declarations of vigilante justice.

Eddie worked from home. The only reason he left his cocoon was for food and alcohol, simplified by the proximity of Walmart, only a few blocks from his house.

Twenty-four-hour markets are a godsend for like-minded night owls. Once a week, between 2 a.m. and 3 a.m., usually Thursdays, Eddie made his way down a still and quiet Maplewood Drive.

The neighbours never caught sight of him, nor he of them. Everyone liked it that way, mostly Eddie. A caseworker would come by, unannounced, to check on him, but that was the only visitor who ever knocked on his door. The sign in his yard did wonders for keeping salesmen and religious zealots at bay.

His parents had disowned him during the trial and never once came to visit him in prison. It was probably for the best, because his parents were strict Apostolic Christians, and Eddie, well Eddie didn't believe in anything. He had nothing in common with them or their beliefs; he simply didn't believe in God or Satan. For him, that dogma was meant to keep children in line, and adult pocketbooks open and giving.

Two years had passed since Eddie moved into his home on Maplewood Drive. Over three years removed from prison, three years without incident, three years absent any interaction with kids, three years of living his life like a hermit on a forgotten mountain in a land that was difficult to pronounce.

What hadn't passed was his desires. Oh no, they were

still there and as strong as ever. But with the internet and the deep web just a few clicks away, Eddie kept his monsters contained (most of the time).

In all the time he had lived on Maplewood Drive, he never saw any neighbourhood children playing near his house. And while this was better for everyone who lived there, especially Eddie, he often dreamed about seeing kids at play. He missed their sounds of running and playing, screaming and shouting, the wide-eyed innocence that only the very young – and the mentally challenged – possess.

Early one Friday morning, as he made his way to Walmart, he noticed a "for sale" sign two houses down and across the street. He knew an elderly couple had lived there, but he could only assume that one or both of them had recently died. He had no one to ask.

After Eddie returned from shopping and was safely locked inside his house, he consulted Zillow to see what information he could gather on the house. Nothing much; it was a typical three-bedroom ranch-style home, where every room was in desperate need of an update. Unless, of course, you appreciated the fustiness of a 1974 home resplendent with dirty earth tone shag carpet, sunken living rooms, depressing yellow linoleum, fake wood panelling, and appliances that were old ages ago. There was a two-car detached garage with a modest work area in the back that appeared cluttered and well-used over the decades. Eddie was mildly annoyed that the house had no swimming pool to attract young families.

He hoped that a family, rather than some empty nesters, would buy the house, but he put it out of his mind. He didn't think about it again until three weeks later, when he heard an 18-wheeler rumbling down the street at 11:30 p.m.

What an odd time to move, he thought. Peering through the shades, he watched as the truck backed up to the open garage. Two large, dark-skinned men jumped out of the cab and immediately started to unload the semitruck. With only a 60-watt outdoor garage light to illuminate their work, Eddie couldn't tell what was being moved in from his position across the street and two houses down. Strain as he might, he simply couldn't see if there was any children's furniture among the contents.

It took only 23 minutes for the men to clear out the truck, get back in the cab and drive away in the opposite direction from which they came. *There is no way they unloaded a full three bedrooms' worth of furniture in just over 20 minutes*, Eddie mused.

The next day, he noticed the "for sale" sign had been taken down, and new blackout shades had been installed in every window of the house. Eddie knew intimately how important privacy was, so he thought nothing of this being the new owners' first priority. For two weeks, he saw no movement in or around the house.

With his late-night work schedule and aversion to people, he assumed he was just missing their comings and goings, and they, his. Finally, Eddie saw a child's jump-rope on the new neighbours' driveway. He could not believe his luck. *Oh please, let it be a little girl*, he pleaded to himself. It struck him as odd that he hadn't noticed it before. Normally, when kids are outside playing, everyone knows it, but Eddie had heard nothing.

Two days passed without any change in the position or location of the jump-rope. When it was time for his weekly trip to Walmart, in an effort to avoid suspicion, he stayed on his side of the street for as long as possible. He only crossed to turn the corner and enter the Walmart parking lot from the side.

He made his normal purchases, with one exception: This time, Eddie purchased a camera with a telephoto lens. He permitted himself to buy the best camera he could afford, but more importantly, he made sure he was getting the most zoom his bank account would allow. He couldn't wait to get home and try it.

Silently walking back home, he crossed the street

five houses early, making sure that if anyone were watching, they would see him on his side of the street (not that anyone would be watching him at 2:45 in the morning). Passing the neighbours' house, he saw that the jump-rope was gone from the driveway!

Of all the bad luck in the world, he fumed. Why did it have to happen when he was gone? Had he not been so upset about who had moved the jump-rope, it may have occurred to him that they did so at 2:30 in the morning. *Damn it, why do I have all the bad luck?*

Eddie couldn't wait to unpackage his new camera. He read the manual from cover to cover, twice, just to make sure he knew exactly how to capture the pictures he was already seeing in his mind. Turning off the lights, he opened the living room window a crack, hoping to hear something, anything. He had to rest his elbow on his knees to steady his shaking hands. He raised the camera to his left eye while closing his right, adjusting the focus, and there she was!

A 6-7-year-old girl was skipping rope in her driveway, humming a tune he couldn't quite make out. *Finally,* Eddie thought, his luck was turning. His camera unflinchingly pointed at her as he watched her skip rope for 10 minutes. Not once did she stop humming, and not once could Eddie decipher it.

His arms were getting tired from holding the camera in place, and just as he set it down, he could have sworn he saw the little girl look in his direction and smile. *Must be my imagination*, he thought. Taking just a moment for the blood to flow back into his arms, Eddie once again lifted the camera to his face. She was gone. The jump-rope was haphazardly strewn on the front lawn, but that was all. His newly found toy had gone inside.

Eddie vigilantly watched for her to appear again for the next four nights. Much to his disappointment, she did not. He was starting to fall behind in his work, spending far too much time looking for her. His anticipation was building, coming on like a fast-moving wave inevitably crashing violently toward a razor sharp, coral encrusted shoreline.

He changed his routine; instead of his normal weekly visit to Walmart, Eddie made two –sometimes three— trips. This enabled him to walk past her house more often, peering out the corner of his eye for any movement.

Finally, it happened. He saw her again! He heard her before he saw her this time, but, once again, he couldn't quite make out the song she was softly singing. From his side of the street, Eddie glanced over; suddenly, she stopped. Holding the jump-rope limply at her side, she stared directly at him. Only the garage light behind her illuminated the scene. Eddie couldn't quite make out her features, but he could see that she was wearing a summer dress, had two shoulder length pigtails, and quite possibly saddle shoes. He didn't have enough time or light to make out any other details.

Eddie turned back to look at her. He didn't break stride. He didn't say a word but felt as if a bolt of lightning had passed through his body as he gazed upon her. By the time he reached his house, he was desperately clinging to the remnants of reason. Up the street, he heard a giggle.

Unlike the pure mirth of a child, this laughter reverberated with a dark resonance that shook Eddie to his core. Back inside the safety of his house, he dropped his packages and quickly grabbed his camera. Lifting one of the blinds, he held up the camera and focused.

She was still there! She wasn't skipping rope any longer; she was facing his house and staring directly at him. He hastily let the blinds drop as he realised he was holding his breath. Ten minutes passed before Eddie dared to look again. The street was now empty, her jump-rope bundled against the garage door.

How on earth could she have seen me, Eddie thought while lying in bed that night. He ran through it over and over. He was careful, as always. He had turned off all the lights, inside and out, and had only lifted one blind an inch or two, at most.

Eddie was transfixed with this young girl. He lay awake staring at his ceiling the rest of the night; sleep finally overtook him at 8 the next morning. At 5 p.m. that day, he finally woke up to the sound of his neighbour mowing the lawn.

Not wanting to draw attention to himself or his house, Eddie peered through the string holes in the blinds to see if *she* was outside. No luck. Eddie wanted nothing more than to see her during the day. Was she a blonde, a brunette or a redhead? Did she have freckles? What colour was her dress? What types of dresses did she wear? Was she dark skinned or light? He had so many questions and so few answers.

Five more agonizing days went by. Eddie felt like he would crawl out of his skin if he didn't see her soon. That night (or more accurately, the next morning) he was looking through his camera when he saw her saunter from behind a tree and pick up her jump-rope. She didn't start skipping, though; she picked it up and walked to the end of the driveway and waved.

Holy Mother of God! She's waving at me, Eddie realised. He almost dropped the camera in his haste to move away from the window. His mind was whirling; he wasn't sure what to do next. Should he go out and actually talk to her, or should he stay inside the safety of his home? Should he peek through the blinds again? He didn't know what to do. Moving to the far left window in his living room, he once again looked through the shades. Eddie was concentrating so hard on her house, he almost didn't see her standing on the sidewalk in front of his!

He froze. There she was, still holding her jump-rope but remaining perfectly still on the sidewalk. He stared at her dreamily. He couldn't make out her features in the darkness. Then she spoke, "Hey mister, want to come out and play?"

There was no mistaking it: She was talking to him, and she wanted him to come outside and join her. What to do? He did not want to go back to prison, but she was right there, within his grasp, if only he could move. *Who would blame me?* Eddie reasoned. Dropping the blind, he moved excitedly toward the front door. Keeping his hand on the doorknob for what seemed an eternity, he finally released the deadbolt, the chain and the door lock. He felt like Dorothy opening her door to find a colourfully magical land awaiting discovery. Slowly, he opened the door and peered outside. She was gone.

Taking a few steps outside, he could see that there

was no one there. The street was empty, as always. Worse, gone was the glorious ray of sunshine in an otherwise abysmally dark and bleak cavern.

Eddie headed back inside, carefully locking the door. Turning, he saw her. She was standing in his house! He gasped, like a 1950s cartoon mother who saw a mouse.

"Whaaat, what are you doing in here?" Eddie asked in a cracked and splintering voice.

"Oh Eddie, you know why I'm here," she responded.

What the hell? How does she know my name, and how did she sneak in here? He thought almost out loud. "I don't understand," Eddie stammered.

"Yes, you do," the little girl said.

"But, I…"

Before he could finish, she started skipping her rope toward him while singing "ashes, ashes, we all fall down." As he backed away, Eddie realised this was not going to end the way he had fantasised.

"Well, Harry, now we have two houses on the block for sale," Fred said. He had cornered Harry as he was stepping out of his car upon returning from a two-week business trip.

"What are you talking about, Fred?" Harry replied

wearily. "The only one for sale is the old Anderson place."

"Oh, you don't know. Four days ago, that sick paedophile killed himself." Laughing, Fred continued, "Ironically enough, he hanged himself with a kids jump-rope."

A Matter of Perception

by Jason Holden

So what if his wife had left him because of it. He was a passionate man, always had been. She had stopped providing him with what he needed, so he found it elsewhere. He could guarantee she missed him more than he missed her, the kids too. No need to be quiet while he had his fun now, no danger of interruption.

Smiling, he looked down at the two women beneath him, they smiled back as the blonde one lifted his shirt, revealing his perfect, bronzed abs. The redhead reached for his trousers, undoing the buttons, and started to caress his underpants where a bulge was growing.

It had been like this since his wife packed her bags and took the kids. He had travelled the world, bedding any woman he took a fancy to. Old, young—sometimes impossibly young—you only had to know where to look; what keywords to know on your search for something out of the ordinary.

He'd lost his job over his hobby. So what! He didn't

need their money; he had everything he needed right here. Looking around the room he found himself in, he was pleased. It was well lit. The women had their makeup done to perfection. Yes, this was a good one.

The show was starting to heat up now, and he looked back down. The redhead had hold of his penis and was about to put her well painted lips around it.

Blackness. No power. Yet that shouldn't be; he kept it plugged in at all times to avoid just this.

It was hard to see after removing the headset. His eyes had to adjust to reality again. Clumsily, he undid the straps and removed the neural network jack from his neck. Stepping from the chair, his body crumpled, so unused were his legs to supporting the weight of his body.

The room was dark, the thick curtains drawn across the tiny window letting in hardly any light as he crawled to the bed. Thin, wasted arms supported his legs as he pushed himself almost upright. His spine had become curved from hours in the chair, and protruded from his back. Rather than reaching for the curtains, he went for the light switch. It clicked but still no light came.

Sweeping the lank hair from his eyes, he climbed onto the bed, almost like a dog would. Two arms first, bracing. Then a hop with the back ones to bring his whole self up. Drawing back the curtains brought a swirl of dust.

It danced in the light as he flinched from the brightness, shielding his eyes with bony hands.

Tossing aside old ready meal trays and filthy clothes, he searched for his phone, panic building inside him. This couldn't happen, he needed electricity. Needed to get back to his women, they needed him. Needed him to please them.

He made his way around the small apartment, supporting himself on various chairs or tables where he could. Nearing the door, a small table tipped over as he leant on it, and he sprawled to the floor sending the letters that lay piled around the base of the door flying with the force of his fall. The letters were all marked with red.

A pounding sounded from the door, followed by a voice.

"This is it, Mr White, you've had plenty of time. You're being evicted."

The lock clicked open as the super used his keys. Strong hands grasped him around the arms, and he was lifted clear of the apartment. It would have been easy, for his body was all but wasted away. Sobbing, he was turned out into the street and the door closed behind him. He missed his girls, so many of them he'd never had. What would he do without his girls?

Mermaid at War

by Jessica Chanese

"The mermaid is rallying her people, Sire," the young page reported from the doorway of Troian's chambers. "They're preparing for battle." Hesitating, he added, "Her people breached our borders, sir. They collected the satyr woman and child. Disposed of three Sorcerers' Guild guards in the process."

The boy's gaze never strayed from his feet when in the Sorcerer King's presence. He didn't see the bony hand before it rapped him hard on the back of his head.

"*People* is an overly generous term, child. They are but creatures. Creatures who exist only because of our race's ingenuity," Kesper chided.

The Sorcerer King's Advisor enjoyed asserting his dominance over the young pages. Troian found Kesper's self-important ramblings tiresome. Settled in his usual spot at the polished walnut table near his room's largest window, Troian pinched the bridge of his nose in annoyance. Kesper never failed to test his patience with his endless posturing. He would have expected his Advisor to have learned his lesson by now—Kesper found himself thrown against the castle's stone walls more than a time or two when Troian's irritation boiled over—but the Sorcerer King's reprimands proved ineffective. Kesper's end would come soon. Once the mermaid was finally *dealt* with, Troian's Advisor would no longer be needed.

Galen strode into Briarwood's library, where the mermaid had established her command center. He found Nia sitting in her desk chair with her legs tucked under her, hips resting on the heels of bare feet. She scowled at documents arrayed across the marble desktop while absentmindedly twirling loose jet-black braids.

Galen waited near the library's entrance for Nia to acknowledge his arrival. He watched as she tugged on her tunic's collar as if it were spun from burlap instead of filmy cotton. She drummed her feet against her chair in a cadence mirroring the splashing of a tail. Every window was thrown open wide, no doubt to usher in the scent of saltwater and occasional misting of sea spray from the waters below. Galen suppressed a chuckle. No matter how well Nia carried herself in her human form, she was of the sea. There was an impression of absurdity in her trying to appear at ease on land.

The mermaid finally looked up from her reports. "What news do you bring?"

"The satyr's family has been returned to their dwelling, Queen Commander. They suffered at the Sorcerers' Guilds hands, but they survived."

The mermaid nodded. "Casualties?"

The head of her elite guard hesitated for an instant. Nia braced herself for his words.

"Injuries, mostly minor. With the exception of two deaths. My people are notifying their families now," Galen informed her.

Nia stood abruptly, shoving her chair aside then stalking to one of the open windows. She stared down at the waves crashing against the cliffs of Rose Isle, breathing deeply as gulls cried in the distance.

"This can't stand, Galen. I need to put an end to the sorcerers' tyranny. I haven't done enough."

"It's only been two months, Nia. Nobody expects you to have brought Dravkar to its knees in such a short time. You've pulled traitors up by their roots, showing them magnanimity while honouring justice. With your guidance, we've uncovered and dismantled a number of Troian's schemes. Your command has seen us through several skirmishes with minimal loss of life. Each day, you spend hours poring over intelligence, planning our best defence. Neris has never been so unified. You're doing all you can, and doing it well at that," Galen reassured her.

Nia's features hardened. "It's not good enough, Galen. Not when our people are losing their lives to the Sorcerers' Guild—*any* of our people. I don't care if the loss is *minimal*," Nia spat the last word as if it tasted bitter on her tongue. Her knuckles lightened as she strengthened her grip on the windowsill. "Not when Troian is still sitting in his tower unscathed, basking in his wealth and power while all but the richest of his people starve," the mermaid continued. "I've had enough of waiting around for the Sorcerers' next move, enough waiting to see what part of Neris they'll attack next."

Nia faced Galen then. "It's time. We're done waiting. Before the new moon, we bring the fight to their door." The mermaid's tone brooked no argument.

Galen knew better than to question his Queen Commander when the call of battle blazed in her eyes. Instead, he bowed in submission, adding, "As you wish, Queen Commander," before making his retreat.

When Nia's temper flared as it had during her exchange with Galen, returning to the sea calmed her like nothing else could. She fled to Briarwood's beach as soon as he'd left her, seeking the seawater's embrace. Gliding through the cool waters of the ocean's deepest pockets, the mermaid lost herself in her thoughts.

Just two months had passed since Queen Saraya's assassination at the hands of one of her own subjects. Barely two cycles of the moon since Saraya named Nia as her successor. Her whole world had changed in one night; her days before Saraya's death were hazy memories of another lifetime.

The mermaid questioned her Queen's decision at first but understood it in time. Defending Neris and serving its people was Nia's lifeblood. There was no one more devoted to the nation of the Alchemia and its ideals, no citizen better equipped to lead Neris as it fought for its sovereignty. Neris' populace validated Saraya's judgment when they voted overwhelmingly for Nia to retain her post as Queen Commander. The election was held after the standard royal mourning period, and by then, Nia had proved herself worthy of the role beyond any doubt. She was the first leader of Neris to hold dual titles as the nation's Queen and the leader of its military. Their slain Queen chose well.

The mermaid's grief for Saraya, her dear friend as well as her Queen, was as fresh as it was the night she'd held the dying royal in her arms. Nia's blood still ran hot when she thought of how the beloved Fae ruler was betrayed by one of her inner circle, but she knew the Dravkar sorcerers were Neris' real enemy. Adding to a centuries-long list of sins against the Alchemia clans, the sorcerers had captured Samuel's family, using them as leverage to assure the Queen's assassination. The mermaid showed the traitor mercy, allowing him to serve a life-sentence in Neris' prison instead of ordering his execution. She also made certain Samuel's wife and son were rescued from the Sorcerers' Guild's clutches. Their extraction cost Nia two soldiers under her command, but saving the boy and his mother was necessary. They were innocents with the misfortune of becoming pawns in Troian's games. She wouldn't let citizens of Neris suffer at the sorcerers' hands, no matter the indiscretions of their kin.

Nia swam for hours, fragments of the recent past— Saraya's face as she lay dying, Samuel crying for mercy at her feet, Galen relaying the ongoing toll of Dravkar's treachery on Neris' people—*Nia's people*— flashing through her consciousness. It was long after dark when she returned to Briarwood. The ocean cooled her battle lust but had done little to brighten her outlook. The mermaid knew she would not be at peace until Neris was

safe from the Sorcerers' Guild's evils, safe from the sadistic machinations of Dravkar's Sorcerer King. Only when Troian no longer lived would Nia's soul find true respite.

"Shall I call for your tonic, my lord? Or, would you prefer relief of a...*different nature*?" Kesper's tone turned lurid, insinuating a closeness with Troian he had not earned. But while his delivery tried Troain's patience, his suggestion was welcomed. Perhaps pleasure of the flesh would help to take his mind off their temporary defeat.

He rewarded his Advisor with a brisk nod, sending Kesper scurrying into the hall to retrieve Troian's concubines. Members of Dravkar's wealthiest families routinely offered themselves to the Sorcerer King. He selected only the most physically perfect among them, and the most compliant, to join his harem. It was a high honour to be chosen to appease Troian's lustful appetites.

Kesper returned followed by two of Troian's favourite consorts, a nubile young woman called Rinalda and a well-built young man named Rheome. They sauntered toward Troian in unison, each taking the sorcerer by the hand and guiding him onto the silken sheets of his bed.

"Leave us!" Troian commanded Kesper.

The Sorcerer King's willing servants disrobed and crawled onto his bed, wasting no time in relieving their master of his robes. Rheome moved behind Troian, massaging his shoulders with sure fingers. Straddling her master, Rinalda's delicate hands urged the old sorcerer to lie back against the hard planes of Rheome's chest.

"We will relieve you of any worries, my lord. Rest and let us serve you," Rinalda purred.

Troian let his eyelids close, concentrating on the sensations of Rinalda's breasts brushing against him; her tongue trailing down his chest, teasing the sensitive skin along his inner thighs; of Rheome's strong hands kneading his tensions away. The Sorcerer King tried to lose himself in the soft flesh and solid muscle of his attendants, but he couldn't shake his fury with the mermaid.

As Rheome and Rinalda worked, the Sorcerer King's thoughts drifted to the insolent creature who somehow thwarted him at each turn. He imagined the mermaid in chains of iron, naked and unable to change forms. His breathing deepened as the image crystallised. Her eyes were empty, her skin dull and cracking, every part of her dry and aching.

Maybe he would keep her prisoner by the sea,

taunting her with refuge so near yet unreachable. How he would delight in her pain; what pleasure he would take from crushing her rebellious spirit. He would break her, Troian promised himself. He would watch her crumble before him, begging for her life and the lives of the cretants under her rule. And when she begged, he would end her.

Troian's breath quickened; his hips thrust in time with Rinalda's ministrations. It was the mermaid's voice he heard escape his concubine's lips when she moaned his name. When the Sorcerer King brought Rheome's mouth crashing onto his, devouring him with teeth and tongue and no care except for his own desires, it was the salt of a mermaid's blood he tasted. When Rinalda cried out as she crested her peak, Troian imagined the mermaid pleading for his mercy. His climax came while envisioning the desperation of the mermaid's last moments.

The mermaid's time was coming; the end of her reign was inevitable. Troian would make sure of it. Then he would bring the repulsive Alchemials to heel, restoring the natural order of things and making their subservience permanent.

The Sorcerer King slept then, sated by his concubines' attentions, and dreamt once more of the mermaid's demise at his hand.

In the still darkness of midnight, Nia, flanked by her personal guard and a band of Neris' top-tier soldiers, boarded the Sorcerers' Guild ship in silence. The mermaid delayed their attack longer than she would have liked in order to align it with Troian's journey by sea to a neighbouring nation he hoped to gain as an ally in Dravkar's war against Neris. He was travelling on a low-level merchant's ship, intending to mislead those who wished him harm, but was unable to evade Neris' intelligence operatives. The advantage of Nia fighting Troian in her element, surrounded by the crashing waves of the sea, couldn't be overstated. It was well worth the wait to make the Sorcerer King's defeat that much more certain.

The mermaid's forces secured the ship's crew and disposed of Troian's guards with lethal efficiency, clearing a path to below deck for their Queen Commander. Only Galen would be accompanying Nia when she confronted the Sorcerer King. The mermaid was adamant she would be the one to dispatch Troian, or die trying.

Nia moved quickly and soundlessly down the steps and through the narrow corridors leading to the Sorcerer

King's sleeping quarters. Galen followed. The reports indicated Troian was travelling with a small entourage consisting of his recently deceased personal security detail, his Advisor, and two concubines. Nia and Galen passed two doors that they believed to be Troian's companions' chambers and the entrance to a galley kitchen before reaching a broad door at the hallway's end. Nia signalled for Galen to fall back and clear the other rooms. She pulled her dagger from its sheath at her waist before kicking down Troian's door and crossing the short distance to the Sorcerer King's bed. She froze when she found only slivers of moonlight streaming onto empty sheets.

"Dammit!" Nia cursed when a sweep of the space confirmed it was uninhabited.

She heard Galen utter a similar sentiment and assumed he, too, had found only empty chambers.

"Queen Commander! Captain! There's a rowboat making an escape!" one of Nia's guards shouted.

Nia sprinted to the top deck, shedding garments and weapons as ran. She vaulted over the ship's rail, transforming in mid-air. The mermaid surged from the waves a few feet from the Sorcerer King's boat, propelling herself above the water and slashing her tail in Troian's direction. The deadly spines protruding from the

Nia's fins caught the light of the moon and stars as they sailed toward their target. Troian roared as the weapons created by his own people raked across his gut.

The blow's force knocked him into the water. Nia dived after him. She was vaguely aware of Galen shouting and Troian's companions shrieking as she swam after her wounded enemy.

Nia caught up to Troian easily, baring her teeth in a terrible smile as she hooked her arm around the Sorcerer King's throat.

As the mermaid descended with the Sorcerer King thrashing against her grasp, two forms appeared in the water above them. A net dragged behind them. Troian's concubines. Nia sensed the iron fibres woven into the net just before they released it directly over her head. The mermaid had to twist and change direction abruptly to avoid being trapped in the poisonous mesh, inadvertently releasing Troian as she did.

By the time Nia swam back to the ocean's surface, Troian's consorts were hoisting him into the rowboat. The Advisor, Kesper, stood in its bow, aiming a crossbow at Nia. She was sure its bolts were iron, and they would be spelled not to miss.

She paused for barely an instant, but it cost her. With water and blood streaming down his body in rivulets,

Troian reached for his staff and swirled it in the air with a word. The rowboat and its passengers vanished, but not before Troian could flash Nia a smile of his own, one promising violence and vengeance.

Fuming, Nia returned to the abandoned Sorcerers' Guild ship. She stood on the deck naked in her human form, trembling with rage. The bastard would pay for this. Neris would not relent until its sovereignty was secured and tyrants like Troian were eliminated. Nia's battle against Troian was only beginning, and she *would* be victorious.

Aramis and Shelby

by Catherine Kenwell

The smell of leather and cologne compelled Dany to glance up from her computer.

"Well, hello," she smiled at the age-chiselled countenance in front of her. "Welcome to Vintage Pearl Custom. How can we help you today?"

"That's my 1966 Shelby out front," the stranger pointed with his thumb. "It needs a paint job—the original colour is Sapphire Blue. Hard to find the service this girl's been used to since I moved to town."

Dany looked over the stranger's shoulder to the vehicle parked at the door. "Wow…nice. Yeah, we can do that for you." Her head felt a little strange, recognising the fragrance of Aramis cologne. An old-gentleman, smoky smell that brought back instant memories she couldn't pinpoint.

"Where you from?" Dany asked. She was mesmerised, but by the stranger or his car, she couldn't determine.

"North Texas," he replied, curling one side of a smile. "Uh, are you ok, ma'am? You look a little flustered."

Dany flushed even more crimson. She felt warm all over, and embarrassingly, it showed.

"Uh yeah, I'm fine," Dany stuttered. "Let me get Tom out to have a word with you."

Hearing the intercom call, Tom came out to reception, wiping his hands on a blue shop towel. "Hi, I'm Tom, and hey, that's your beauty out there?" he glanced to the car and gave a short wolf whistle.

"Hi Tom, nice to meet you, I'm Chuck. I was just telling this lovely young lady what I had in mind…for a paint job and a solid once-over." He reached out to shake Tom's hand.

The two walked outside to have a closer look, and Dany watched while one and then the other pointed and smiled at the features of the Shelby. Tom opened the driver's door and slid into the leather bucket seat, reaching up to acknowledge the car's unusual dash tachometer. One of the cool features of her dream car, she smiled to herself. God, what she would do for a car like that.

Tom and Chuck chatted as they returned to reception. Dany knew Tom loved the 60s Mustangs too, so no doubt they'd had an animated conversation.

"Dany, let's get Chuck's Shelby in sometime

towards the end of next week," he said to her. Turning to Chuck, he continued, "Chuck, you'll have to leave her with us for five or six days, for the paint and the rest of the work."

The guys shook hands again and Tom headed back to the shop.

"I'm sorry, let me formally introduce myself," Chuck bowed slightly. "It's so lovely to meet you. So tell me, when will I be seeing you again? Next week?"

Dany forced her eyes onto the computer screen. "Yes, it looks like next Thursday will work. You ok for leaving the car over the weekend?"

"Well, sure, as long as she gets the loving care and attention she needs," he smiled disarmingly.

Dany already looked forward to seeing Chuck again. When Thursday afternoon arrived, she was bent over peering at an invoice item when her heart fluttered. Aramis. That earthy, musky fragrance. She glanced up to see him, dangling a key in front of her.

"Ready or not, here we go!" Chuck laughed as he handed her the key. "Don't mind me if I'm a little nervous…she's the only lady in my life and it's kinda hard to let her out of my sight. I'm sensitive about who touches her when I'm not around."

"I'll keep an extra careful eye while it's here in the

shop," Dany smiled. "You don't need to worry about a thing. Just leave everything in my hands."

Dany wanted that car in her hands…she wanted to sit behind the wheel, feeling the leather against her skin…

Suddenly she snapped to attention, the daydream over. "Oh, and thanks, Chuck. I'll call you when it's ready," she waved as he walked out the front door.

Tom started prepping the Shelby for painting on Thursday afternoon, taping the windshield and door handles for protection, then gently sanding the paint surfaces. On Friday afternoon, he did a little tinkering under the hood; from Dany's vantage point at the front desk, it appeared there wasn't much to be done. He gently released the hood to click it shut.

"We're all ready to paint first thing Monday morning," Tom told Dany, a little chuckle escaping. "I'm excited. She's like the Mona Lisa, a real enigma…and Chuck says he's the original owner, but working on her…I just feel there's an odd history to this one. Boy, I wouldn't mind hanging on to her for longer, but we'd better get it back to Chuck. He's the kinda guy we want in this shop!"

Oh yeah, reckoned Dany, *we want him, alright.*

Chuck, and his ageless handsomeness, his Shelby, his Aramis. She squirmed in her seat when she thought of him. So unlike her, this lustful desire. The shop serviced more exquisite cars belonging to rich, powerful, good-looking men, yet she'd never felt the strange attraction she did with Chuck and his Shelby.

As dusk settled in, Tom headed out through the shop's back door. "I'll leave locking up to you, Dany, and I'll see you Monday morning. Enjoy your weekend!"

"Yep, you too!" she replied. "See you Monday."

Dany watched Tom pull around the front of the shop and exit the driveway. She smiled as the '58 Chevy truck receded into the twilight. He called her Merle, a strange name for a bright red stunner. "Good night, Merle," she whispered as she turned off the OPEN sign and double-locked the door.

Tucking her purse under her arm, she reached for and clicked off the front office light. Walking into the back of the shop, she switched on the night lighting and adjusted her eyes to the dimness. *One more look at that dream car*, she thought. *Maybe I will dream myself a Shelby tonight*, she laughed to herself.

Dany placed her hand on the driver's side door, and ran her palm along the smooth, cool metal. She slowly circled the Shelby, closing her eyes to better memorise its curves and breathing in every inch. Returning to the driver's side, she reached for the handle and opened it. She'd have to ensure she replaced the tape covering it just so, or else Tom would wonder what she'd been up to. But she simply wanted to sit in the driver's seat.

Her right foot propelled her as she slipped into the driver's seat, and the smell of leather and cologne enveloped her in an embrace. She fit perfectly into the bucket seat, like it had been hers all along. Squirming a bit to settle in, her skirt bunched up and the bare backs of her thighs were against the soft-worn animal skin. When she realised how good it felt, she wiggled a little more to increase the skin to skin contact. She relaxed her head against the headrest and placed her right palm on the gearshift. Left hand, gripping the cool steering wheel. This was her ultimate desire, unleashing the power of a Cobra high-performance V8.

Dany felt possessed, full of urges she couldn't control. The Shelby's power over her was beginning to overwhelm, and her entire body began to throb. Her right hand found its way from the gearshift to the inside of her burning thighs. She caressed the ribbed leather beneath her and brought her fingers back to her wetness. Squeezing her eyes tight, she rocked in rhythm, drinking in as much of the musky car-and-cologne as she could.

Suddenly, Dany heard a metallic click, and snapped open her eyes to a blinding bright. Someone turned on the lights! She gasped, trying to catch her breath and freezing motionless. Who was here? Her eyes shifted in the direction of the slowly advancing clip-clip-clip footsteps. If she remained still enough, whoever it was might overlook her.

The footsteps halted. Somewhere near the back of the Shelby. Had she been seen? Dany held her breath.

The intruder popped open the trunk latch and rattled around inside. Another metallic clunk, and then, silence. She stifled a gasp.

Clip, clip…Dany's glance shifted to the window, where she set her eyes on a waist, belt buckle, denim jeans. A glimpse of torso, bending in half to frame a face. Chuck.

"Well now, Dany, what might you be up to in my treasured baby?" His voice rang with a surprised humour, but he wasn't smiling.

Dany froze, feeling as awkward as a child who'd been caught doing something unbearably naughty.

"Now, Dany, don't be embarrassed," Chuck reassured her. "This isn't the first time this has happened…not at all. You're not the first woman I've come across quenching her lustful desires in my Shelby. I told you I'm sensitive about who touches her when I'm not around. This…is why."

Dany smiled weakly, still unable to speak.

"I've been in 29 states already, and it's happened every time I take her in for care."

Breathing an embarrassed sigh of relief, Dany brightened and started to speak. Chuck stopped her.

"Why do you think we've come all the way from North Texas, young lady?" he asked. "Every time, some little trollop takes it upon herself to sully my true love. Goddamn it, I know she's irresistible, but…come on, pull yourself together and we'll just pretend this never happened."

Chuck opened the door and gallantly reached for Dany's hand to help her out of the car. "There you go, miss. You can be on your way now."

Dany bent down to grab her purse, glancing at the telltale wet spot on the driver's seat as she did so. *Ugh, I hope he doesn't tell Tom*, she thought. She just couldn't face the shame, and anyway, she'd probably be fired. Maybe she'd just offer up her resignation before the shit hit the fan.

Turning to walk away, she could feel Chuck's eyes burning into the back of her head. She twisted slightly towards him, to apologise.

"Oh Chuck, I'm so sorr—"

Chuck raised the tire iron above his head. Clunk. Whacked Dany square on the back of the skull. A sickening crack, before she knew what hit her.

Dany crumpled to the floor and dark crimson began to puddle around her head.

After 29 states and almost 60 years, he was drained. The routine repeated itself—first, the sacrilege, the cleansing, then fire and brimstone. Another carnal disgrace he'd have to take care of.

"Damn," Chuck shook his head, muttering to himself. "So unbecoming, this depraved lust. You'd think they'd learn to show some respect."

L'amour L'mort

by Jo Seysener

She speared her way through the crowd. They parted for her in a great wave, bowing in deference. One had the audacity to peek up at her—*to wink*—and her lips curved. Full and dripping of promise, she fed from his anticipation, his knowing that she would deal with him later.

I watched as I always did, standing above, waiting for the carnage below. Well, it wasn't, not yet. But it would be, later.

"Like she'll be in your bed, tonight," a courtesan whispered disdainfully in the ear of the one she'd marked. He shrugged her off, irritated. She would choose tonight, just one. He needed it to be him.

That was her gift; they all believed the dream.

The mob murmured, pulling after her in a wave. Our queen. Following her was an avenue of death, but still, we lived for her. We want to die young, not to live the lives of the old. Be younger forever in the tiny death, that is the end of this life.

But she would never let us go, even after we'd given

all she asked.

Our queen was skilled in the arts of torture.

She mounted the dais, arms wide as she sucked away their life. Their dreams. But most of all, their love, their desire for her.

The void, the blackness after—heaven or hell, it doesn't matter. We love, we live, we obsess. Dance, twirling in a night that will never end. Indulging in all we want, but never may have. We are the sins.

A waiter topped my glass, never empty. Everything I could ever want. I was as jaded as the crowd, but just as obsessed as they. I was pathetic, in my lust of what they still had. I sipped my drink without tasting the flavour, observing the show below.

"You're not down there, brother, showing your…sacrifice to our beloved?"

I snorted, bubbles frothing the top of my bloodwine.

"I can only die once, *brother*. And that was many moons ago."

He smiled, drifting away to devour some poor soul who thought this would be the end of their torment, of their lust for death.

Beneath me, bodies sank into the checkerboard floor, into the soul cells below. She would feed off them tonight, every night. Some, like me, she would resurrect.

I watched her, the most beautiful thing in the world, slither up the staircase. My desire for what she held knew no bounds. I would do anything for something she would never give, though I knelt, crawled toward her. Pressed my lips to the toe of the boot she offered.

Her smile was pure decadence as she revelled in my submission. I worked my way up her boot, but she flicked the toe, rolling me like a dog. And I did it all, begging, for what she could give but would never offer.

Our queen. The greatest gift she gives is life to those who crave only death at her side.

And we live for nothing.

Lust for *Life*, or *No Job for an Ordinary Woman*

by John H. Dromey

Sandy's hair had that new car smell. Either she was fresh off the assembly line or had been hermetically-sealed in a showcase prior to deployment.

The captain euphemistically referred to her as a morale booster. He should know. She was confined to his quarters.

Subsequently, the rest of the deep-space crew had urgent needs which—according to the ship's engineer—only Sandy could satisfy.

Her first spacewalk was a one-way trip. Her android hips and attached synthetic tissue plugged the gaping hole created by a meteor striking the hull.

Safe access was restored to the galley and food storage compartments.

Lucifer's Lament

by Lyndsey Ellis-Holloway

A heavenly breeze carried the sweet scent of honeysuckle, caressing Lucifer's face with a lover's touch. A shiver of pleasure ran down his spine, and he let out a contented sigh, smiling at the memories such pleasant smells brought to him.

Her hair always carried the scent of honeysuckle. It reminded him of the first time he had seen her. Her golden skin blinding in the bright sun, glistening as she stepped out of the lake she bathed in. Droplets trickled down her curvy frame and down her long legs—even now he found himself aroused at the thought of it. A flick of her head had sent silken, raven coloured hair over her shoulder, and she had looked him dead in the eye, no fear upon her face whatsoever, as she stepped out of the water towards him.

Her dark brown eyes, mischievous and enticing, had taken hold of him and left him weaker than he would have liked to admit. Intrigued by her, intoxicated by her, Lucifer's whole world eaten away by the very thought of her. His body ached to be near her, to hear her voice and feel her fingertips against his skin. He bit his bottom lip, smiling as he let out a soft moan, imagining her hands against his stomach.

Lucifer had told her who he was, but that did not frighten her; it seemed to excite her all the more, to know that she was sleeping with the Morningstar, God's favourite son. It made everything in their interactions seem to catch fire, burning brighter, with a passion that Lucifer had never experienced before, not even with Raegul.

Raegul. His poor beloved mate, it was the guilt he felt that drove him home, that brought him back from Earth to Heaven. Raegul had suffered enough at Gabriel's hands because of him. Gabriel had pulled off her wings, because of the choice she made in becoming *his* mate, and not Gabriel's. Yet he longed to be on Earth, away from the Host and his obligations, with a woman who knew what he was but expected nothing of him.

"I'm surprised to find you here Lucifer, for a moment I wondered if you would return home at all," Raegul's tone was soft, and he flinched, noting that she had called him by his name, rather than 'my love'.

His hands moved to his lap, in an attempt to hide his body's reaction to thoughts of his lover. Lucifer refused to meet Raegul's eyes as she moved to sit beside him, his heart in his throat as he heard her sigh.

"My eyesight might be failing me Lucifer, but I am not yet blind, nor am I unobservant. You were thinking of her again, your Lilith," there was a change in tone, more scathing than usual, and Lucifer had heard the way she referred to his lover as 'your'. "Father was looking for you, he seemed to think I might know where you were, given we chose one another," she added flatly.

"Raegul." Her name on his lips felt like a betrayal, the full weight of what he must have been putting her through, hitting him like an avalanche.

"Every time you go to her, there's that niggling doubt in my mind, that this time you won't come home. I know you feel the same way, but I know you better than you know yourself Lucifer," she interjected, before he could formulate an excuse, "You don't love her. I know that. You do too, though you haven't admitted it to yourself yet, let alone to her. It's why I've tolerated your tryst— why I've never said a word—because I know you will always come home to me."

He let out a small sob, touched, and somewhat broken, by her forgiveness. Which he did not deserve. He could not look her in the eye, opting instead to lean over, resting his head upon her shoulder. His heart ached, he had hurt her—badly from the way she spoke to him—but she still loved him. Raegul was right, she always was, all of their family knew she was wisest of them, God had chosen his Angel of Judgement well.

"My poor, foolish, star," Raegul sighed, "you take your role as Light Bringer too literally my heart. You shine so brightly, that all want to be close to you. I cannot blame her for wanting you, I weep for the day when I will not be able to look into your eyes with my own. You get so swept up in living, in wishing to experience everything. Father told you to love them, to hold them dear, and I cannot blame you for spending time amongst them, and doing what he told you to," she placed her fingers under his chin, forcing him to look at her, his heart in his throat as she smiled at him. "But you've blinded yourself in the process my love, that's why you are drawn to her, so desperate to be accepted by them, you cannot see the danger you are in yourself by lowering your defences and giving into your desire for her."

Lucifer sighed, entwining his fingers with hers, raising her hand to kiss her wrist. "I do not deserve you."

"No, you bloody do not, and don't you forget it Morningstar," she chuckled.

"What did Father want, anyway?" He asked, hoping to change the subject and distract himself from the storm of emotions within his stomach.

"He didn't say, though I have a feeling that it might

have something to do with our brothers and sisters being at one another's throats. If we don't find a way to calm their fury, we will be breaking up more than just scuffles."

"I may have an idea of how to fix that, but it means me asking more from you than I already have,"

Raegul chuckled and rolled her eyes, placing a hand against his cheek, "I've never been able to deny you anything, why start now?"

"Come on, I'll tell you my plan on the way to Father."

Lilith ran the pure white feather through her fingers, eyes closed as she imagined the feel of the wings it came from. She had plucked the feather from Lucifer's wing when he slept; for an immortal being of Heaven, he did like to sleep after they made love, an almost human response to a night of passion. That amused the woman at first, though it also presented her the opportunity to take the feather, something that she could keep with her always. A part of him, for when he left her alone.

She was used to his absence, used to long periods of not seeing him, he was an Archangel, God's most favoured son, he could not ignore his duties entirely, not for her. Not yet.

Lilith hated the absences, loathed the times when he was not with her. He was unlike any man she had ever met, and rightly so given his Divinity, it was what drew her to him. The sense of power emanating from him had been palpable, and she desired it as much as she desired him.

He'd been gone far longer than usual. Lilith grew anxious at first, but that had given way to anger. He'd not even bothered to send word to her, to let her know when he would return. What of all the promises he'd made to her? He had promised to give her the world, to pull her from the poverty she lived in and ensure she lived happily. That he would show her the world and give her all she could ever want.

Lilith opened her eyes to glare at the feather in her hands. He'd abandoned her, just as Adam had. She swore, ever since her exile from the Garden, that she would find a way back to Eden, or find something better for herself. To spite her former lover, just as much as God. Ironic, that she should have fallen for God's favourite son, when God hated her so.

Lucifer promised her everything and left her with nothing. He'd been her way out of the squalor, to the power and privilege that she desired that she deserved. Her skills as a witch could only take her so far, she had to be careful, or else she would have been called out and killed, but Lucifer could have given her what she wanted without the risk!

"Lucifer! You promised me, you swore that you would help me rise from the mud! Do the words of the Morningstar mean nothing?!" she screamed, her beauty lost to her anger as she stared at the ceiling of her hut.

"I cannot give you what you want Lilith, the power you crave is not meant for humans, I was blinded by desire for you, but we were nothing more than a passing dream, a feather in the wind. We were never permanent. I am Divine, I will not age, but you will, I'm sorry."

His words echoed through her mind, but all they did was fuel her rage. He could not be with her because he was Divine? Well, she had a part of his Divinity, and she would consume it just as *she* had been consumed by *him*.

Eyes wild, Lilith stuffed the feather into her mouth, snapping the shaft with her teeth and choking down the vane. She looked almost rabid, devouring the memento she'd taken from her lover, but already she could feel the power from it, could feel his power inside her.

She swallowed it all, licking her lips and sighing in satisfaction. As it began to make its way to her stomach, Lilith could feel its warm glow from within, already feeling the difference in herself. Sadly, that euphoric feeling was short lived. Her throat felt as though it were on fire, and her eyes went wide as she began to panic. Pain roared to life from her stomach, and she felt as though she'd swallowed a hot coal.

Gasping, spluttering, Lilith clawed at her mouth, thrusting her fingers into her throat as though she could catch the feather and drag it back out. But it was too late, the damage was done. The power she longed for was hers, but not in the way she'd anticipated. The immortality she sought was hers also, but not in the way she'd desired. Her anger and hatred towards Lucifer, her sinful desire for that which was not her own, had twisted and perverted the Divinity from the feather, just as it now twisted and perverted her form. Lilith screamed as her body began to change, she might remain beautiful, but she was no longer human, she was becoming something else. Eden was lost to her forever.

Raegul and Lucifer stood, hand in hand, unseen by the tortured woman. Together they watched, witnessing the birth of something entirely new, hidden by their powers, so that Lilith was not alone, but remained unaware of her audience.

"She is no longer human, nor will she be again," Raegul said softly, "What will you call her? She is your creation after all, and even she deserves a name with which to identify herself with."

Lucifer sighed heavily, his eyes sorrowful as he watched his former lover writhe upon the floor, weeping and screaming as her bones cracked and stretched, while horns grew from beneath her raven coloured hair, and a tail sprouted from her perfectly shaped backside. Even now, with her body contorting and moulding into a new shape, he found himself aroused by her; it was difficult to cast his desire for Lilith aside.

"Demon, that is what she will be called. She will be the first of many to come, this is the fate that awaits all humans consumed by Sin."

"Demon. Will it be enough? To unite the others?"

"It will have to be. Or else what is to come will all be for nothing."

The pair stood in silence and watched Lilith's transformation a while longer. Once the changes had ceased, and the woman's wails had subsided, the Archangels turned to leave, Lucifer wrapping his arms about his mate's waist, to return them home together.

With a flick of his wings, Lucifer cast down a handful of his feathers for Lilith to find. He knew she would use them, either to strengthen herself or to change others out of spite. It was what was required if they were going to unite Heaven; their brothers and sisters required a common enemy.

Him.

It was what he deserved, his penance, for his lust for flesh and for allowing Lilith to lust for his power. Raegul would suffer, but she was prepared for that. He would have time to reflect upon his Sins, and hopefully, in some way or another, he would atone for what he had done.

The Archangel dared to look back at his lover, his gaze meeting Lilith's, time standing still as the two former lovers' eyes met. One beat of a wing, and she was gone, but the image of her anger would last an eternity, as would his sorrow.

Sanguine Enamel
by M.J. Christie

You sink canines into flesh, feel the artery pop, taste the gush of thick, red blood saturating your mouth. Your tongue laps frantically, relishing every viscous drop pumping from her sainted throat through maleficent lips.

"Lick me," she gasps. Draws her knees up, wraps her spreading legs around you, arches her back. She wants you. All of you. "Lick me, faster. Faster." Frenzied pleas you have every intention of fulfilling.

Deeper you go, above and below. You thrust and tug; engorged nipples press against you; exploring fingers bring a growl.

She will be yours. Completely. Forever.

This, you already know.

Sexcapades

by Dawn DeBraal

Avery walked past him, smelling of summer and sunshine—all things good—and Roger wanted nothing more than to destroy that light in her.

Avery lived next door to Roger in Pole's Mobile Home Park; Roger lived in lot thirteen, Avery, in twelve. There was only twenty feet between units. No trees. The sun beat down on them all day. There wasn't much to do at Poles. The swimming pool had been closed due to leaks and never repaired. From a distance it looked like the pool was still a part of Poles Mobile Home Park, but it had long since dried up.

Roger worked at an electronics store, selling computers and televisions. It was odd that he would meet his neighbour that way; she bought a laptop computer from him. When he took her credit card and read the address, he remarked that they were neighbours. Avery was a little unsettled about that, like she had lost her anonymity or something. Roger whispered to her that he could load all her programs for free, she didn't need to spend the extra three hundred dollars. He could come over that night and do it for her.

Avery again looked a little suspicious, and she told Roger she would wait and pay for the store versions.

Roger sighed. He thought he could get his foot in the door of her mobile, and maybe a little extra for his offer of free software. She seemed quite stand-offish, so Roger installed everything while she waited, charging her the additional three hundred dollars. She thanked him and politely walked out the door.

It could have been because Avery held him at arm's length…the reason she drove Roger crazy. He never understood why he lusted after her so. She brought out the worse in him. He watched her day after day like a buzzard watching roadkill, waiting for the moment he could swoop down and take her. Roger had a girlfriend—well, he *had* a girlfriend up until a couple of weeks ago; Tamara broke it off. She told him he was a chauvinistic bastard and he treated women as if they were objects. He hadn't agreed at the time, but now that there was distance between them, he realised he should have been more thoughtful. He never did anything nice for Tamara. Just had her come over to satisfy his needs. He never took her anywhere or gave her anything other than his "Johnson." Perhaps that was selfish—he didn't think so at the time, but now, with some reflection, maybe he hadn't treated her right. Standing there, watching Avery walk by having not had sex with anyone but himself for several weeks, Roger desired her more than anything he had ever wanted in his life. Avery became the sole object of his focus. The more he tried to get in that door, the tighter she held it shut.

Whenever he tried to see her, she told him she would not get involved with a neighbour; if something were to happen and she had to live next door to an ex-boyfriend, it would be a disaster. She asked him to step away from her and move back into the neighbour zone, to which Roger agreed, but he was still doing subtle little things to spark Avery. Avery knew this, and she resented him for it.

Avery walked down her driveway in that little summer dress, chiffon swirling around her, caressing her knees. The tight bodice and flowing sleeves made him drool. Roger had to suck saliva back into his mouth. She was on her way to work and Roger said, "Good morning," as she passed. She waved back unenthusiastically and gave a wan smile.

This torqued Roger off. *I'm being neighbourly darn it, what was wrong with this woman?* Most women found him extremely good looking. He was over six feet, but not freakishly so. He worked out at the gym. He learned early on, the rule of a good salesman is to be good-looking and friendly. The women loved him. He was the highest selling salesman at Circuit Land.

He was going to find a way to woo Avery Adams if it killed him.

Roger was high on his sales commissions; today had been a great day. Maybe the moon was in the right position, or perhaps his stars were aligned, but he had made hundreds of dollars in commissions. His boss told him it was the highest of any salesman, ever. Roger was beside himself with pride and excitement. He kind of wished he was still dating Tamara, because there was no one to share his success with…and he also needed a good *rogering*—that's what he called sex these days. Which was why he'd decided to pick up a bottle of wine and share it with Avery, celebrate his success.

She was home, her car parked in the carport next to the mobile. He knocked on the door holding the bottle of wine.

"Hi! I want to celebrate. I made the largest commission of my career at Circuit Land!"

Avery opened the door wide and took the bottle of wine. "Well that's nice. Thank you! Congratulations," she said, closing the door behind her.

Roger heard the dead bolt and then the chain slide across the door and was stunned. *What the hell just happened? She did not, just do that to me.* He put his fist up to pound on the door, but then thought better of it. Some small part of Roger knew this was not the way to get Avery to look at him. Perhaps grabbing the wine had been a prelude to a romance? She had accepted a gift from him. What did he know?

Instead, he called Tamara. She hung up on him. Tamara knew the only reason Roger wanted her was for sex. And kinky sex. He wasn't just happy with the good old missionary position. It's not that Tamara was a prude. She had been willing to go the extra mile for Roger at the time she was dating him, but it got more demeaning every time she was with him. Roger liked to see her submit to him, but Tamara was a proud woman.

Roger was sad when Tamara hung up on him. He was going to have to search elsewhere for a hook up, so he took himself to Thaddy's, a local bar where many young people hung out.

She sat alone at the bar, her head hanging over her drink. He'd seen women like that before; desperate women who thought they'd lost everything. He sat down next to her.

"Can I buy you a drink?" he asked politely. Her head shot up, her eyes penetrating his. He shrank back in his mind. *Wow, she is beautiful…but freaky.* She leaned her elbow on the bar to hold up her head.

"Sure. You can buy me a drink." She'd been drinking a tap beer, but now she ordered a martini with two olives. Roger didn't mind, if he could pick her up, the expensive drink was worth it.

"Roger." He offered his hand.

"Thelma." She limply took it. They started the dance, back and forth. He told her about his great day and wanting to share it with someone. She told him about the lousy day she'd had and how she didn't want to be alone. Roger's ears perked up on that one. One drink led to a couple, and the next thing he knew, Thelma was driving to his house behind him. He was excited—she was almost as beautiful as Avery. Almost.

In his van, Roger turned on some music, wincing when he realised Avery had taken the wine he'd purchased. He looked in the fridge. Beer, was all he had. Thelma was perched on the couch with her shoes off and her legs drawn up under her, her arm draping the back of the couch in such a way that, when Roger sat down next to her, he was encompassed by it. He liked a woman who knew what she wanted.

"Sorry. All I have is beer," he said.

"Beer is fine." Thelma cracked open the can and took a long drink. The woman could hold her liquor, that was for sure. She put her hand on Roger's thigh; he almost jumped but was suave enough to use his startle to grab a kiss. She responded appropriately. Roger knew if he played his cards right, Thelma was going to be a willing participant in his little sex games. She seemed desperate, which excited Roger a little bit. He started stroking her arm with his fore finger, and she looked him in the eyes, allowing him to continue with his roaming finger. He poked it closer into her armpit to try and cop a feel of her breast. Thelma kept her eyes on Roger, intense and never flinching. She accepted his kisses and his grinding, and moaning, they moved it to the bedroom.

"Wait, I have to get my stuff, it's in the car." Thelma left him erect and breathless. She must have had some lady stuff to attend do, because, upon her return, she spent a lot of time in the bathroom preparing herself. Roger had long since lost his little soldier.

"Are you ready?" Thelma called out.

"Yes," he said, noticing a stir in his loins. Thelma came out of the bathroom wearing black fishnet stockings attached to garters, a laced leather corset, booty shorts and black seven-inch heeled patent leather boots. It was the whip that caught his eye. Roger was both frightened and excited.

"Please, no more," Roger cried as Thelma whacked him with her whip again.

"Shut up." Roger had already missed three days of work. They were calling him every few hours now, but he hadn't been able to pick up the phone—the handcuffs held his hands to the headboard, the leg irons securing his feet.

Thelma was insatiable. She was relentless. She came complete with her own little blue pills that somehow worked, despite his unwillingness to participate in her sick sexual games anymore. Thelma had broken him. It had taken her three days, but Roger would never lust after a woman again. Thelma pulled the choke chain around his neck, and he was helpless to stop her moves.

"Please, Thelma, I don't want to do this anymore. Let me go," Roger pleaded. Tears rolled down his face; he was exhausted and humiliated. He couldn't have been more ashamed of himself. She made him beg—something he'd made Tamara do—and Thelma laughed at him. Now that Roger was on the receiving end, it wasn't as much fun.

Roger tried to think of Avery whenever Thelma tried to arouse him, but he didn't want to suffer at the end of Thelma's whip again.

Avery chuckled. She could hear Roger begging Thelma for her to stop the *sexcapades* as Thelma called them. When Avery looked out the window a few days ago and saw her cousin Thelma's car parked in Roger's driveway, she was giddy. After Thelma was done with him, Roger wouldn't lust after another woman ever. What Thelma did to her men in the privacy of their bedrooms was for Thelma's eyes only. Avery would have to thank her cousin for breaking her neighbour. Thelma had gone to Thaddy's whenever Avery saw Roger leave in the evenings. She knew Thaddy's Bar was Roger's hang out. It was only a matter of time before Roger would meet and hook up with her cousin—Thelma was beautiful and liked it kinky, a combination Roger would not be able to pass up. Avery knew that after another day or two of sexcapades, Roger' bad habit of lusting after women would be broken.

Tiger Nut Sweets

by Maura Yzmore

I am Iah, the Moon. King's Daughter. Beloved King's Mother.

For my brother and husband—the now-dead man who was briefly King—I bore two children, my only true loves, both sweeter than tiger nut sweets.

You are Neferu, the Beauty. King's Daughter. And mine.

Tomorrow you marry your brother, our new King. At night, when he looks at you with the ember eyes of a stranger, your wedding dress sliding off like the cool waters of Nile, know that the moonlight on your skin is me sending you comfort, praying your daughter never has to become her brother's wife.

Unplugged

by M. Sydnor Jr.

Alone. Empty Office. Busy mind. Can't leave. Why? Seven, that's why.

Without trying, she held him hostage. Unable to enjoy lunch with his colleague. Unable to satisfy his growling stomach. Her desk, the receptionist's desk, guarded the exit. She sat, waiting. He hid, pacing.

Should've never looked at her. Should've never talked to her. Should've never unplugged her.

Gary peered out from the conference room at the back of the office and saw his friend return from lunch.

"Trev," he whispered and waved.

His friend stood from his chair and walked over, shrugging, "What're you doing in here, dude?"

Gary pulled his friend in the room and closed the door. "I messed up, man. I messed up really bad."

Trev sat in a chair and watched his buddy pant, pace, sweat, and stammer.

"I-I-I don't know what to do."

"Slow down and tell me what's up."

But Gary couldn't chill, his anxiety was through the

roof. So much, that his childhood friend, Trev, hardly recognised him.

"CeCe? Did something happen something to CeCe?" Trev asked of Gary's wife.

"No, no, no, no, no. She's fine—well, for now. Until she finds out what I've done."

"And what did you do?" Trev leaned back in his chair and crossed his arms.

Gary stopped pacing. He took a deep breath, then scratched his head. He was hesitant at first, but ultimately decided to spill the beans. "Seven."

"The receptionist?"

"Yeah."

"What about it?"

"I fucked her."

Trev uncrossed his arms and leaned forward. "You what?"

"I…I…" Gary started moving again, shaking his head, "After…after work Friday, after everyone had left, I took her to my car and we…we just…one thing led to another."

"And you're talking about Seven?"

"When she first started here, I couldn't stop myself from looking at her. The shape of her eyes, the thickness of her lips, and when I got a closer look, seeing her body,

I...I mean she's perfect. She reminds me of CeCe when we first met."

"Wait, wait, wait, wait, wait..." Trev erupted from his chair. "Seven? The receptionist? The fucking android out there?" he pointed to the closed blinds that could look out to the front desk if opened.

"Yes. Are you listening?"

Now it was Trev stammering and pacing. "Ha— How do you even... How does that even happen?"

"Would you just listen to me? I'm trying to tell you."

Trev scoffed, then plopped back in the chair, rubbing his head.

"CeCe and I have been having trouble for the past year..." Gary sat in a chair across from Trev and sighed. "I-I mean we're good. I love her to death. But we've just had trouble in the bedroom. I don't know if I'm just not physically attracted to her anymore or if something is wrong with me. I just haven't been able to perform—"

"Yo, this is way too much information. Maybe you should see someone."

"Would you just listen, man. Shit. This is serious."

"Okay."

"So, last Monday when the boss brought her in, I was like *whatever, we have a new robot at the desk, a female android instead of a male.* I remember thinking *upgrade,* because this one looked more human than the last, y'know?"

"Right," Trev agreed, shifting in the chair, looking for a comfortable spot.

"Then, as I left that Monday afternoon, I talked to her. Just to introduce myself and immediately I got this feeling. This strange sensation. This massive erection. I mean, she's incredibly hot, anyone with eyes could see that. But I was at her desk, in broad fucking daylight, poking out of my slacks. I swear it was an out-of-body experience almost. Like my dick had control of the car and I was locked in the trunk.

"So, I went home with this massive hard-on that I haven't had in months. I grabbed my wife, kissed her, made-out and we had the best sex that we've ever had. The next night, same thing, right? But I had to close my eyes and think of Seven. A fucking robot, can you believe it? But I had to keep it up, because I was pleasing my wife.

"And then Thursday night. Same tune, thinking Seven was riding me, scratching my chest, moaning my name. I actually screamed out *Seven* as I…as I finished. Can't remember how she reacted, but I made up some bullshit about us going seven times all week or something like that."

"Gary?" Trev sighed like he'd heard enough, still

shifting in his chair.

"Just wait a minute. Hear me out." Gary rose to his feet, pacing again. Couldn't look his friend in the face anymore, so, he projected the regretful images that plagued his mind onto the empty walls as he told this story. "So, Friday, I decided to act on it. Told my wife that I'd be home late with the intention of..well…you know…"

"Fucking a robot."

"Well, yeah." Gary decided to look at his friend, face the shame, and he saw Trev shaking his head. "So, after everyone left, I approached her and—"

"How did you even get her from the desk? Isn't she, like, plugged into the wall or something?"

"See, that's what I thought, too. Even Seven. She had told me that she wished she wouldn't be stuck at the desk every day, all night. To get out and interact with everyone. But all I did was unplug her. They must've put it in her head that she couldn't leave, ya know? They can't have a robot roaming the streets."

"Right."

"So, she stood up and walked out with me."

"Then you fucked a robot?"

"It's not as crazy as it sounds, dude. Seven, they…they made her like…like a woman. A real woman.

Inside and out. Every detail, and I mean every single detail. From her lips, to her nipples, to her ass cheeks. I mean, there was no foreplay, we went straight to business. Seems like she wanted me as much as I wanted her."

"She's a robot, Gary. She doesn't have wants."

"Well, she pulled me inside of her."

"Okay, I've heard enough, man."

"When I got inside of her, I immediately felt like the biggest piece of shit on the planet. I regretted the very moment. As I was penetrating her, it just wasn't at all what I imagined. And on top of her, going in and out, I had to close my eyes and think of CeCe. Can you believe that? The fucking irony."

Trev must've blinked a hundred times as he stuttered. "I-I-I mean. I guess you have to ask yourself if it's cheating, since it's a machine and all." He laughed. Gary didn't. "Think of her like a giant sex toy. You don't even have to tell CeCe about it. Hell, I wouldn't." Trev slapped his thighs and stood with a tight face, holding back his laughter it seemed. "Seems as the issue resolved itself, though. You fucked up, just ignore the thing and get on with your life. It's a computer for Christ's sake."

"But that's not all." Gary walked over to his friend and grabbed his shoulders. "After we finished—after I finished. She looked me in the eyes and told me that she loved me."

"She what?" Trev snorted.

Gary let him go and walked around the room. "She fucking said she loved me. Then her eyes went black and she shut down. I tell you, man, I've never been so freaked out in my life. Had to carry her back to her desk and plug her back in."

"Then what happened?"

"I got the hell out of there, that's what happened."

"Maybe it was just a malfunction or something," Trev said. "Just a random response embedded in her system."

Gary shook his head, "No, it's more than that. Saturday morning, she called my cell phone, dude. I answered and immediately hung up when she told me who she was. But she kept on calling. Must've been fifty times that day. Leaving me creepy ass voicemails, like *I love you, Gary. Call me back, Gary. I need you, Gary. Please call me, Gary. I can't wait to see you Monday, Gary.* Shit like that. Fucking crazy, dude. I had to sneak in here this morning. And she's still been calling me. I had to disconnect my work phone before I came in here."

"Fuck."

"Yeah! Fuck!"

Trev peeked out the blinds and looked at Seven,

"What're you going to do?"

"I don't know."

Then a knock interrupted them, followed by the door swinging open. Gary nearly jumped out of his skin until he saw that it was just another colleague. "Excuse me, guys. I need this room," the co-worker said.

"Right. We'll get out of your hair," Trev spoke for them and pulled Gary out of the room to face the outside. Everyone was returning from lunch as they walked back to their desks.

Four hours left of his shift. All he had to do was not look up. No big deal. Eventually he would have to walk past the front desk to go home, but he would worry about that later. Now, he had to focus on work. Or anything to look like he was busy.

Head down. Mind busy. Working. Focusing. *Fuck, gotta pee.*

He almost made it. Three and a half hours in and all that water he drank forced him outside his six-by-six world. The closest bathroom was across the front desk, of course. So, he took a deep breath, stood, and looked to the front. But she was gone. The desk was empty.

Did they take her away? Did Trev tell the boss about

it and they unplugged her? He figured it wasn't his problem anymore, so he walked to the bathroom, sort of skipped there, full of joy, and did his business.

The mystery surrounding Seven's disappearance fell into the darkness of his mind. His main concern was his marriage and how to fix it. *A do-over.* He couldn't wait to get home to his wife and shower her with his love and affection. To treat her like a Queen and make love to her all night, on his terms.

At the end of the work day, he packed up his things, got in his car, and drove away. On the way home, he sang tunes from a playlist he and his wife used to enjoy early in their marriage when they would take road trips. An hour later, he pulled into the driveway of his two-story home and saw that the front door was cracked open. With no real caution, he left his car and walked up the steps.

"Babe?" He called out as he pushed on the front door. There was no answer.

He crept up the hallway, peeked in the kitchen, checked the bathroom and then he came upon the living room at the end of the house. The back of her head poked out the top of her favourite rocking chair as her favourite TV show played on the tube.

"Babe, what the hell? You left the door open."

She stood and turned to face him. It was CeCe

alright. Well, her face at least. "Hi honey. You're home." But it was Seven's voice, speaking from behind the CeCe mask. The fucking thing was still dripping blood, Seven's naked body was covered in it.

With this frightening sight, Gary stumbled forward and saw his wife's headless body lying in the middle of the floor. He gasped, fell to his knees and wailed.

As he started to crawl to his wife's lifeless body, Seven grabbed him in her arms and shushed him. "It's okay, it's okay. We can be together now, don't you see." With her strength, she forced him around to sit on his butt and she pulled his face toward hers. "You can be with both of us now."

"No," he screamed and pushed away. "No." he swung his arms as she tried to grab him again. Then, he ran in the opposite direction, but she was faster and appeared in front of him in seconds.

"Calm down, Gary. Baby, it's just me." She took CeCe's face off her head and tossed it at his feet. "See. It's just me—Seven." She raised her palms to calm him.

"What the fuck did you do?" He was afraid to look at his wife.

Tears covered his face. Chills ruled his bones. Anger filled his heart. All that emotion weighed him down because she grabbed him before he could attempt an escape. She held him, pulled him down to the ground, rocked him like a baby. Shushed him. He struggled. She squeezed.

So hard that his fighting stopped.

So long that his breathing ended.

Taming the Beast

by Maxine Churchman

"Aw, come on, man! I've got a raging thirst. Let's just find a pub and get a pint."

Gerry was tempted. A cold beer would certainly slake his thirst, but it wouldn't satisfy that deep down gnawing sensation. He'd gone past the tetchy stage and was seriously worried he would lose it completely soon. His friend of seven years didn't realise what could happen, and he wanted to keep it that way. Only a good cup of tea would calm the beast within. He was up to eight cups of tea a day, but he hadn't had any since they left yesterday afternoon. He regretted leaving the camp stove behind. There wasn't room in the car for the gas canister, and Ralph convinced him they wouldn't need it anyway.

"It's only two nights. There will be plenty of places to eat and drink."

They had spent the evening in a nice cosy pub downing shots and pints like a couple of teenagers. Shortly before closing, the gnawing had started in the pit of his stomach and he made his way to the bar.

"A pint of the local and a cup of tea please," he

ordered.

The barmaid looked at him with one eyebrow raised. It wasn't a good look. What had happened to all the pretty barmaids? They used to be buxom and blond, a lure to bring you into the pub and a distraction so you didn't notice how much you were spending while you were there. This barmaid scraped her dyed-black hair up into an unflattering knot on top of her head. She wore harsh black makeup around her eyes and vivid purple lipstick. Tattoos and piercings completed the "don't fuck with me" look.

"I suppose I could make you a coffee" she said, but he could tell from her tone that she didn't want to.

"Just the beer then." Coffee wouldn't do and he didn't fancy his chances if he pissed her off.

During the night he had to keep getting up for a pee. He couldn't be bothered to walk to the toilet block each time, so he relieved himself against the wheel of Ralph's motor. The gnawing made it difficult to sleep; morning couldn't come quickly enough.

They walked into town first thing and ate breakfast in a little greasy spoon café. His tea had been delivered in a cardboard cup with a plastic lid.

"What's this?" he asked the owner. "I want a proper cup or mug."

"Sorry mate. We've only got disposable cups." He didn't sound sorry at all and Gerry felt like punching him. The gnawing was making him tetchy, but it was still manageable; he took a deep breath to calm down.

The food wasn't great—the tea was undrinkable. It had obviously been made with dried milk.

They spent the next couple of hours looking for a tea shop. There were plenty of coffee shops but, in Gerry's experience, they couldn't make a decent cup of tea. They offered swanky teas with lemon juice and sugar, or – heaven forbid – iced tea!

"What kind of a town is this where you can't get a decent cup of tea? If we were in France or the US, I could understand it, but we're in the heart of England. I just want a good, strong, English breakfast tea with some fresh semi-skimmed cow's milk," he moaned.

"What is it with you and tea anyway?" asked Ralph. "You're like a crack-head who can't get a fix. Christ man! It's only tea. Surely you can go without just for the rest of the day. Tomorrow, you can join the old ladies drinking tea at Julia's before the wedding. This is supposed to be our lads' weekend since we missed the stag. Let's get a beer and a bite to eat. It's nearly lunchtime."

Gerry could see a pub on the corner and pointed to it. "You go ahead. I'll meet you in there shortly."

Ralph sighed and shook his head. "You'd better. And don't call me shortly."

Gerry watched him walk away before crossing to some public toilets. He looked closely at his brown eyes in the mirror. The gold flecks were starting to appear. He pushed back his sleeves to reveal his forearms. The dark hairs were definitely thicker and the veins in his wrists had started to bulge and pulse. He covered them up quickly and splashed cold water on his face.

Alone and away from the distractions of the town, he could sense the gnawing spreading throughout his body. He had to satisfy his lust for tea before it was too late.

As he emerged from the toilets, he noticed a small insignificant shop on the other side of the street. People passed it without a second look, but the sign over the door made his heart race. "Dagmar's Dreams" it read. After all these years, could this be the one?

He hurried across and pushed the door open. A bell tinkled merrily to announce his arrival. He had to stoop to get through the opening into the dimly lit room.

Yes! This was it. He sat on one of the two chairs placed either side of a small round table. Dagmar emerged through a curtain of black beads that rattled and jiggled before settling back in place. She placed a tea tray on the table and sat in the other chair. The china cups were exquisitely patterned with little blue flowers. She hadn't aged at all. Her dark hair was still thick and glossy, framing her almond-shaped face and softening the sharpness of her nose and chin.

Gerry reached for the milk jug, but Dagmar slapped his hand away and scowled at him.

His skin was tingling now from head to toe as his hairs thickened and more broke through. His eyes throbbed but he resisted the urge to rub them.

"So, Gerruphin, how have you enjoyed your years on Earth?" Dagmar asked him with a sly smile.

"It's been hell and you know it." His voice had lowered several octaves, and he stumbled over the words as his teeth lengthened and his tongue split.

Dagmar cackled. She was enjoying his discomfort. "Everywhere is the hell of your own making," she said.

"No, this was the hell you made for me." He reached again for the milk jug, but his hands were clumsy and he knocked it over. "Please Dagmar. Help me."

"You still haven't learnt your lesson, have you? You must control your lust. All this time you have been giving in to it. A lust for tea harms no one, but the consequences of not controlling your desires are just as dangerous. You become a monster. Now pull yourself together while I get more milk."

She left the room with the jug. Had he missed the point of Dagmar's spell all this time? He had been a fool. He thought she had just banished him because of the way he lusted after the water nymphs. Would she let him return if he could control himself?

He closed his eyes and concentrated hard, willing the gnawing to stop. He heard the curtain rattle again as Dagmar came back. He kept his eyes closed as she settled into the chair. He listened as she poured the milk; it would be fresh and cold. The hot brown tea gurgled up the spout and splashed into the milk; he could hear it creeping up the sides of the delicate china cup, making it sing. He visualised picking up the cup, holding the diminutive handle between his finger and thumb, his pinkie sticking out, as he raised the cup to his lips. He imagined the comforting warmth as the liquid slid down his throat, the aromatic smell of the infusion. He had never wanted a cup of tea more in his life, but he now realised that he had to resist the temptation. This was a test and he needed to pass it; something big was at stake.

He opened his eyes and looked at Dagmar. She smiled coyly at him over her steaming cup. "There now! I knew you could do it."

He looked down at his hands and felt his face. He was normal.

"Tea?" she offered.

"No thanks. I will give it a miss. Can I return now?"

"Not yet. You still need to prove yourself. I will be back in another seven years. This is your last chance. If you resist all temptation, you will be able to return, but if you can't control yourself, you will be banished to Hell. Just beware though; tea may not be your downfall next time."

Dagmar and the shop disappeared in a fireball that scorched his flesh, and he found himself standing outside on the street again. He walked towards the pub, thinking about the nice cold beer Ralph would have ordered already, and he had a sudden hankering for a hot curry.

Blooming Day

by N.M. Brown

"Millie, wake up! Come on, it's your birthday! Today's a very special day! You're 18! Mum's working so you get to spend the whole day with me. Meet me in the living room when you're ready." My sister Elena sings cheerfully at me while shaking my mattress.

I get out of bed and stare in my mirror with a disheartening annoyance. My mousy brown hair lays as limp as death and my eyes are so unremarkable that barely anyone knows what colour they are. My spindly frame, flat like a boy, leaves a lot to be desired.

All the other women in my family carry an elegant, ageless quality to them. Mothers are mistaken for sisters; grandmothers are met with shock and disbelief at their age. Maybe I'll grow into it.

But anyway, needless to say, I'm not the prettiest of girls where I come from, and definitely not as beautiful as Elena. She's twenty-seven and has been perfect since well before I was born. Every hair and curve perfectly in place. I don't hate her for it like some sisters would. She's always been more like a confidante and mother figure to me.

I trudge down the stairs and pour some cereal into a bowl. Elena's perched on a chair, her eyes brimming with excitement. She starts in before I even sit down. "Okay, Millie, what I'm going to tell you may sound strange, but today your life changes completely."

"Yeah, yeah I know. Today I'm legally an *adult*. I'm now legally able to be held accountable for all of my decisions. Along with the tidal wave of credit card offers that could suck me into debt."

Elena's face gets serious. "No. Well…I mean, yes…but that's not what I'm talking about. Now…you know the women in our family have always been a little different, right?"

I nod in agreement. It's true, the lineage of women we come from were all strikingly beautiful, independent and strong willed. I don't see what that has to do with this though.

She continues, "Well, every Valentine's Day after our eighteenth birthdays, something called the Blooming takes place. It sounds weird, but hear me out. You were born on February 13th so there's not much time to teach you everything."

Once again, I interrupt her; it's a habit of mine. "Elena, what are you talking about? I'm too tired for this right now. Stop being so cryptic and weird."

I've exhausted my sister's patience. "Millie, I'm serious, dammit. Listen to me!" She pounds her fist down on the table in front of me, then smooths out the tablecloth, trying to soften the gesture. "Go out tomorrow and find the right man. If you feel one drawing your spirit near, that's the one you want," she says, despite my incredulous expression.

"Meet him for a date and let him take you home. Make sure he lives alone, there are several ways to find out without being obvious. Let nature take its course and call me the next day. Tell me everything." I say something to her about my first time being special with someone I loved. By this point she has her hands on my shoulders and is looking into my eyes. So…I did as she told me.

A tall, handsome man catches my eye the next night. I pretend that today is still my birthday. I'm amazed at how easy this is, he seems captivated by everything I say. The lines flow smoothly off my tongue. My giggles are provocatively placed with perfection. After some slight prodding, I find out that he lives alone, so I let him take me home.

Our chemistry continues to build and, as these things

do, nature took its course. It's one hundred percent new to me, yet my body knows exactly what to do—what I like and don't like…being able to know what his body liked— it was euphoric. The floods of pleasure do well to mask the initial sting of pain.

I wake up the next day a bit sore but happy. He's still lying there beside me peacefully, his back facing me. I snuggle him and he feels like cold marble against my skin. I roll him over and uncover him. Eyes open, no pulse, he looks withered like a grape left in the hot sun. This hulking man from last night was reduced to such frailty, his skin almost dust like. A slight smile rests on his thin, mummified lips.

Not knowing what else to do, I call Elena in a panic and give her the address. Hey, she told me she wanted to hear all about it afterwards. Besides, my sister's the one who told me to do this in the first place, this is her problem too now. If anyone knows how to help me, it's her. I can't go to Mom with this or call the police. What would I even say? I'd be known as the dead lay girl for the rest of my existence, and that's *if* I manage to avoid a murder charge. I'm losing it.

There's a knock at the door. After checking the peephole and seeing my sister's face, I open it. Elena is smiling wide, completely calm. Tears are streaming down my face in horror. "Elena, help me! What did I do wrong? I did exactly what you told me to do! What's wrong with me. My life is over!" I start clawing at my hair, my voice becoming unrecognisable with hysteria.

She gathers me into a hug and starts to chuckle. "No, it's not. His is. And nothing! You did exactly what you were supposed to do." I look at her, even more confused. I start to yell and scream at her, but this time she's the one to interrupt me. "Millie, stop…go look in the mirror."

I go into his bathroom and look at myself. My eyes are blue like the Caribbean, my hair a flowing mane of chestnut curls, and my body curvaceous and beautiful. I understand now; I understand everything.

I'll always have a newfound appreciation for sex. The best thing is, I'm starting to gain control of it.

I can literally sleep with whoever I want. Each body given over in pleasure to me adds vitality and zeal to mine. Men will throw rationality out the window when it comes to getting attention between their legs.

There are three dates planned just this week alone. I'm really getting the hang of it now, and things are going to be so much fun.

My Girl

by Nicola Currie

After two hundred and thirty-five women, sixty-two men, two hermaphrodites, three thousand and sixty-four shags, eight thousand, two hundred and eleven orgasms, seven hundred and one blowjobs, fifty-three orgies, eighteen public dogging sessions and seven sex tapes, I thought I might have a problem.

"That's above average for someone not yet thirty, isn't it?" I asked the therapist I had to see now, after a police officer caught me wanking in my car when I couldn't help myself and had to pull over on a busy highway, my under-dash jostlings more obvious to the slow-moving traffic than I had realised.

My therapist couldn't reply, his mouth gaping like a sex doll before he snapped it closed, like he was afraid of what I might suggest putting into it.

It wasn't like I didn't love it anymore. I loved everything about it, apart from the chaffing, itself my biggest clue that perhaps I needed a break. That and losing Tiffany.

My girl since school, Tiffany had put up with a lot.

Far more than she knew, actually. She'd caught me cheating on only a handful of occasions, but after the second or third time, she started to care less and less, until I was the only one shedding tears when she finally walked out.

I told myself it was good—now, I could fuck with abandon, as though I wasn't already. But then something odd happened. For the last few years, whenever it happened to actually be Tiffany I was having sex with, she was the last thing I would think about. I even started to insist I only shag her from behind. I told her it was because it felt best but really it was so I could close my eyes and fantasise—about other girls, other guys and a variety of tangle-limbed combinations. It became as though I wasn't with Tiffany at all, not really. No wonder she left, when I had already in my mind.

Now she was gone, I couldn't fantasise about anybody else. Thinking about her and her strawberry blonde curls, her freckled skin, her tits so small they were basically all nipple, was the only thing that could get me off. It didn't matter who I was with or how dirty we got. A regular fuck of mine, Sally, an ex-porn star with gold medal stamina, couldn't make me cum and got so offended she kicked me in the nuts. Neither could DirtyDevil89, the girl (guy?) I found online but never met face-to-face, only cock-to-face via the glory hole of the squalid public toilets near the train station, and she (he? they?) never wavered in their ability to perform a perfect blowjob. Even Tiffany's cousin, with the same strawberry curls and freckles, couldn't get me off, not even when I switched positions with him. I wasn't giving or receiving anything.

The thing was, Tiff was quiet in bed, the opposite of a screamer. I'd loved that about her – it made it so easy to go wherever I wanted to in my sordid mind. But now I only wanted to think about Tiffany and her silence, which was something of a problem. My fellow pervs, sluts and nymphos were far from silent, even with their mouths full, so cumming with anyone else became impossible. I was reduced to finding release only with the most juvenile of orgasms—alone, in my bathroom, wrist aching as I thought about the girl from school.

For the first time, I felt sad afterwards. Lonely. I thought if I could just see her… I didn't mean to scare her, I just wanted to watch through her window as I touched... I would never hurt her, she knew that, but she called the police anyway.

"It must be painful," my therapist said. "To have to force yourself away from someone you are obsessively drawn to. But you know you have to, right?"

"I know," I answered, not too proud to cry. "But it's like you are saying I have to stop myself breathing."

That was the first time my therapist looked at me with something like sympathy in his eyes.

"There might be something that could help," he said. "I work with lots of people with sexual issues. Some would be a danger to the public without support. There are…tools."

"What do you mean by 'tools'," I asked. He waffled on about preventative action and replacement activities but didn't clarify. Instead, he handed me a card and told me that would get me what I needed.

Fornidroid Therapeutic Services. I booked an appointment a few days later. I was expecting something shady, that the building would have blacked-out windows and a discrete entrance around the back, like the 'private shops' I often frequented.

But it looked like any other clinic. Harsh lighting and squeaky floors. Middle-aged receptionist on the front desk. White-coated consultants barging briskly down long corridors, through mysterious double doors.

Some guy let out a groan from inside one of the consulting rooms. Jesus, what was happening in there? I was starting to worry that by 'preventative action' and 'tools' my counsellor had meant more than meditation and a fleshlight. What if he meant some kind of hi-tech castration—some cock-ring/Taser combi that shocked you at the beginnings of a semi? My mind raced with a hundred genitally-horrific possibilities. *That's it*, I thought. *I'm out of here.*

"You must be my referral," a stern-faced white-haired woman said. She kind of looked like my mum and suddenly I felt like a naughty little boy, waiting to be punished. "Follow me."

I did as I was told and followed. A guy about my age, also in a white coat, nodded from his computer as we entered a small room.

"Take a seat," the doctor said. She pointed to a chair with a helmet covered in wires suspended above it. "When you are comfortable, we will lower the scanner over your head. It will only take moments."

"Scanner?" I said, hunkering low as I sat down. "Scanning for what, exactly?"

The woman huffed. "Not again. Has no one explained?"

I shook my head. *No, mummy,* I thought, in a way that was inappropriate for a pervert who was about to get his brain scanned.

"Of course not," the woman huffed again. "In simple terms, we need to scan the erogenous zones of your brain to determine your sexual preferences. We'll use the data generated to calibrate your sexual proxy droid to your individual predilections."

"Sexual proxy dr… I'm getting a sex robot?!"

The doctor frowned in the same way my mother did. "We aren't giving you a present. This is a psychological tool to treat your addiction, to protect yourself and, more consequentially, others from more damaging behaviours. This is medicine and your decision to accept this treatment should be a considered one."

"Of course, doctor," I said, with solemnity on my face and wood in my pants. "How does the scanning work?"

"The headset will flash a stream of images and sounds that cover a variety of appearances, personalities and characteristics. This will happen quickly, at a subliminal level, so you will only experience a continuous blur and white noise. The headset will test your reactions to these stimuli. As mentioned, your droid will be modulated based on these results."

It's not that that didn't sound pretty cool, but it wasn't necessary. I only wanted Tiff.

"I already know what the perfect droid for me would be like. I have pictures and videos of my ex on my phone. Could you use those?"

"That would be breaking Human Copyright laws. It would be illegal and immoral to replicate a real person, even with their consent. I assure you your droid will be perfectly suitable for you."

I started to protest but there was a knock at the door. Another doctor stuck her head in.

"Excuse me," my doctor said. "My colleague needs to consult with me."

When she left the room, I smiled politely at the younger dude doctor, who was typing away. I jumped as the headset above me whirred and shifted suddenly.

"Do you use Cashy?" the guy said without preamble.

"The money transfer app?" Of course I did. Most prostitutes used it, not trusting their johns wouldn't beat them up and take their money back afterwards. I had great relationships with all my professional lovers whenever I had had use for them, but still, it was payment by Cashy or blue balls.

"If you have a grand ready to send and the videos and images you say, I can get you the best ex-girlfriend replica droid you could ever imagine. We have about five minutes before Doctor Cockblock comes back. Decide now."

I said yes without hesitation. I'd have paid a million to have Tiff back.

"We have to move quickly," the guy said as soon as I had transferred the money. "Give me your phone. I'll replace all the images and audio in the subliminal stream with images of your girl on loop. Give me her social media handles and I'll pull whatever I can from there too. While the scan runs, it'll help if you think about the things you liked most about her. This will help manipulate the data so the droid exhibits similar qualities. Oh, and buddy? Mention that I hacked the scan to anyone, and I'll reprogram your droid remotely. She'll cut your dick off while you sleep."

By the time mother doctor returned, everything was set. As she gave the order to lower the headset, I thought of Tiffany. Of course, my first thoughts were about how much I wanted her, how beautiful she was. But then I thought of things I hadn't expected, things I had forgotten. How she was a really good cook. How she had this wicked grin. How, before my infidelity broke her, she would get jealous of other women and that made me feel loved.

Two weeks later, I returned.

"Hi Hun," Tiffany 2.0 said, as I entered the consulting room, with that glimmer-eyed smile of hers.

I came right there and then. Groaning.

We barely left the house for a week. You'd think it would be weird, awkward, but it wasn't. It felt so natural, I forgot she wasn't human, wasn't Tiffany.

Each day was the same, like the beginning, when Tiff and I first lived together. We fucked the day away then alternated cooking for each other—her pro-quality Thai and French dishes, for my baked beans on toast. Afterwards, we cuddled as we watched second-rate horror films, laughing at the ridiculous deaths of endless idiotic victims. I'd forgotten how she would tilt her head up at me from where she lay on my chest and give me the cutest of devilish smiles.

The first time I had to leave her, I was nervous. The clinic had told me there were two options when it came to proxies. They could be programmed to hibernate when left alone, or, if I wanted the girlfriend experience, to mimic humans—they could go get groceries or shopping for clothes; to movies, to the gym, the library; they could do almost all the things a human girlfriend could do, but they would come home to me, guaranteed, and tell me about their day. Of course, I wanted that. I wanted Tiff entire, complete, absolute.

Still, I was worried the first time we parted would be

the last time I would see her. If she was really like Tiff, then she would leave me. But we couldn't be chained together forever, so we agreed to meet at Bonacci's, our favourite restaurant, where I knew she loved the risotto. I had my final therapy session first and Tiff would go shopping. We hadn't had much need for clothes the past week, but new Tiff could only manage on the few clothes old Tiff left behind for so long. My heart re-broke a little as I watched her walk away.

My final hour with my therapist passed slowly but positively. He was pleased the 'tool' I had now was working so well. I told him how grateful I was and could have kissed the man. I probably would have done, if my therapy had not been so successful.

I raced to the restaurant, flooding with anxiety as I approached the door. What if she wasn't there?

But I saw her the moment I entered, sat at a table alone, glass of wine in hand, gazing off into the distance. She took my breath away. She'd transformed herself in only an hour. Her hair was cut into a wavy bob that highlighted the cuteness of her delicate, pixie face. There was something fresher, freer about her. Her first outing without me had obviously done her some good.

"You are so beautiful," I said as I reached the table. I expected her to giggle, but her face fell.

"What the hell are you doing here?" she said, her eyes afire. "You can't come anywhere near me."

I was confused for a moment then realised, as panic ran its talons down my spine. This was her. The real Tiff.

Her face went white as someone tapped me on the shoulder. I turned. Shit!

"Hi Hun," new Tiff, still long-haired, said with a forced smile. "Who's your friend?"

She had the same iced-eyed look real Tiff always got when she suspected I was fucking someone else. Except it was far more intense, her stare far colder than any look the real Tiff could ever be capable of giving. For the first time, Tiff 2 did not look human.

I remembered how I'd thought about Tiff's jealousy in the scanner. Maybe focussing on that personality trait had magnified it, distorted the data used to make Tiff 2. She fixed her eyes on the real Tiff and didn't blink.

"She's no one," I said to Tiff 2, ignoring the real Tiff's stuttering shock behind me. I wanted nothing more than to go to her, to tell her I was sorry, to explain that it was her, only her, I wanted. But I had to get Tiff 2 out before something kicked off. "Just someone who looks a bit like you. Isn't that funny?"

Tiff 2's eyes thawed a little. I had no choice but to ignore Tiff—my Tiffany, my oldest friend, my girl—and usher Tiff 2 away as far as I could.

By the time we were home, Tiff 2 was cheery and I relaxed. I could fix this. As she made us homemade risotto instead, I texted my Tiffany.

"I'm sorry. I needed you so badly."

I made the mistake of leaving my phone on the table as we ate. It pinged and Tiff 2 picked it up before I had a chance. The phone was locked but she could see the incoming message.

"What have you done? How? Who is she?" Tiff 2 read aloud. "Whose Tiffany?" she asked.

"Just an old friend," I said, with my most reassuring smile. "She saw us in the street earlier and can't believe how I managed to pull a girl like you."

Tiff 2 didn't question me further but some of the ice in her eyes returned. We held each other again as we watched another slasher, but it didn't feel right. Like I was trying to hold a ghost, a phantom. Like I was holding something that wasn't real, that haunted me anyway.

It was strange to watch a horror film and wish you were in the movie rather than your own living room. I was clammy, nervous. My phone pinged again in my pocket and my pulse raced. Sweat ran down my face.

"Aren't you going to check that? Tiff said, turning her head over on my chest. I could have screamed to have

those eyes so close to me.

"It'll be no one important."

Her eyes didn't change. The corners of her mouth were pinched with fury.

"Yeah, well, you stink of BO. Go take a bath and I'll do the dishes, as usual." She pushed herself up off me and stomped off to the kitchen. I followed, but by the time I got there, she already had the vegetable knife in her hands, plunging it into the sink. I figured a bath was best after all. Behind a locked door.

I ran the water and pulled off my clothes, not even bothering to take my phone from my pocket. I couldn't face Tiff's texts yet. How could I explain?

I sank beneath the water. *Be rational*, I told myself. *Tiff 2 is not trying to kill you. Anyway, she's no stronger than a regular woman. You'll be fine.*

By the time I broke the surface, I had reassured myself and lay back. I was half-dozing when I heard the doorbell ring.

"Tiff?" I said, sitting up. "Who is it?"

There was no reply.

"Tiff?"

"No one, Hun," she said cheerily, moments later. "Wrong address."

At least she didn't sound so pissed off with me. I

chuckled at how much I had managed to spook myself.

"Hey Hun, you coming down soon?" Tiff 2 said. "I have a surprise for you."

I got out and towelled myself off. When I dumped my clothes in the laundry basket, I remembered my phone. Shivers ran down my spine when I finally looked at Tiff's second message.

I'm coming over.

I pulled on my sweaty clothes and rushed to the stairs.

"Tiff," I called as I raced down them. "I need to go out. Something's come up, I need to…"

Tiff 2 stood at the bottom of the stairs, holding a bloodied knife in her hand. In the other was my Tiffany's head.

"No one will bother us now," she said, with her devilish grin. "I'm all yours…"

In silent shock, I felt something deep inside me break. I knew I would never lust or love again.

"…and you're all mine."

Local Girls Are Waiting for You

by Raven Corinn Carluk

Lilyth made a show of licking her fingers, lingering on each one, moving closer to the camera. She moaned loudly, rolling her eyes closed, and listened to the little dings of incoming tips.

The succubus finally opened her eyes and looked directly into the webcam. She pushed just a touch of her power into the watching crowd, opening them to her. Lilyth would be able to feed on them for many more hours, without having to be signed on. "Until next time." She blew a kiss and pressed disconnect.

Waves of energy caressed her skin, and she sighed. She'd felt them during the entire session, had just been too busy performing to properly appreciate them. Warm and tingly, sharp and delicious, filling her to the core with heat.

She'd never felt so sated in her life.

Lilyth rose and stretched, purring to herself. In her three centuries of existence, she'd never felt so good.

Even working in a brothel hadn't given her raw sexual energy like performing as a camgirl. It certainly hadn't been as lucrative with such varied clientele.

The last of the tips were still coming in, but the total was currently over two grand. Not her best night, but she hadn't put on a particularly exotic show. A few direct messages waited for her, most likely requesting full nudes. Maybe a private show. Lilyth always had someone willing to pay big for even more of her.

And without having to use more than a fraction of her seductive powers.

She rose, leaving the computer running and her toys out. She'd clean up her playroom later, after she'd taken care of herself. Lilyth looked forward to a long soak in rose-scented bubbles, sipping wine and reading a horror novel. Maybe plan her next show, maybe just watch something online.

The doorbell rang. Lilyth wasn't expecting anyone, certainly not at two in the morning, but she was more curious than wary. Anyone attempting to attack her would find themselves in for a world of pleasure and pain.

She let her hair down as she walked, then loosened her corset. Nothing like a little extra flesh to make sure her unknown visitor was off-guard and distracted. Lilyth didn't bother with the peephole, just jerked the door open and stared down at the man on her stoop.

He hunched, scruffy and thin, dared only look at her from the corner of his eye. Approaching forty with sallow skin, he reminded her of a whipped puppy. "Mistress Lilyth," he said softly. "I enjoyed your show tonight."

The succubus stared down her nose at him, one brow raised sharply. Lilyth didn't know this man in particular, but she'd known men like him. Broken, pathetic, caught up in their desire for her, thinking only with base hormones.

When she didn't send him away, he took it as permission to continue. Squaring his shoulders but keeping his eyes down, he spoke. "I wanted to leave you some coins, but my wife got the credit cards to block the site, so I can't spend any money there. Had to make a new account to even log in to watch tonight."

He paused, wringing his hands and licking his lips before his next set of rambling words. "She had my last gift charged back, so I decided to stop and get you something special. Since I'm meeting you in real life, and everything." He fumbled in his back pocket and retrieved a long jewellery box.

Lilyth remained still, unblinking. What to do with this one? He was resourceful enough to find her location, and obsessed enough to defy his wife just to bring her a necklace. Should she have sex with him *then* kill him? Or simply use him for all he was worth until he was tapped out and wanted to die? Both sounded equally appealing.

She held out one well-manicured hand, staring wordlessly.

He glanced up for the briefest of looks, almost too quick to be called eye contact. He stepped forward and laid the jewellery box in her hand before retreating to a respectful distance, ducking his head, hands behind his back.

Lilyth opened the velvet box and stared down at the diamond and ruby necklace. Far too many karats to estimate, some of the gems the size of her fingernails, gleaming in the porchlight. Gold and platinum chain and settings, almost as valuable as the larger stones.

"This is decidedly more than just something special." There was no price tag, but she knew it wasn't cheap. "You would give me more gifts like this?"

He fell to his knees and gazed up at her adoringly. "Yes, Mistress Lilyth. Anything you want, as much as you want." His voice quavered with emotions and his eyes glistened with unshed tears.

The succubus stared down at the human man, drinking in his fear and desire. He clearly had money and a willingness to spend it on her. Though she used it sparingly during her shows, her power had driven this man deep into his baser side, making him a slave in need of her flesh. She'd kept men like this in the past, could do with one again.

But he had a wife—someone who controlled their finances—rendering him nothing more than a potential body slave for the succubus.

Lilyth smirked, lifting the necklace from the container, holding it to the light. Her decision was easy. Almost made for her. "Come inside," she said, stepping aside.

The Stranger

by Rhiannon Bird

Jeremy scuffed his boots against the stairs as he always did and stashed his rifle under the third floorboard of the deck. He raised his hand to knock on the door and froze. It was ajar. The door with five locks was sitting ajar. Jeremy pulled his knife out of the sheath on the back of his belt. He pushed the door slowly and it swung inwards. A very feminine laugh floated towards him, and he furrowed his eyebrows. There wasn't much light inside the house, the boarded windows saw to that, but it was enough to make out two distinct figures on the couch.

"Elton?" Jeremy asked carefully, not moving the knife from out of his hand.

"Jeremy," he answered loudly bounding off the couch. "We have a guest." He stood in front of him and whispered, "Play nice." Jeremey frowned. The girl turned towards him and smiled lightly. The kind of smile that shouldn't have survived through the war. Her blonde hair swung softly at her shoulders and her clothes sat perfectly. She looked too clean and too perfect to be here, it made Jeremy wary. She batted her eyes and tucked her hair behind her ear.

Jeremy twisted the knife through the air to make sure that she saw it, before tucking it back into the sheath. "I said, play nice." Elton said out of the corner of his mouth.

"This is as nice as I get." He grunted.

"I'm Rose," the girl bounced over to him, "it's nice to meet you." She held out a hand, and he eyed it disdainfully.

"I'm not sure you should say that yet." He crossed his arms.

"Just one second," Elton said, and he pulled Jeremey away from her. "Dude, what are you doing?"

"What do you think I'm doing? She's a stranger." He turned away and roughly relocked all five locks of the door.

"A very sexy stranger who wants our help." Elton watched her from where they stood.

Jeremy clicked his fingers in front of Elton's eyes. "Pay attention."

Elton gave him an annoyed glance, "What?"

"We can't trust anyone."

"And where has that mentality gotten us so far. I haven't seen a woman in forever, and I don't know about you, but I can think of a million things I could do to her." Elton bit his lip while his eyes drifted back over to Rose.

"Nothing worth dying for. Grow up." Jeremey rolled his eyes.

"Me getting laid will not kill us."

Jeremy spun to face the same direction as Elton. "Look at her, I mean really look at her. How does someone live through world war III and still looks that innocent? Plus, her clothes are too perfect; no dirt and no rips at all. It all screams dodgy to me."

Elton sighed, "For once, don't be paranoid. Rose is staying, and there is nothing that you can say that will change my mind." Elton clapped him on the back and walked to the girl. Jeremy crossed his arms and watched them with narrowed eyes.

Jeremy punched the pillow under his head and turned over on the couch. His back was forced at the wrong angle and there was a very mysterious lump under the cushion. He'd moved to get away from the sounds from the room next to him, but he still couldn't sleep. Every time he closed his eyes, he swore that he could hear footsteps. It didn't take long for him to decide that he wasn't going to be getting anymore sleep.

Jeremy crept down to the basement door and punched in the code. The door hissed and swung open.

The bunker was stocked full of more food then they needed. He sorted through all the canned goods. There was mango here somewhere.

"What's this place?" Jeremy jumped so high that he hit his head on the wire shelving.

"Shit." He turned to see Rose standing in the doorway in Elton's shirt. "What the hell are you doing down here?" Anger leaked into his voice as he shuffled her out and locked the bunker.

"There are people out there starving and you have so much food in there," she said, shocked.

It was the first time since he'd met her that she sounded real and genuine. He eyed her for a second, "That's none of your business."

The mask snapped straight back into place. "Can't sleep?"

"You're a detective." He rolled his eyes and pushed past her, back to the couch.

"Maybe I could help with that." She slid a hand onto his shoulder, and Jeremy jumped up and backed away from her.

"Stay back, woman." He glared at her, "I don't know what you are planning, but know that I'm not fooled by this act." She gave him a long hard look before withdrawing and padding back upstairs.

Jeremy didn't move until he was sure that she wasn't coming back. Then he sat back on the couch and waited until morning. At least that was what he intended to do. Somewhere along the way, he passed out into a deep sleep, deeper than he'd had in a while.

Jeremy startled himself awake.

"About time. I've been kicking you for five minutes," Elton hissed beside him. His eyes were still bleary, and when he tried to move his hands, he found them tied together. That pulled him into focus. They were both sprawled in the corner of the lounge room and bound. In front of them stood two burly men with guns, while two more people sat on the couch.

"Fuck," he breathed, and the two turned to stare at them. A girl stood up, and it was a moment before he recognised her. Rose looked very different in practical clothes; the flowy dress now gone. Her face had a raw hardness about it that only came from years of fighting for her life, and her hair was pulled back into a sloppy bun to keep the hair out of her face. Her combat boots slapped on the ground as she walked over to them.

"What's the combination for the bunker?" she asked.

Jeremy turned to Elton. "This is your fault, if you

didn't think with your dick this would not have happened." Elton just shrugged sheepishly. Rose kicked Jeremy's foot to get his attention again. "I don't know," he said slowly.

She nodded. "If you aren't going to cooperate, that's your own agenda." With that she turned on her heel and walked back over to the couch.

"I liked her better before," Elton grumbled.

"I respect her more now," Jeremy said as he tested the strength of the knots around his wrists.

"Little late to say that now," Elton muttered sarcastically. He slid himself closer to Jeremy and began to untie the knots binding his hands. "Almost there," he whispered. The other one on the couch glanced at them and for a moment Jeremy felt his heart stop. Then their eyes glided away from them. "Done." Elton slid smoothly back to where he had been sitting.

"Did you have a plan, beyond that?"

"That's where you come in." He flashed Jeremy a smile. Rose walked over to them and Jeremy tensed, holding his arms completely still. "Why are you doing this?" Elton asked tightly, the hurt leaking into his voice.

"Sweet Elton," she smiled at him, "We live in a world of thieves; I don't know what you expected." She then dragged him up and towards the bunker door. Jeremy chewed his lip. This was just getting harder and harder. One of the gunmen followed Rose and Elton, leaving only one, standing with his back to Jeremy.

He sucked in a deep breath and kicked out a leg. The gunman fell unceremoniously to the floor, and Jeremy dived for the gun. He scooped it up and fired. One in the thigh of the gunman, and then another into the stomach of Rose's friend. He scurried across the room, ducking as bullets whizzed past him. He sat on the floor with his back against the couch, two seconds. He had two seconds to recollect himself. One. He breathed in and out rapidly. Two. The other two intruders still lay on the floor groaning.

Jeremy rolled out to the side of the couch and fired straight into the shoulder of the second gunman. The man fell quickly, and Jeremy scrambled forward, grabbing the gun away. Rose faced him smugly, Elton in front of her with a knife pressed to his neck.

"You recognise this knife?" she asked.

Jeremy remained on his knees with the gun cocked and ready. "Yes," he ground out. It was the same knife he'd attempted to scare her with when she first got here. "It's not right to seduce people then rob them."

She shrugged, "I use the gifts I was given. It's not my fault that people are gullible. All you need to be is beautiful and people assume you're innocent."

"Let him go."

"But I was having so much fun just chatting." She smiled deviously. He pursed his lips and didn't reply. "Fine," she sighed, "If you don't want to be any fun. Give me the code and I'll let Elton leave in one piece."

"No." Elton's eyes widened.

Rose laughed. "Aren't you cute. You think I'm bluffing." She pressed the knife harder, and a thin layer of blood ran down Elton's neck. He squeezed his eyes shut and his body was starting to shake. "I grew up in this world, I hardly remember what it was like before. I have seen things you wouldn't imagine. I am a thief who steals from other thieves. Do not underestimate me, house boy."

Jeremy narrowed his eyes and there was a tense silence. The only sound was Elton's rapid breathing.

"8673," he said finally, and Elton slackened in her arms.

"I'm checking that," she said and pulled Elton along with her down the stairs. Jeremy walked to the top of the staircase, his gun still at the ready. She punched in the numbers and the door hissed open.

"Let him go now," Jeremy said, his finger hovering over the trigger.

"Of course." She pushed Elton onto the stairs just as

Jeremy pulled the trigger and the bullet pinged off the bunker door as it swung shut. He pounded down the stairs, leaping over Elton, and entered the code. The door didn't move.

"Shit." Jeremy hit his fist on the wall.

"What happened?" Elton asked, pushing himself to his feet.

"She's changed the code from the other side of the door. We aren't going to be able to get in there." He bent down to pick up his knife and clicked his tongue in disgust. She was taunting them. He used it to cut Elton's hands free and then tucked it back into his belt.

"We should get out of here," he said, glancing one last time at the locked door.

"But this is our home," Elton said as they picked their way out of the house.

"We had to face the music some time. We've been locked in that house for far too long."

"Then what are we going to do now?" Elton asked as they stood on the deck, looking out at the barren landscape.

Jeremy sighed. "You heard the woman; it's a world of thieves." He pulled his rifle out from under the deck and handed it to Elton. "To survive, we have to become them."

Some Body

by Robin Braid

I was somebody. They just couldn't see it yet. Level Cs are supposed to accept their lot without complaint, cursed by genetic inheritance to stay down and keep their mouths shut. The District Director may as well have had nothing on me; I was data irrelevant, just another slob treading water. If it wasn't for my stupid face and misshapen body, I would have been climbing the ladder of success long ago, chasing my dreams without fear of hindrance.

Then one day, a ray of hope broke through the grim chrysalis of disappointment in which I'd lain all my life. High up in my block, the Level As reside in the Sky Suites, and as I was heading down the staircase to my apartment, I looked up to see one of the glass elevators descending. Within was a vision of beauty so striking that it caused me to misstep and lunge to grab the handrail. An angel in red. I fell for her right there.

My friend, Pearce, works for the postal service and has licence to visit the upper floors. When I asked him about the beautiful woman, he said straight away it must be Zima. I lay in bed that night thinking of Zima and how we could meet. Picturing her smiling face as I introduced myself. Imagining all the wonderful times that would follow, where we would go, what we would do, how we would spend the rest of our lives together. Inter-level relationships were not impossible, but first she would have to invite me into her company. I just had to catch her eye somehow. In the social zones, I'm stuck in level C, far from the velvet rope, and what lay beyond was not for me, not yet. Approaching her on the street was also out of the question, if she got spooked and set off her Body-Alarm, my chance would be blown for good.

In the morning, I stared at my face in the bathroom mirror for a long time. Was this a face Zima could love? If I was an A, I'd have access to all the complimentary services I'd need. They can get nipped, tucked, pinched and polished to perfection. The rest of us had to work a bit harder. I just had to go that extra mile to get to where I needed to be.

When I wasn't at work, I started loitering in the lobby, trying to look inconspicuous as I watched the elevators, waiting for Zima to appear. On the third day, my wish was granted. She was dressed in black this time, and her hair was different, I almost didn't recognise her, but my heart wasn't fooled. As she stepped out of the elevator, I rushed to the C exit and around the front of the building. I made it just in time to see her merge into the crowd on the street. Such grace, such class in how she moved, I was so entranced I almost lost sight of her and had to hurry to keep in range. I followed for a few blocks, trying to pick an opportunity to get ahead so she could see me and start to know me. I began to get a little anxious I was going to miss my chance though, and my desperation must have been obvious to the Street-Cams. As we reached the corner before the Park, an Officer stepped out and called to me, and I panicked and took off. I dare not try that again, and I can only hope Zima didn't turn around to see me skulk off like a common thief.

Yesterday, Zima was at the station waiting for the Bullet. I could see her through the glass talking to a guy in the A Lounge. He was shaped like an athlete, tanned and confident, and Zima was smiling and laughing a lot. I knew then what I had to aim for. Soon I'd be that guy making her smile, I really believed that. If I didn't, I may as well curl up and die.

I took a mouthful from the Black Spirit bottle and dreamed. I pressed my forehead against my little rain-streaked windowpane and peered up to street level. An endless parade of feet rushed by. People with places to go, things to do, somebody to love. With every petite pair of heels that passed, beautiful, sweet Zima glided through my orbit, almost close enough to touch. Desire swelled in me. To bury my face in her hair. To tell her how much she meant to me and how happy I could make her, we could make each other. She was my light at the end of the dark tunnel I'd been crawling around in for years and I would be the hero to pluck her from her gilded cage.

Everything I needed to achieve my goal was now in my possession. I had the Black Spirit to numb me and give me the confidence to see it through. I had some scissors and rope I'd stolen from work; they wouldn't be missed—my boss was a silver spoon sucking moron. Pearce gave me the pills, I didn't know exactly what they were—they were unlabelled—but he'd been prescribed them by the District after he was pushed down an escalator by an angry A and he was sure I could use them. In a small cardboard box, wrapped in a smooth, white rag, was a collection of steak knives. The one thing my father had bequeathed to me. He did nothing for me in life, but in death he had provided me with the tools I needed to transform into something he could only have dreamt of being.

I bit down hard on the rag then stuck the knife straight in and started sawing downward. It felt as though something was tugging at my side, but I felt no pain. My

hands weren't steady, but if I moved slowly enough, I could just about maintain enough concentration to do the job. The tugging stopped, and I heard something wet and heavy hit the floor. I instinctively kicked it, like a damp, discarded towel, towards the corner of the room and set to work on the other side.

When I was done, I wrapped my midriff in an old, grey bedsheet, then slowly wound the rope around and knotted it in front to hold everything in place. My feet felt very heavy as I stepped towards the mirror, and my face seemed to pop and swirl before my eyes, but I couldn't stop now. The scissors were in my hand, and I raised them up and cut quickly. The nose, the chin, the jowls. I hated it all, it was going to be so much better now.

A warm, wet scarf serenely enveloped my neck, and I struggled to keep my footing on the slick floor. Slowly, I made my way to the couch, then collapsed onto my back. My fingers pressed into the worn fabric as I felt myself sinking down, Zima's body on mine, our souls entwined. I felt happier than I ever remembered being.

They'd all know now. I am somebody.

Good Intentions

by Sandy Butchers

I often wonder what on God's Earth I have done to end up like this; sitting beside a creature I cannot describe by name, and holding his—yes, *his*—hand while waiting for him to stop breathing. Because of his appearance, there were few who understood that his intentions were all but hostile. But what am I saying? Good intentions are mother to all fuck-ups. Ethan was a wonderful guy, someone with true character. His only problem was that he wanted to love—and be loved—so badly…it drove him bonkers.

You see, the thing is, when someone suffers the wrath of magic and is left deserted with nothing but a promise for everything to go back to normal as soon as he finds true love, you will understand that this search for love will turn to lust in the blink of an eye. Damn fairies and their magic!

Looking back at everything that has happened to me during the past few months, I can only ask myself how I—of all people—ended up being the love interest for a creature with savage looks and a beastly appearance.

Maybe it was meant to happen like this. Perhaps I was meant to end his suffering, to be the one to release him from the magic that had tortured him for years. How was I supposed to know that it would kill him?

Eight months ago, my father had broken his arm in a freak accident. It had gotten stuck between a tree and a rock while he was taking out the honeycombs from the cove. A branch had broken off, had crashed down, and had clamped my father's arm between its wood and the rocky ridge. When he had managed to wriggle himself free, he came home with his arm snapped like a twig. My mother braced it between two wooden boards, but this didn't leave my father capable of providing his family with the food we needed. So, it was up to me to hunt for food. I had been out hunting with my father several times, so I knew the basic tactics. Setting traps and snares was easy for me. My dad would point out which traps to take and where to put them, and I, being the good girl I was, armed them.

One evening, I'd gone out to empty the snares and found that one of them was gone. I had followed the trail of blood that started from the point where I had set it.

Today I would have screamed at myself that I was

being stupid, and that I shouldn't go after something large enough to drag a full-sized snare behind itself, without bringing any weapons to take it down with me. But at that time, I was convinced that my torch was more than I needed. Surely, whatever had stepped into that snare would have bled to death by now? It will not surprise you that today's me was more right than I ever could have imagined back then. For when I found my snare several miles out from where I had armed it, I saw something I had never seen before in my life.

Amidst the thick growth of the forest, I had heard deep snarls and growling. I'd known for a fact that it wasn't the sound of any wolf, so, curious me got closer to have a look at what I had caught. In the light of my flickering torch, I saw human eyes stare at me pleadingly. That being said, I think his eyes were the only thing human about him. His mouth was filled with yellowed fangs, and his hands were set with dagger-like claws. From his head had grown antlers, and from his back unfolded wings large enough to take him into the air with but a single beat of them.

His legs were bent and crooked, clawed, and covered in fur like the legs of some wild animal. But there he was, and more human than I thought, for the moment he saw me, he started to talk.

"Can you help me?" he asked, trying hard to push back the sound of the growls in his voice—trying his best to sound as human as possible. He pointed at the snare that had clamped its jagged teeth into his beastly leg.

I stood perplexed, looking around—to see if the creature in front of me was indeed speaking to me—like a fool. Of course he was talking to me! But the moment I realised that I was the only one to be spoken to in a radius of miles and miles, I also realised that this beast in front of me was intelligent…most likely intelligent enough to know that it was *my* trap as soon as he'd see me disarm it.

"Please, this thing is killing me," he pleaded as I stood there, considering my options.

"Uhm…yes," I stammered as I walked closer, "hold this." I handed him my torch, careful not to touch his claws, and kneeled down by his side to disarm the snare. He was bleeding badly.

I quickly took the key from my pocket and opened the lock. With all my strength, I pushed open the iron jaws and released the creature from its grasp. That's when my world turned black.

I found myself lying on a bed of hay in a small room of a wooden cottage—hovel, rather. I had no clue how many days had passed or if it was only the next morning, but the way I could feel my heartbeat throbbing in my head, I knew I had been smacked well, most likely with the end of my torch.

"Don't try to escape," I heard his voice from the corner of the room.

"What are you?" I asked.

"It's *who,* not *what.*" His answer was a low, guttural rumbling.

"My question remains."

"Ethan."

"Ember." I wasn't sure if giving him my name was going to be of any help, but there I was, giving it to him. For all I knew, he could have been the one who saved me from whatever hit my head.

"That's a beautiful name," Ethan said. "Tell me, Ember, why did you set those traps?"

He sounded friendly, alright. "I needed food for my family," I answered.

"And you couldn't have snared a rabbit? You had to set a trap large enough to capture a bear?"

"My father told me to put it there."

"Ah, so I should blame your father for this?" He stood up and showed me his furry leg. A hideous scar had formed on his flesh.

"My God, how long have I been out?" I cried, shocked by both the sight of his leg and the realisation that

I must have spent months in this bed already.

"A couple of hours," Ethan said.

I cried even harder. What on earth was he trying to tell me? That his leg had healed in some hours? I had seen the wound, watched him bleed. "That's impossible!"

"On the contrary," Ethan continued, "I find you rather impossible." He spoke with such civility.

"How is that?" I was stupefied.

"I had nearly given up hope that I would ever turn back to my human form. I was already resigned to spending the rest of my days looking like this."

"You mean you were human once?" I suppressed the pity I suddenly felt for him.

"Yes. I suppose what happened to me is very much like what is happening to you."

"What? Please, I don't want to look like you! Let me go!" I struggled to get out of bed, but my head was still spinning. Ethan caught me before I hit the floor and put me back on the pile of compressed hay.

"Easy now," he said, "I am not going to turn you into anything. Well, I might turn you into my wife, but let's talk about that some other time."

I lost my shit there and then in a form of hysteria I had never witnessed before. "What do you mean *making me your wife*?" I screamed. "What the hell are you? How is what happened to you similar to what is happening to me? Look at me, I look nothing like you, you hideous freak!" I looked at his claws as I ranted, ignoring the fear for them slashing me to shreds.

He cringed. "It is similar in how we both caught a creature that was never meant to be caught. One day I found a fairy in one of my traps, and she cursed me for it. Now here I am, caught in yours. I bet you never expected to find *me* in it."

"You're damn right, I didn't," I sneered. "What do you want from me?"

"Your love."

I snorted. "Right. Enough of this, let me go."

Ethan bent over me and smelled my hair.

I shivered to my bones. "Listen, my family is most likely already looking for me. There will be dogs, there will be swords and pitchforks. They'll light this place up like a candle at Christmas when they find me." I spat the words in his face. "Keeping me here is pointless, you will only endanger yourself."

"I'm sorry…but I cannot let someone as pretty as you slip through my fingers. You will love me, and you will break my curse."

For those of you who have been paying attention to my memoirs so far, this all happened eight months ago. My family never came to rescue me. Those dogs I told Ethan would shred him to ribbons never showed up. No sword or pitchfork ever gleamed in the moonlight as I waited…and waited.

The first few weeks made me feel terrible about this. Why wasn't I worthy enough to be saved? What had I ever done to deserve this exile in this god-awful place, with some man-beast who wanted to marry me?

The worst part is that today I am not even sure anymore of what I find the most disturbing thought in all of this; the fact that my family had left me for dead, or the fact that—despite him trying to force himself onto me, time and time again—I was starting to see that Ethan's actions were desperate. If he would simply stop trying to bed me, if he would stop trying to wed me, he really wouldn't be so bad. By now, I can get past his antlers, past his crooked legs and claws. In fact, he has been rather hospitable, despite his occasional snarls. Protective and caring. He has been the only one willing to ensure my survival. I couldn't say this much of my family.

Today marks the two-hundred and fifth day of my

stay with Ethan. I have lost count of the times he has tried to seduce me into sleeping with him. Not a day has goes by where he doesn't shower me with compliments and words of love. Not a day has passed that he hasn't walked into my bedroom naked, hoping he could peel off my clothes as well. It annoys me, and yet at the same time, I find it rather funny. He said he is centuries old, yet he behaves like a fourteen-year-old boy who claims to have found the love of his life.

I have asked myself if it's truly love he is seeking, or if it's only lust that drives his actions. But the more I think about it, the more I am starting to see how those two are tearing at him from deep inside. He wants what he can't have, yet he deserves so much more.

During our dinners together, we often talk about his past. About who he was before he was turned into this creature. I ask him to tell me all about his curse, again and again. At night, in my bed, I would repeat the story to myself, searching for a clue that could make his suffering end. I mean, I know the answer is obvious—he needs someone to love him—but be honest, could you love someone, if all that person sees is your flesh, not who you actually are? Could you have warm feelings for someone—even if that someone would be completely human – whose sole purpose is to tear the clothes from you and have your bodies tangled together like some organic puzzle?

Now ask yourself this: would you be able to see through that, and understand that to someone like Ethan, love and lust have become the very same thing?

It occurred to me that, most likely, I was going to stay here for a good, long time. I figured that I might as well give him a chance to prove himself to me. Judge me if you want, but compared to all those men and women who had left me to rot out here in the forest, Ethan was the most decent man I knew.

And so, I slowly undressed myself.

Ethan did not even blink. He must have been stupefied that, after all these days, I had finally decided to give in to his persistence. He picked me up—careful not to graze my face with his antlers or cut me with his claws—and gently placed me onto his bed.

But right when he was starting to see the shape of my body, surrender to the warmth I gave him, hear my heart pound in my throat…the door of the cottage creaked open.

I told Ethan to hide and that I would go and see who came in.

"Please, don't run," he whispered.

"I promise, I won't leave." I walked to the door, forgetting to put clothes on, surprised as I was by the

sudden event.

There, amidst the broken and ravaged interior of the cottage, stood my father—stupefied and crying.

"Ember," he sobbed, "what are you doing here?"

"Father, I—" I quickly grasped a blanket from the chair at the fireplace and wrapped myself in it. "Your arm looks better," was all I managed to say.

"I've been searching for you for months!"

My mouth fell open.

"Come with me."

Like an arrow shot from a bow, Ethan jumped from behind the door and bared his teeth. "You will not take her from me!" he snarled.

"My God!" My father screamed, "What are you?"

"Dad, this is Ethan. He won't hurt you. Please, stay calm." I turned to Ethan, gesturing to him to calm his temper.

"Wait…were you…did he?" my father stammered from behind me.

I'm not sure what I saw in his eyes, but I knew things were even more messed up than they had been the moment I decided to surrender myself to Ethan.

My father ran. He turned and slammed the door behind him. All I could think of was to stop Ethan before he would chase him down like a rabbit and turn him into stew. I grasped his wrist and drew him near, kissing his lips and wrapping my arms around him. It worked, yet I knew that this distraction was not going to save him from what was coming.

I had been so wrong! My father had been looking for me from the day I left home, and now he had found me. Suddenly I realised that my family—those dogs and swords and pitchforks—were coming after all. "Listen, Ethan," I said as I took his head between my hands, "they will come for you now."

"Why? I have done nothing wrong!"

I swear to god, I could see the fear in his eyes. Yes, being the creature gave him certain strength and abilities, but even he knew that he didn't stand a chance against the men that would gather at his door. I could already hear the dogs outside.

"We are surrounded," Ethan sighed as he walked to the door.

"What are you doing?" I asked.

"I'm going to end this…"

It all happened so fast. Within minutes, a small garrison had gathered around the cottage, swords drawn and—as I predicted—pitchforks at the ready.

"You disgusting creature!" One of the men yelled when he saw Ethan in the doorway.

"You beast!"

"You monster!"

I ran outside and placed myself in front of Ethan. "Leave him alone. You have nothing to fear from him!"

"Ember, come here. You'll be safe with us."

"Haven't I been safe for the past eight months without you?" I asked. "Truly, he will do you no harm!"

I heard several bows drawn to tension.

"This beast wants nothing but your flesh. Step away, Ember."

I remained quiet. Perhaps I thought that he was right. Perhaps only now did I realise that I had let Ethan crawl into my mind. I turned to face him, but what I saw in his eyes made me certain: his intentions had never been hostile... I kissed him—knowing it was going to be his last—and heard the arrows whistle through the air.

Shot by true marksmen, each of them missed me as I was but a small creature compared to him. Instead, they pierced Ethan straight through his chest.

Ethan sank to his knees, gasping for air. I cried when I saw him slowly turn into the man he once was. He was beautiful. And now he was dying. I kneeled beside him and held his hand. "It's over," I whispered, "You are free from your bounds of lust. Now love…for you are loved."

I watched the life slowly drain away from his eyes.

I wonder…what on God's earth have I done to end up like this: sitting beside a man whose beauty I cannot describe with words, holding his hand in his final moment.

Digits of Doom

by Serena Jayne

The red digits of doom on Gerald's alarm clock displayed the time: 10:08 AM. Deadly rays of sunshine cast a laser beam lightshow on the beige bedroom walls. He glared at the ill-fitting blackout blinds. It would be hours until nontoxic moonlight replaced the scorching sunlight.

"Get up already!" Mitzi, his ball and chain, banged her fist on the doorframe. With her cherry-red lipstick, pale foundation, and frumpy frock, she was the embodiment of a crazed circus clown.

He wanted to bite Mitzi. Needed her blood to slake his raging thirst and rekindle his blissful buzz. She'd been his burden for eight awful years. Years that had turned his hair grey and his heart hard. Her blood would be bitter. Sour. Caustic.

"I'm not moving until dark." His tone sounded toddler-denied-a-lollypop whiny, not big, bad vampire bold.

She sighed. "Shrinks are too damned expensive. The Wilkinsons are sending their daughter over to psychoanalyse you to your senses. Cindy got a B+ in Psychology 101 at the community college."

"No." He shuddered. "No visitors." Gerald couldn't have guests. It wasn't safe. He wasn't safe.

"Should've married Richard." She patted her lacklustre locks. "Then I could afford salon services instead of drugstore dye."

Gerald gritted his teeth. Richard had a high paying job. Richard was hung like a stallion. Mitzi's parents loved Richard. Richard. Richard. Richard. The cow always wielded the name like a knife. Stab. Stab. Stab.

"You mention that jerk's junk again, I'm gonna…"

"You're gonna what? Shoot me the stink eye? Whoopty do." She rolled her eyes. "You're a whole lotta talk and zero action."

"If your darling Dick would take you off my hands, I'd wrap myself in a blanket and drive you to his McMansion right now, but he doesn't want you. He collects pert, pretty, perfect trophy wives. You're no looker, Mitzi. At best, you're a booby prize. A saggy one at that."

Mitzi's lower lip quivered. "Big words for a 'fraidy cat who's too chicken to get out of bed."

Her childish taunt sparked memories of the grade school bullies whose chants of "Jerky Gerry" gouged his

psyche. For twenty-two years, he had regretted his inaction. He refused to begin his undead life racking up more remorse.

He leapt up and shoved his wife onto the scratchy carpet.

She slapped and shrieked and clawed.

He banged her head against the floor until her struggles stopped and her cries ceased.

His canine teeth ripped into her neck, releasing the nectar inside. He lapped up her briny blood, gagging at the metallic taste.

With a burp, he stood and waited for the return of the magical high. The promised side effect of ingesting human blood.

Instead of euphoria lighting up his brain, loneliness made his belly ache.

He'd stolen a vial of serum from the blonde brick-house-built hooker who'd revved his libido before injecting him with the concoction that made his blood sing and turned him into a creature of the night. Enough serum to create an undead companion.

Living forever and getting buzzed on blood were well worth the ten grand he'd paid the prostitute. In movies, vampires weren't created using fluid from a vial with a pharmaceutical company label, but this was real life, not some fantasy flick.

Maybe he should turn Mitzi. Having a harpy by his side beat being alone. He couldn't spend eternity with her running her mouth, but with a slight alteration, Mitzi could be a manageable mate.

Unholy fire scorched his arm. He darted away from the sneaky sunlight and reached into his nightstand drawer.

Just as his fingers closed on the cool metal handle of the scissors, the doorbell rang.

Cindy. Young, beautiful Cindy with her luscious lips, gravity-defying rack, and sweet ass.

Unlike Mitzi, he wouldn't need to cut out her tongue to stomach her companionship. If he had a hot piece of tail, other men would respect Gerald for his prowess with the ladies. Every night, he and Cindy could make mad love in the blood of their victims. With her by his side, he could not only indulge his lust for her, but cultivate a lust for life.

Licking his lips, he dropped the scissors, stepped over Mitzi's body, and flipped his middle finger at the red 10:33 AM on his alarm clock.

So what if it was still morning. So what if the sun still shone bright. Big, bad vampires didn't allow a little sunlight and a few dastardly digits keep them from their destiny.

Damned

by Stephanie Scissom

Lucifer stepped inside her apartment and pulled the door shut behind him. Abigail stood looking out the window, hugging herself. She turned to face him, tears shining in her eyes.

He faltered, feeling strangely awkward and unsure in front of her; the one who knew him better than anyone. A tear slid down her cheek and, automatically, he reached for her. With a sob, she held up a hand to stop him. Then she turned away.

Not knowing what to do, Lucifer slid open the glass door to the balcony and stepped outside. Scarlet and copper leaves danced in the crisp October wind. He smelled the earthy scent of their decay, and of the coming rain. Although autumn was his favourite season, he felt a hint of the coming winter in the breeze, and it made him sad. Winter meant coldness, loneliness. This one meant goodbye. She probably hated him, now that she remembered everything. It was just as well. The best thing he could do for her was still the one thing he never wanted to do. He had to walk away—*really* walk away. No contact, no watching. He had to let her go, had to stop being so fucking selfish. The thought broke his heart. Michael wanted to punish him, but nothing could torture him as badly as the curse of an eternity without her. He lit a cigarette and wished he could just die. To feel nothing, to be nothing…how much he craved peace and a release from the guilt that crippled him.

As he finished his second cigarette, Abigail joined him on the balcony. They stood shoulder-to-shoulder, but he couldn't meet her eyes. Finally, he turned his hand over, palm up. She slid her hand inside his. The contact broke his composure. How could she even stand here after all he'd done to her? After all she'd suffered because of him? He pulled her into his arms, burying his face in her hair.

"I'm sorry!" he gasped. "I'm so sorry! Avery—the reason I let her do that to you—"

"I know," Abigail interrupted. "I know. Shhh. I know. She told me."

She pulled back and took his face in her hands, making him look at her. "I'm glad she did it."

Tears fell from her eyes, but she was smiling. *Smiling*. He didn't understand.

"It was so good to relieve those days with our babies. With you. We were so happy. You were the best father.

The best husband."

Somehow this was worse than her anger, or her pain. Lucifer's gut clenched. "Abi—"

"You were!" she insisted. "All this guilt ... you didn't do this to us. *He* did. We were *happy*. I'm sorry I blamed you."

"I should've told you what I was. Maybe—"

"It wouldn't have made a difference. I would've wanted you anyway."

She kissed him.

The feel of her warm, soft lips—of her hunger—caught Lucifer off-guard. Suddenly, he felt like he had back then, thousands of years ago, when everything was right and everything was good and no sorrow had ever touched them. When it was just her and him and the fire that had raged between them since the moment they laid eyes on each other. He seized the back of her head, deepening the kiss. The wind carried the scent of her shampoo. With some irony, he realized she smelled like apples. The apple of temptation, the apple of his eye. Her cool hands slipped under his shirt, teasing him, caressing him, stroking him.

And there he was, as lost and fallen as he'd ever been, prisoner to a passion even the devil himself couldn't resist.

Lucifer couldn't think; he couldn't stop. All there was was Abigail. Her heady, demanding kiss, her cool, greedy hands, her dangerous curves beneath her soft, clean-scented flannel shirt.

His lips were on her throat. He was drowning in the sweet, salty taste of her skin. The pulse throbbing in her neck matched the fever pitch pounding of his heart. His hands gripped her denim clad hips, pushing her back against the brick, pinning her with his body. Then they slipped under her shirt, skimmed up her smooth, flat stomach. She wore no bra.

His breath abandoned him as he cupped her soft, full breasts in his rough palms. Gently, he kneaded them, enjoying their weight, their perfect heft. She gasped when he caught her nipples between his thumbs and forefinger and squeezed.

Her hips rocked against his erection, making him groan. His mouth found hers again as his hands slid back down her body. He cradled her ass through her shorts, grinding against her. Then he reached behind her to open the sliding door and push her inside.

His fingers fumbled with her zipper, but then he had it. Her shorts pooled at her feet and she stepped out of them. He slid his hand between her legs. Her thin panties were a flimsy barrier. He felt her heat, her dampness, the

crease of her sex. He slipped his fingers inside the hem.

Wet. So wet.

Lucifer closed his eyes as he stroked her. He knew this body as well as he knew his own, knew when to speed up, when to slow down. She clutched him, burying her face against his neck as her legs began to shake.

Her nails dug into his shoulders, and her breathless little moans in his ear were driving him insane. He wanted more. He wanted all of her.

He scooped her up and carried her to her bed.

She laughed when he threw her unceremoniously on the bed, her beautiful eyes glowing. He crawled up the bed, up her body, trailing kisses from her ankle to the inside of her thigh.

He pressed his face against the transparent fabric of her panties, then raked his tongue over her cleft. She cried out and lifted her hips, as if he needed any urging. He yanked her panties off and threw them over his shoulder before burying his face in her smooth mound.

He took her to the edge with his tongue, then pulled back when her legs started to tremble. She groaned in frustration and he hid his smile, knowing the payoff would earn forgiveness.

Slowly, he unbuttoned her shirt and opened it like a present. He kissed his way up her abdomen to her breasts.

Lucifer looked in her eyes as he took one hard, pebbly nipple in his mouth.

Eye contact was a big thing with Abigail, and she'd taught him to love it, too. So intimate, so raw. The look on her face right now was all that he could stand. He sucked her hard, and she cried out, bucking against him.

"Please," she gasped. "I want you inside me."

He stripped off his pants and positioned himself between her thighs. He rubbed his tip along those lips, teasing, stroking her, but she wasn't having any more of that. She arched her hips, plunging him inside her. Lucifer sucked in a breath at the feel of her, so tight and warm, encasing him.

Too long. It had been too damn long.

She smiled, then she started doing that thing she did that drove him wild, gripping and releasing him with her pelvic muscles. In all these years, he wasn't the only one who'd learned how to tease.

He knelt there motionless, enjoying the sensation, the triumph in her eyes, until he couldn't take the stimulation anymore. He snatched one of the pillows from the bed and shoved it underneath her ass. Then he grabbed her legs, placing them on his shoulders. Lucifer began to thrust.

From the look on her face, he knew he'd found the right angle. He pounded against her, each thrust hitting

that sweet spot.

"Don't stop, don't stop, don't stop!" she begged, and he couldn't have, even if he'd wanted to. So tight. He lost himself in the delicious friction of her and it was all he could do to keep his eyes open, to watch her beautiful face as she came.

Abigail shattered around him. The ripple of her muscles destroyed his control. Clutching her ankles, he gave two final thrusts before he exploded inside her.

A Warned You

by Stephen Herczeg

"Dude, now don't kill me, but..." started Jake.

"What?" said Ted.

"I put you on Sex0rzt, you know that dating app," Jake said, stifling a small snort of laughter.

Ted's face was a mask of horror.

"What? Are you fucking mad?" he said.

"No man, but think about it. Nothing will probably happen, but if it does, hooboy, it might ever pay off and you'll be in heaven," Jake said. "Though you've got to get over the whole you thing."

"Fuck you," said Ted, "I've got more chance than you. At least I'm not a virgin."

"Yeah, you keep saying that, but I still don't believe it," said Jake, a big smile on his face. "Anyway, I've seen my fair share."

"When?"

"Well, there was that time—"

Ted cut him off, "Give it a rest dude, the only time you've ever seen anything is when you walked in on your sister in the shower. And that was just sick."

Jake, looked downcast. "Yeah, I know, but you've got to dream, I suppose."

A sly grin crossed Ted's face. "But did you really see anything?"

"Dude, now you're being sick," said Jake.

Suddenly, Jake's phone beeped. Jake picked it up and opened to the front screen. A small notification icon showed in the top left corner.

"Fuck, that's the Sex0rzt popup," he said.

Ted looked hesitant.

"Seriously, that quickly?"

Jake's finger reached for the Sex0rzt icon. He wavered for a second.

"Well, hit the stupid thing," said Ted.

The app opened up and showed a small heart with a three inside. Jake tapped the love heart and several notes appeared. He read them for a moment then looked up at Ted with a wide grin on his face.

"Dude, you've got a hit," he said.

Ted, his face a mask of suspicion, said, "Bull, show me." He leaned in and shouldered Jake out of the way.

Jake tapped the message. The name, "Angela," showed on the top of the message with a profile picture of a raven-haired girl. The message said, "Love your pic, wanna meet up? PM me."

"Oh, fuck," said Ted.

"Yeah, well that's the general idea," said Jake.

Ted pulled out his phone and opened the Play store.

"How do I log into this thing?" he said, searching for the Sex0rzt app and beginning to install it.

"Oh, now you're interested," Jake said.

"Damn straight, she's gorgeous," he said.

Jake smiled and helped Ted log into the app.

"Dude, we're meeting up on Saturday night. There's a party or something. In the country at her Uncle's estate. Sounds huge. I was hoping for something a bit quieter, but she said there'll be tons of people," Ted said into his phone.

"Fine, well I'm glad I was able to make your week. Hope you manage to go all the way," said Jake, his heart a little shattered by how well his plan had gone.

Ted chuckled, "Don't worry, I passed your name onto her. You might get some tags from one of her friends."

"Oh, now you're playing matchmaker, excellent, that makes me feel more of a man," said Jake.

"Hey, it's how many not how," said Ted.

Jake thought for a moment. A smile crossed his face,

"True that."

A short beep rang through both phones.

"You gotta 'nother call?" asked Ted.

"No," Jake said, pulling the phone away from his ear and looking at the screen, "Oh, crap, I got a Sex0rzt tag."

"Sweet," said Ted, suddenly to no-one as Jake checked the app. He waited for a moment, then a high-pitched whooping came back through the ether before Jake spoke again.

"Dude, we're going on a double date," he said.

Ted pulled his beat-up mustang off the small country road and onto the gravel driveway. His lights lit up the darkened tree-lined track that wound its way towards a well-lit mansion visible through the grove.

The little wood gave out onto a wide circular driveway. The mustang crunched its way along and Ted parked it beside a group of similarly aged cars. He looked towards the opposite side and noticed a line of late model limousines, their drivers congregating in a small group to one side.

"Dude, this is freaky. There's a mix of crap cars like mine, and look at those beautiful rides over there," said Ted pointing across at the limousines.

Jake looked one way then the other.

"Cars, who cares, I'm more concerned about something else," he said, a wide grin beaming across his face.

"Dude, it's a party, nothing like that's gonna happen. At least not for a few hours yet. We gotta meet these girls first. I'm sure they'll take one look at us and split," he said.

"Well, one look at you," said Jake with a snigger, "Me, on the other hand."

"Fuck you," said Ted.

"Not my type," said Jake, "Otherwise I would have made a move a long time ago."

Ted grimaced, "Dude."

They left the car and walked up the front steps to the mansion entrance. It was a sprawling three story affair. The owner was either from an old, well-established family, or one of the newer internet-based tycoons.

"This place looks like something Steve Jobs would have owned," Jake said.

"Doubt it, he was all new and minimalistic. I'm thinking Bezos," replied Ted.

"Not likely, maybe his wife," said Jake.

"Maybe she's running the party. She's single now, and rich," said Ted.

"And a babe," said Jake.

"With that much money, I wouldn't care if she looked like Mike Tyson," said Ted.

"Fair point," said Jake.

They both shut up as they reached the top of the staircase and were confronted by two footmen, both dressed in period costume.

"May I take your name?" asked one.

"Only if you give it back," said Jake.

Ted and the two footmen grimaced at the horrible joke.

"Dude, sometimes you are really lame," said Ted.

The footman smiled and said, "Oh, Sir is very droll."

Ted cut in and answered, "I do apologise for my troglodyte friend. I'm Ted Masters and this is Jake Spencer."

The footman looked on his small tablet, moving a list up and down until his face brightened.

"Ah, yes, all is in order. Please go through and enjoy yourselves. The ballroom is to the left, the facilities at the rear to the right. There is a coat room just inside to the right as well," he said.

The other footman opened the door and allowed the two to enter.

They stepped through and into another world.

The entry foyer was a wide-open expanse, with two winding staircases leading up to a first-floor landing. To the left, another large set of doors was manned by two more footmen. To the right was the coat room with a young woman in attendance. They quickly left their jackets and stepped up to the ballroom entrance.

As they checked each other's appearance, Jake grimaced at Ted.

"You could have tried harder," he said.

"Dude, I look almost identical to you," Ted said.

"It will have to do."

The footmen hid their smirks and opened the doors for the two. What greeted them almost knocked them over.

The ballroom beyond was a long, cavernous chamber with a high ceiling, stretching up for a full three storeys. It was exquisitely finished with marble columns wrapped in gold gilding and a floor covered in dark wooden parquet. A string orchestra played at the far end, to a room full of dancing, twirling couples.

It was the couples that grabbed the boys' attention. The girls were all gorgeous, seductively dressed in the minimum that would be allowed in polite company. They were statuesque with long tresses of blonde, brunette and red hair. Their bodies honed to athletic perfection, their skin as clear as porcelain, but hued in as many shades as the tribes of the world.

The partners were another matter altogether. Jake and Ted could have swapped places with every single man dancing on the floor. Each one had a similar gawky look about them. Each looked as though their mother had dressed them whilst drunk. Each one appeared lost in the arms of their dance partner, but out of place at the same time.

"It's a total nerd fest," said Jake.

"Totally," said Ted.

Suddenly, they both began to have second thoughts. They looked at each other and started to turn when their names echoed across the room. They spun back and saw two of the most beautiful women they had ever laid eyes on approaching.

The pictures of Angela from Sex0rzt did nothing to prepare the mind for the image of Angela in physical form. Ted's compulsion to leave vaporised as soon as he saw her. He tried to peer at Jake but couldn't drag his eyes away from his date.

Jake, himself, was lost in the whirlwind of splendour that was Heather. Long, curling blonde tresses ran down across her shoulders and flanked an artist's model face and body. He tried to speak, but his brain couldn't cope with forming words as well as drinking in Heather's magnificence.

"We're so glad the two of you finally arrived," said Angela.

"We thought you'd bailed on us before we'd even got started," said Heather, a smile lighting up her face.

Ted tried to form a reply but was interrupted by the arrival of a waiter. He held his tray out with four drinks atop it. The girls took two drinks each and deftly placed one in each of the boy's right hands.

"We have a lot to talk about tonight, I want to know everything there is to know about you," said Angela into Ted's ear. She raised her glass and waited until he mirrored her action. When Ted's glass was at his lips, she downed her own and watched as his disappeared.

"Good, that should calm your nerves a little," she said.

As Jake and Heather finished their drinks, the waiter accepted the glasses back and disappeared from view.

"Let's dance," Angela said, nodding to Heather who grinned in return.

"Let's," she said.

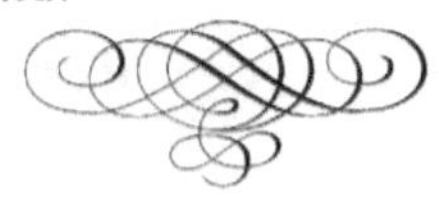

Ted's eyes fluttered open. One of the last things he

remembered was dancing with Angela. He only had eyes for her, and it seemed, she only had them for him. She wrapped herself around him on the dance floor, gyrating and grinding into him as much as the fabric of their clothes would allow. Finally, she whispered in his ear that there were vacant rooms upstairs.

She took his hand, led him from the ballroom and up the winding staircase. They found an empty room and Angela turned the lock, ensuring they wouldn't be disturbed.

She edged up to Ted and ran her fingers through his hair and looked deep into his eyes before pushing him onto the bed. He felt like he was flying as time slowed down and his brain drank in the incredible sensations on offer. This was a dream the likes he'd never managed in his life, to find himself in a lavish bedroom, with a beautiful woman, about to engage in some carnal pleasure. Heaven had found him on Earth.

He landed and stared back at Angela. She began to slowly unfasten her dress and let it slide down, revealing a body clad in the sheerest of underwear.

Ted's consciousness started to fade and try as he might to stay awake his mind flew away into the dark recesses of the void.

Now, his sight concentrated on focusing on the

ceiling above. His thoughts raced. Had they made love? Had he fallen asleep? Had he failed to keep himself in check?

Flickering light dashed across his vision as it regained focus. The ceiling was corrugated and angular. It seemed made of rock or dirt with what looked like plant roots hanging down at intermittent intervals.

He realised he wasn't in the bedroom anymore. He tried to rise. His arms and legs wouldn't respond. His head was immovable as well.

He peered around and almost screamed.

He was in some sort of cave. Rock walls lined the area. Primitive flaming torches jutted out of the walls at odd intervals. The orange fire casting a yellow pall across the scene.

A bizarre melodic chant filled the room. Straining, Ted managed to see the figures producing it. There were dozens. All wearing strange robes, with hoods that concealed their faces from view.

He glanced the other way and saw Jake.

Finally, he screamed.

Jake's dead eyes stared past him into space, his face frozen in a rictus of pain, a trickle of blood-soaked drool ran from his open mouth. His hands and feet were attached by ropes to a flat stone altar, Ted immediately realised he was bound to something similar.

It was then Ted noticed the shape standing behind Jake's corpse. He wore the same brown robe, but the hood was thrown back revealing his face. He was an older man, with a shock of grey hair and a long white beard. His arms were upheld, beseeching the heavens.

He spoke in a deep, resonant tone, "Ashtaroth, take this virginal soul that we have cast into the abyss for your pleasure. Grant us your favour as we grant you this gift."

The old man dropped his hands and pulled a bone-handled dagger from Jake's chest, flinging drops of red across the body. He cast his eyes down towards Ted. A sly grin broke across his face.

"Ashtaroth, the night is still young, we have another virgin offering, so that you may bless us and keep us in your thoughts," he said.

Ted realised what he meant. He shouted in fear, but then realised what the man had said.

"I'm not a virgin. I'm no good to you," he cried.

The old man stepped around Jake's altar and approached Ted. The combination of his face and smile was both wicked and kindly at the same time.

"Honest, I've had sex. Dozens of times," Ted pleaded, "I'm no good to you."

The priest stopped at the foot of Ted's altar. He

strained to look at the man, fearful that the blade would fall before he could plead his case.

As the priest stepped closer, a warm hand patted Ted on the forehead, and he turned to look at the owner and saw Angela standing beside him.

"Angela, get me out of here, this man's crazy, he killed Jake, he..."

Ted realised Angela was wearing the same type of brown robe. She was one of them. She smiled and caressed his brow.

"I know, Ted, I know. It's okay," she said.

"No, tell him, we had sex, didn't we? I remember clearly. In that bedroom. You and me. We.."

Angela smiled, a gentle, condescending smile.

"I know that's what you think," she said shaking her head, "But, no. You were drugged. You fell asleep. That's all."

"But, I'm not a virgin, I've slept with other girls. Really, I have."

Angela smiled, chuckled to herself and shook her head again. "No. No, you haven't. I would know."

She leaned forward and gently sniffed.

"I can smell it on you. It's a talent. A gift from Ashtaroth. It's never failed me," she said.

Tears welled in Ted's eyes and ran down his face.

"But, but…"

"Be comforted. Your death will serve a purpose, more than your life ever would," she said backing away and joining the adherents behind her. She replaced her hood and merged with the other devotees.

"I'm not a virgin, honest," Ted entreated Angela, but through his tear-soaked eyes he lost sight of her.

He turned his head away and gasped in shock when he saw the old priest towering above him. The man smiled gleefully down at him, soaking up the boy's pain and sorrow like a balm.

"You don't need to do this?" Ted pleaded, "I'm not what you think I am."

The old man raised his head to the ceiling and shouted, "Ashtaroth. We commit to you another unsullied soul. Dine well and bless us with your darkness. Your approval only spurs us on to even greater service. Our desires are matched by your desires in an endless cycle. Grant us our yearnings so that we may serve."

Ted tried to make one final appeal, but only croaked out a short squeal of pain as the dagger slammed deep into his heart. His head flopped to one side as his eyes glazed over, forever staring into the distance.

A deep, booming voice echoed all around the cave, driving into the very hearts and souls of the assembly.

"What is this insult? This one is tainted. You have failed me," it said.

Suddenly, the walls and floor of the cavern began to shake. A thunderous cacophony echoed through the chamber. Dust rained down and massive cracks appeared in the ceiling. Ted and Jake's bodies were tossed to the ground as the stone altars collapsed under the onslaught of the floor's upheaval.

Great fissures opened beneath the feet of the advocates, sucking them down to the hell they so fervently worshipped.

The old priest stared across at Angela, his face a mask of terror and fury.

"What have you done?" he screamed at the young woman. His anger short lived as a great rent appeared in the ground beneath him, dragging him into the bowels of the Earth.

Angela turned and pushed her way through the crowd. As one they all followed and rushed for the exits. A sudden cracking above brought tons of Earth and rubble down upon their heads, bringing their fight for freedom to an abrupt end.

Within moments, it was over. The congregation was no more.

Amidst the settling dust, a lone translucent form

hovered. Ted's spirit examined the death and destruction before it. A smile crossed its spectral face. A hollow voice whispered across the chamber.

"I warned you I wasn't a virgin," it said.

A Got a Message for You

by Sue Marie St. Lee

Nina examined her new breasts and nipples in front of the mirror, opened a tube of dark-pink lipstick and applied colour around and onto the tautly-pulled skin the plastic surgeon fashioned to replicate nipples. *I hope the tattoo artist can do this good.* From the bedroom doorway a long, loud, wolf-whistle broke her thoughts.

"Hellllo!" Troy reached out to caress Nina, his libido engaged for action.

"Troy, not now," Nina protested, pulling away from him.

Troy did not back down, his tongue probed her ear to the nape of her neck while caressing her plump bosoms.

"Damn it! Troy! No!"

Quickly releasing his hug, he spoke in anger, "Damn it, Troy? What the fuck? *Troy* has done *without* for nearly six months while you transitioned through this breast cancer. *Troy* worried during the five-hour bilateral mastectomy, the expansion surgery, every fill of the expansions, the replacement of the faulty expansion, the implant surgery, every visit to the oncologist. *Troy* was there.

"I haven't *bothered* you for sex. I understood—or tried to understand your fears, what you might be feeling. I've been faithful. When the hell are you going to understand that you're still a woman? I want you!"

"You don't understand, you say you do, but you don't." Nina began dressing, "Everything may look normal but there's no *feeling*." She bounced her breasts in her hands, "These have no feeling. If you want to suck my nipples," she pulled on the nipple protrusions, "these are *not* nipples! All of the sensual nerves are gone! I'll never feel the exhilaration of your mouth upon them again. My boobs are dead and gone."

Nina sank her face into her hands and cried. Troy hugged her close and strong, "I'm sorry. I didn't know this. I'm so sorry."

Still holding her, Troy pulled his face back to look into her eyes and asked, "You're meeting the tattoo artist today? Maybe he can put you in touch with women who've gone through this. Maybe someone can offer help on how they got through this."

"Yes, I'm meeting *her* in a couple hours. I want to see pictures of her past work and I have questions for her."

"Sounds good." Troy looked at his watch, "I've got to run now. Are you okay? If you want, I'll re-schedule the meeting for another day and I'll go with you."

"No, I'm okay, I just needed to cry."

With a warm kiss and hug, Troy left for work.

An hour later, Nina walked into the tattoo parlour. The room was bright with sunshine streaming through the wall of windows. Reggae music accompanied with Pomegranate incense wafted through the air. Four ink-beds were positioned beyond the half-wall of the waiting area.

Nina stood at the lavish front counter carved from Haitian guayacan wood. Masterful carvings of ancient symbols were embedded with shiny stones.

"Hi there!" The only female tattoo artist called out, "You must be Nina. Please sign in and have a seat, I'll be finished with Sam in about ten minutes. There's coffee, water, and cookies. Help yourself."

"Thanks." Nina grabbed a black coffee and sat facing the arena of artists. She studied her surroundings. Statues from another culture stared at her from their wall-pocket pedestals. Posters, displaying award-winning tattoo designs and artists, hung in frames made from the same carved guayacan wood.

Upon the back wall, a life-sized portrait of a

gorgeous man caught Nina's attention. The man was the epitome of tall, dark, and handsome. Dreadlocks framed his bronze face and flowed down, beyond his broad shoulders. His face was of perfection; the jawline of a sculptured Greek god outlined a strong, cleft chin. Above it, an inviting, gentle smile gave way to dimpled cheeks. But, his eyes, his eyes were ethereal with the strangest colour of turquoise projecting a look that could pierce your soul. Framing those exotic eyes were expressive, thick eyebrows. Nina was transfixed, lost in her curiosity of the man.

"Okay, Sam, you're done. How d'ya like it?" the female artist asked.

"Great, Sugar!" Sam rose from the ink-bed and made way for the door, nodding his head as he passed Nina.

Sugar followed Sam to the waiting area, "Thanks for waiting, Nina. Let's go to the office for privacy and we can talk. Oh, by the way, my name is Sugar."

The office was to the right of the portrait. Nina stopped to read the engraved plate upon it, it had one word—*Antoine*.

"Oh, that's Antoine. Everyone stops to stare, but you kind of get used to him if you're a regular here. He's gorgeous, isn't he?"

"He's definitely unusual. Who was he?"

"*Was?* He owns this place! I swear, there's some kind of magic in his work. You'll probably meet him; a lot of our breast reconstruction clients go to him after their tattoos heal."

At her desk, Sugar opened a folder named *Nipples*, flipped the laptop to face Nina, and they scrolled through before-and-after photos of women who went through what Nina was about to embark.

"None of these photos look like tattoos, they look like real nipples!"

Sugar smiled, "We are the only tattoo salon in the state that actually inks in 3-D."

"I'm convinced. But I have another problem. Even after the colouration, I know these nipples won't have any sensation. How do other women cope?"

"That's where Antoine does his magic. Every woman who chose to have him do the Regeneration has been very pleased."

"Really? I'd like to talk to some of these women."

"Sure. I can't give their names or numbers to you, but I'll text a few of them with your contact information and they'll call you. Do you want to wait for the 3D tattoos after you see these women?"

"No. I'm convinced that I want you to do the 3D tattoos; I'll meet with these women during the healing phase." Nina signed the contract for the procedure and to be contacted by the other women.

"How soon can we get started?"

Sugar pulled up her calendar, "I'm free tomorrow afternoon. How about one o'clock?"

"Okay, I'll see you tomorrow."

"Don't wear any lotion on those nipples."

The next day, Sugar worked her artistic 3D magic on Nina's nipples and held up the mirror for Nina's approval. "What d'ya think?"

"They look better than the real ones! I can't believe there's no charge for this!"

"Oh, never a charge for ladies who've fought breast cancer. Y'all have been through enough. Antoine insists on contributing in this way. He'll be calling you in a week to set up your Regeneration procedure."

Over the next week, Nina visited several women who attested to Antoine's abilities. She was convinced that he held the key to making her hopes a reality and waited for his call.

Exactly seven days after Nina was inked, Antoine called.

"Hello?" Nina answered.

"Hello, is this Nina?" Antoine's baritone voice sent a powerful chill through Nina.

"This is Nina."

"Sugar mentioned you'd like my service to regenerate your nipples." Antoine's Cajun accent was heavy, but not difficult to understand.

"Yes. I hope you can help me. I've been so depressed."

"Yes, the time for pleasure is soon for you. Seven days from today, you're healing will be finished. Meet me at my clinic. I'll explain everything and you'll tell me if you want to go ahead. Okay?"

Antoine agreed to a two o'clock afternoon appointment and gave his address to Nina.

That evening, Troy took Nina out for a romantic dinner at one of Chicago's finest restaurants to celebrate the final stretch of Nina's breast and nipple reconstruction.

"So, this guy can get the feeling back in your nipples?"

"Yes, he can! I talked with some of his clients and they are in absolute heaven. They even said that their libido intensified. I am so looking forward to this!" Glancing from side to side making sure no one could hear her, she whispered, "I can't wait to fuck your brains out!"

"Me too!" Troy's leg rubbed against Nina's under the table, "This is gonna be better than our honeymoon fuck-fest."

"Hey, I'm gonna make reservations for us at Le Palais de L'amour. We'll spend the weekend making mad, passionate love."

The following week, Troy went to *Aramis' Arousals & Aphrodisiacs* to buy sexy apparel, lotions, and an aphrodisiac for Nina. A tall, dark, handsome man with dreadlocks greeted Troy. "Hello. I'm Aramis. Welcome to my hut of pleasures. Anything you need for love-making is here."

Troy smiled and explained what he was looking for, especially the aphrodisiac.

"You have come to the right place. I have just the thing to keep your lady wanting more cock." Troy followed Aramis to a wall stocked with tiny bottles labelled with strange names. Aramis reached for a pink bottle labelled *Toorpaclluks*.

"This will keep your lady begging for sex. Just put a little drop in her cocktail."

Troy paid for the potion, sex toys, and lingerie. Next, he made the reservation at Le Palais de L'amour for the following weekend and arranged limousine pick-up for Nina.

Nina arrived at Antoine's clinic half an hour early and rang the doorbell. Antoine opened the door, appearing as ethereal as the painting. Nina was spellbound.

"Hello, Nina." Antoine flashed a gleaming smile. "Welcome to my hut of wonders where your troubles will be transformed to pleasures.

"Come in, come in. Don't stand in the cold!" Antoine waved his hand for Nina to enter. The entire first floor of the building resembled where you might find a voodoo priest practising his art.

The room was filled with statues, woven baskets, and clay pots within them. Crosses of every size, made from tree branches and twine, hung from the ceiling, walls, and rested against statues. Shelve-covered walls were stocked with liquid-filled antique bottles.

An odd sepia haze veiled everything. The only colour visible was Antoine's turquoise eyes. Nina felt uneasy. Antoine sensed Nina's discomfort, "I apologise—the lights. I'll switch to daylight. Yes?"

Without waiting for a reply, Antoine remotely changed the lighting to daylight quality. "Better?"

"Thank you."

"Follow me." Nina followed Antoine to an area

behind a wardrobe screen.

"Come, sit here." Antoine pointed to a leather recliner. Alongside it was a rolling stool and hospital cart, on its top shelf lay sealed needles, syringes, rubbing alcohol and gauze pads.

From the counter behind Antoine, he grabbed a white candle, lit it and recited strange words, ending with Nina's name. "The blessing is done. The ceremony is begun. Next, I take a little blood from you, a little blood from me and mix it into one blood. That is what makes the magic. Then, I inject into your new nipples."

Antoine withdrew three millimetres of blood from Nina's arm, transferred it to a fresh syringe barrel, and repeated the process with his own blood. He twisted a sterile needle to the tip of the syringe, swirled it, closed his eyes and whispered strange words with the reverence of one saying a prayer.

"Remove your top now. The blood is blessed."

"Will it hurt?" Nina had been quiet until this moment of no return.

"Your flesh has no feeling *yet*. As the syringe empties, your feeling will return and there will be pain, like someone sticking a needle into the nipples you had before the cancer surgery."

With precision of a skilled surgeon, Antoine held

Nina's left breast and with his right hand, began injecting the blood into her nipple, circling in one centimetre increments until the syringe was half-emptied.

"That hurt! Oh my God! That nipple has feeling again!" Tears of happiness filled Nina's eyes.

"Of course, what'd you expect? Now, be still, there is one more to do."

In minutes, regeneration of the left nipple was also complete.

"Okay, we're done. All feeling is restored. Your nipples will even protrude or contract responding to heat, cold or stimulation."

Nina, still sitting in the recliner, fondled her breasts. She was oblivious to Antoine' comments. Her hand slipped into her jeans, between her legs—she moaned and writhed while pleasing herself.

"No!" Antoine scolded, "You must celebrate this blessed gift with the man you love, with your husband."

Nina gave Antoine a crazed look, rose from the recliner while shedding her jeans.

"I want you. I've wanted you from the first time I saw you in that painting." Nudging closer to him, Nina reached for his balls and began caressing them while rubbing her body catlike against his.

Antoine pushed her away. "No! I don't have sex with

my clients. That is against the law of the magic. You must go. Now!"

"I don't *want* to go! I want *you*!"

Turning to the counter, Antoine opened a basket, pulled a clump of moss-like twigs out and held it above the white candle which was still burning. Chanting strange words, he used his breath to blow the smoke in Nina's direction. Within minutes, Nina's nymphomania subsided.

"Why am I naked? What the fuck did you do to me?" Nina had no recollection of her actions.

"You had a reaction to the blood-magic. I've only seen this once before. You're alright now. Dress and go home."

"Wait a minute. What do you mean *had a reaction*? What kind of fuckin' reaction? Why did it happen? Is it gonna happen again?" Nina retrieved her clothes and began to dress while Antoine answered.

"No. You had intense vexation from abstinence, it manifested and sought satisfaction. You pleasured yourself then wanted for me to pleasure you. I blessed you with burning Skullcap Root to strengthen the fidelity in your marriage. You will be fine as long as you never take Toorpaclluks, an aphrodisiac potion that counteracts fidelity for twenty-four hours. Now, go to your husband."

"That's weird. I mean, I don't remember any of that. It's like a blackout."

"No worries. You will make lots of love with your husband. Now, go."

Nina arrived home, showered, slipped on a sexy black dress with stilettos, pulled her long blonde hair into a sexy, twisted updo then packed a small bag with toiletries for herself and Troy. Downstairs in the living room, she drank a glass of wine and paced, waiting for the limousine.

Troy waited for Nina in the lounge at Le Palais de L'amour. When Nina entered the lounge, every man in the room ogled her provocative beauty. Troy raised his hand to draw her attention as he stood to walk toward her. He put his arm around her and escorted her to the table where he had been sitting, "You are ravishing. How about a drink to start our weekend? How'd it go?"

"It went great, it worked! I'd like a whiskey sour."

"Fan-fuckin'tastic! Okay, Babe I'll bring the drinks and hors d'oeuvres then we'll go to the dining room."

After a couple of drinks and dinner, the couple headed to their room. Todd went to the bar, cracked open the champagne, took the aphrodisiac from his pocket and poured its entire contents into Nina's glass. "Let's toast this special occasion." Nina downed her entire drink in large, unladylike gulps. The fuck-fest began and carried into the wee hours of morning with moaning, groaning, licking of edible panties, jock straps—sex toys were strewn about the room. Before passing out, Troy plead with Nina, "I can't stay awake any more. I need sleep." Nina was not ready for sleep, she wanted more—more sex.

She dressed, tidied her make-up and hair and set out for the lounge. There was one patron sitting at the bar. Nina headed to sit next to him when the bartender appeared from the back room and her attention was diverted. She screamed, "Antoine!"

The bartender turned to look at her. "Ma'am, my name is Aramis."

"No, it's not. I know you. You are Antoine. I was at your clinic this afternoon. You blessed me."

Aramis' mind raced with lightning speed. *She thinks I'm Antoine. I don't know what's going on between them, but she looks horny.*

"Lady, you have me confused with my identical twin brother."

"I don't care who you say you are, in my eyes, you *are* him and I want you." Nina reached over the bar to grab his face and kissed his mouth deep and wet.

The bar patron butted in with a hiccup, "Hey Lady,

my name's Antoine!"

"Chuck, it's time to go. Get outta here." Aramis took Chuck's glass away, pointed to the door and grabbed a tiny blue bottle from under the counter. He put it to his lips and drank the entire bottle in one gulp.

Chuck stumbled toward the exit. Nina paid no attention to either of the men; she slithered on top of the bar, wrapped her legs around Aramis' and began humping his still-clothed body.

Aramis flicked the lights off, held Nina and carried her to the back room. They tore each other's clothes off fucked, licked, sucked and ate each other until daylight when Aramis heard rustling in the outer lounge.

He pulled away from Nina just as the door swung open and a woman yelled, "What the fuck do you think you're doin' you bastard! You been fuckin' this floozy all night while I been tryin' to call you?"

"You missed our date. I called, and called, and all I got was *leave a message*! Now I got a message for you, you lying asshole pimp!" The woman pulled out a pistol and began shooting. "And for you, you slut whore!"

Alarms sounded, the woman knew that police would arrive soon, so she wiped the gun of her fingerprints, put the gun in Aramis' hand, pointed at Nina and shot again. She grabbed a bottle of vodka, smashed it open and poured it on her hands to rid them of gun powder residue, then lay down beside Aramis, crying and screaming.

That night's headlines read: Two Shot in Lover's Quarrel at Le Palais de L'amour—Both Expected to Survive.

Podcast of the Dead

by Mark Mackey

My name is Hailey Cavenforth.

It's the day before Halloween. I'm sitting behind my desk in the dorm room that I share with Arya Markstone at Haven-Bracers Women's college, recording this podcast as a warning of what has befallen Haven-Bracers.

Arya hasn't kept the fact secret she desperately lusts after me, and I feel the same way about her. Unfortunately for Arya, she was the first casualty of the zombies' lust.

As I sit implanted in this chair, I can hear the door being pounded on furiously by these zombies, my roommate now one of them—desperate to use me to satisfy their lust for human flesh. It won't be long before they burst in and I suffer the same fate as Arya.

I graduated Valedictorian from Wavercrest High School and jumped right into student life at Haven-Bracers Women's college after summer break. After all, gaining further education has always held appeal to me.

Even though I'd got on pretty well with the

roommates I'd had throughout my years here, the best one by far is Arya. She and I are so much alike, and we have such desperate affection for each other, I wouldn't trade her for the world.

Anyway, enough about that. Let me explain in detail how it all unfolded. Unbelievable as it sounds, an infectious virus from some corner in the dark depths of space is to blame for

the zombie invasion. I don't have a clue how it arrived, but I suspect it may have been dropped down around the same time someone in Havencrest, where Haven-Bracers is located, reported seeing a UFO. It doesn't matter how it arrived, the point is, it did, and now the same Illinois town is paying the price for it.

The first citizen to be struck with the virus—patient zero as it's termed—was a teenage girl, a cheerleader squad captain; Jade Handerfield. She spread it to her fellow cheerleaders, through biting the crap out of them— guess they won't be cheering anymore. In turn, they spread it to their families, and so on.

Within hours, Havencrest had become Zombie Town, USA.

Once all of the town's citizens were turned into zombies, they began to make their way towards Haven-Bracers, pulling the unsuspecting students into their

undead ranks. If I had known what was happening, and zombies were on the way, I would have dragged Arya with me and rush from the dorm room; jumped into my car and drove as far away as possible. I didn't, however.

As they made their arrival, like now, I was sitting at my desk, studying for a test. And Arya, well, she was taking it easy on her bed, reading one of her romance novels. She's obsessed with them.

"Hey, I'm in desperate need of some coffee, you want some?" Arya asked in the middle of her reading.

"Yeah, I could go for some," I replied, turning to face her.

"I'll be right back," Arya said, tossing her book down and scrambling off her bed.

A few minutes after she stepped out, I was distracted from studying by my roommate's scream.

Concerned for Arya, I stood up and headed for the door to investigate.

I pulled it open, stepped out, and that's when I saw it.

Them.

The women I had become friends with and associated with over the years had now become the living dead. It was like my worst nightmare come to life. Worse, Arya, the woman who had my heart, stood among them, her white blouse soaked with blood, and like the rest, her eyes had a vacant emptiness to them; full indication she tragically fell victim to these zombies' lust for flesh.

It took me only a second to realise it would be in my best interests to get back into my dorm room as quick as possible and lock the door to savor the last few minutes alive before I ended up like Arya. Turning back around in a rush, this is exactly what I did.

Sitting back at my desk, I could barely bring myself to believe that over just a few minutes, not only my roommate, but the entire floor had become zombies.

They've broken down the door and Arya's leading them in. They're rushing for me to seal my fate.

The sound of fabric ripping.

A blood-curdling scream.

Imminent death.

Silence.

The sickening sounds of zombies eating flesh.

Pi

by Ximena Escobar

The school shoe bounced nervously under the chair. "She's such a bitch," moaned the girl (even if her knees were comfortably apart, the dough of her flesh met in the middle, under her skirt.) She raised her voice. "Said I'm a whore because I pose for you!"

She lost her shoe as the metal legs lifted off the ground, resting her head on the painted white bricks. "Pi?"

Dust stirred in the beam of sunshine filtering through the skylight. Pi circled his rock like a *torero*, wiping the sweat on his brow with his pirate sleeve.

"What do you think I should say to her?"

But his eyes stayed fixed on the rock, absorbed in contemplation.

Kate swung forward to a standing position. The shoe eluded her as she slipped her foot back in, but she trapped it under her heel. She pulled her skirt straight. "I'm telling her to go fuck herself."

Pi opened his hand at her abruptly. With the other, he traced a charcoal line loosely over the porous surface all the way to the edge; it skimmed off the stone like a seagull. He looked like a sculpture; graceful yet dominant with his rigid policeman hand on one side, and his other arm raised beautifully like a flamenco dancer, fingertips holding the chalk like a seagull about to shoot down for its feed. It did, landing precisely on the charcoal line from which he began to shadow the rock desperately, more like a starved hawk when it devours its kill.

Kate treaded softly, waiting quietly until he'd shadowed the whole area below the line. He didn't turn around, but he tossed the chalk when he finished, on one of the many sketches scattered on his workbench. She picked it up, causing it to roll onto the other drawings. She swept the black dust off as she examined it.

"My hair isn't like that, you know." Her hair appeared longer on the page, and of a different quality. It spiralled into the air like serpents talking around her head. "I mean… Were you drunk or something?"

Greek goddesses were everywhere on the papers; wrapped in sheets that hung below the hips, some holding instruments, others with venomous tongues curving out of their mouths, or lying on their backs with legs parted as their casual hands pretended not to know they were blocking the view of the sexes.

Pi turned around, sticking his fingers under the bandage around his palm.

"I only do goddesses."

He pulled at the gauze and his hand began to circle itself out.

"Why do you ask *me* to pose then?"

"It's time you went back to your mother."

The gauze unravelled silently.

"I don't want to."

"Back to your friends..."

"They're idiots," she said.

"You're an idiot," said Pi, lifting his pupils to meet hers.

Kate recognised his sudden desire. He tossed the gauze on the workbench without taking his eyes off her.

"Close the door."

She took a step back, unbuttoning her shirt before scampering to the garage door, pulling it down with a thunderous rattle. Hurrying back, she stopped her feet a distance from Pi.

He took a step closer, and another, drying his sweaty palms on his shirt and his jeans. Kate's chest heaved in anticipation, awaiting the pull that brought their bodies together as his finger hooked the bridge of her bra.

He opened her mouth with his. He pushed his tongue stiffly down her throat, squeezing her arms with his hard hands. He pushed her down to a squat, pressing the bulge of his jeans against her face.

She felt the roughness of the denim on her lips. She felt her scalp stretch as he tangled his fingers in her hair, rolling them into a fist. He pulled her head back.

"Turn around."

Kate obeyed.

Pi knelt behind her, lifting her skirt with his sculptor's hand—his hard hand, on her soft ass.

Hooking the G-string with his finger, he pulled it up as his warm steamy breath permeated through her ear.

"Don't you understand I need to work…"

Kate's mouth sank into her elbow as she waited for the strike of his palm. It hovered upon her for a long circular instant before it hit, sending shock waves to her breasts; nipples sprouting, mouths opening. Redness spreading and lingering.

"Lie on your back."

"Like this?"

"Shut up."

"You want me to talk dirty?"

"Just keep the fuck quiet."

"Ok. Ok, Pi."

He rose up like a tower above her, his sex standing as erect as him, his hands on his waist.

"You want me to suck it for you?"

The cock heard and wriggled—like the hair of the Medusa in the sketch—but came to hang loosely.

"What is it, babe? Don't you fancy me?"

Pi's lips tensed thin. "Yeah, I fancy you."

"You do?"

"Yeah."

He slapped her with his semi-flaccid worm, shoving the mass of sex into her mouth, her moans rolling and warm. He pulled her away, looking at her blotchy face.

"You exist too much."

"Huh?"

Pi reached for his chisel, tossing her back onto the rug.

She waited on her elbows, the sharp point of the chisel skimming down her chest, between the mount of breasts rising, deflating, rising. Pubic hairs protruded from under the thin cotton layer that covered her sex like a warm white pillow. He pressed the stem of the chisel there, as he'd done on her lips. He hooked the elastic with the point, pulling it to as he pierced her eyes with his stare. He leaned over, but a kiss away from her mouth.

"If you don't go home, I'm gonna fuck you with this."

The little slut. The mindless, ignorant barking. The insolent distraction. The animal separating us from god, enslaving us to flesh, to children; turning us into a cog, a spiritless machine, a wheel suspended in a vacuum of mediocrity. The beast pulling us away from the breast and throwing us into abandon; a river of death where the heavenly forests of creation bypass us; always falling prey just when we're about to reach the sky through the sacredness of our skill...

A long black hair lay disgustingly on the rug. Let that be the last he ever saw of her.

Pi looked at his rock. Aphrodite, the goddess of love, was waiting within it for the touch of his hands. He pulled his fingers in preparation. A predator shimmered in his eyes; the goddess was also, first and foremost, a woman. He needed to find the marrow of the woman. Find it as the sole purpose of the first hit of the chisel, straight from the surface, so the woman would never be anything other.

He chalked his hands, wrapping the gauze around his palm. He squatted, holding its expanse, and sliding his hands in and out with circular strokes like he'd done on Kate's roundness. Reaching down, he felt the unexposed dark roughness underneath with his fingertips.

He began to carve in the middle. He chiselled for hours; hours that became days. His hand, sweating on the grip of the chisel, carved with the strength of his muscle as he listened to the will of his genius; a beat that kept him going like warrior horses treading the earth.

Reach the human quality of Aphrodite. Scrape out her perfection with your hooves; the sacredness, the geometry. Give it dents that deserve slapping, a sadness that needs to be smacked out. Something that inspires in us action—to stomp, to piss on, to sow.

Pi's stiff sex bulged under the denim. His shirt stuck translucently to his wet chest, panting as it chased the ever-elusive light in the periphery; the divinity in the sideline. Let that goddess in the horizon of every motion take precedence. Let that bridge in my song take over completely; bring the love perceived in the beginning, the lie that nourished our sense-of-self, let it sweep over the whore and bury it. Let in the fantasy, the perfection, find the beauty of curves. Love it, care for it with calloused hands that polish our wounds, release it with fingertips that free music out of strings. Rub and dig the groin like a fossilised streambed; feel it like a desert snake; slither up and down the smooth channel; smooth and sanded; warm like the beach under the white light that beams through the ceiling; warm like the sand you lie on with your eyes closed, in the redness of darkness; a dune to the cave where everything is lost.

There was his masterpiece! There was The Aphrodite! Love and beauty in the accurate shape and essence of a woman. Oh my! She was perfect. She was complete.

Emotion flooded his chest. Treasures cannot be stripped of the risk of losing them. He surrendered, the salt of his tears absorbing into the stone like the blood of fallen men.

Something moved. A slow soft touch gliding upon him like a breeze, spiralling around his hair, his temple, his jaw. He dwelled in that touch, listening to the calming sweeping sound of fingers in his ear.

Aphrodite was looking at him! She was looking at him with seeing eyes. She was looking at him like eternity, like timelessness, soundlessly—but Pi could hear her! What joy! What ecstasy! Her voice was amorphous, like light—wordless, illegible—but it enveloped him like the exquisite disintegration of his skin; Pi, who had extracted life from the grit of the earth, was one with the whole.

"You have shaped me to the image and likeness of your incompleteness," said the goddess.

A want opened in his chest. A want that relentlessly carved itself in his heart. He had indeed shaped her to the likeness of his need—her breasts to fit the cup of his hands, her mouth to fit his sex, shed light on his blindness. She was his balance. She was his perfection.

"Speak again, my angel!"

But Aphrodite stood cold and silent as stone.

His hands gripped her shoulders as he looked, desperately, for a glimmer of life in her eyes; but there was no stamp of his miracle; just the futility of his grasp.

The impossibility of reliving that sacred climax he had experienced, mocked him. She was treacherous! The whore at the chore had risen in the horizon of his realisation, like the slut she was first and foremost. And he couldn't destroy her. He couldn't dig his fingers into her flesh and mark her skin with shame; undo her without only undoing himself; his mastery. He couldn't make her a reflection of his fear; open a window into her self-doubt nor give her the light that quivers in a bitch's eyes, under the threat of a fist. His tongue pounced on the statue's nipple, like a leash pulling a dog's neck.

He forcefully closed his eyes, trying to dissolve the ridiculous sight of himself; a brute pumping his lust against a statue—just a little faster, just a little further, just a little bit less mind. He hopelessly ignored the stubborn memory of Kate's sad ass fuelling him, open for his disdain—her face, her stupid face—as the goddess disappeared under the imprint of the memory of her flesh.

The long black hair looked at Pi from the rug. He caught it between the hardness of his fingertips, letting it glide into the paper basket.

That's when he decided to kill her. He scanned the room for the phone.

First published in World of Myth Magazine, May 2019

Coitus Interruptus

by Thomas Kearnes

Danny was lying nude on the vinyl couch when he first heard the chant. An insipid dance track played, hardly a song at all, just a lockstep bass beat accompanied by shrill whistles and a smoky-voiced diva's moans. All the men listened to this tripe. Like the other men of his tribe, he lacked the imagination to escape it. He heard something simmer beneath the thuds from the speakers tucked in the high corners of the room.

The voice in the song was breathy, almost too high to discern, but Danny knew what he'd heard.

The time is now, the time has come

Join us in the high kingdom

From the rear of the house a running shower echoed; Brandon, their host, was still cleaning his anus in preparation for the next round of sex doomed to wither in their memories before sunrise. All the men had agreed to this psychic hobbling, they'd agreed to ostracise any man insisting on affection.

Danny swung his feet onto the floorboards and walked to the stereo. He pressed a button, and the CD skipped to the next track. Another thudding bass beat, the same voices schilling artificial ecstasy. He glared at a speaker, waiting to hear the chant again. The teasing voice began its rhyme, and Danny's bloodshot, dilated eyes grew wider. He recoiled from the speaker like it was a decaying corpse hurled down from the heavens. He'd smoked too much but not nearly enough. Spent, he couldn't corral his thoughts.

The time is now, the time has come

Join us in the high kingdom

He listened a few moments, focused. If he concentrated hard enough, perhaps this snatch of song would vaporise, an auditory hallucination from the crystal meth. With each repetition, however, the chant emerged more fully from the dance track, a siren slicing through morning traffic. This wouldn't be happening if I hadn't enjoyed my cousin raping me the summer after kindergarten, he told himself.

Afraid to be alone, Danny headed peeked into the bedroom and saw Curtis perched atop the bed, masturbating to porn—another download of men too high to refuse sex stimulating more men too high to refuse sex. Curtis may have been tall, may have had flinty eyes. He might have been the man Danny would finally and forever love.

Curtis numbly stroked himself. Loneliness is safer in numbers than in isolation—more common, too.

"What you doing?" Danny asked at the doorway. He remembered to smile.

"Watching this," Curtis replied in a dead voice. He might have been dead, but he might have been waiting to live again.

Danny stepped forward to see the laptop screen. They watched two men, a built blond and a slender brunette, simultaneously penetrate the ass of an older, bearded man while he writhed atop them. These men always managed to reduce sex to a circus act. The bearded man's face wrenched in spooky wonderment. The men's skins were tan and hairless: their bodies moved with the dull precision of knitting needles. Danny found himself enraptured, forgetting the chant. At that moment, no amount of sex could satisfy him. He could not imagine, however, any man he wouldn't despise the moment after orgasm. Finally, he said, "Brandon showed me this one before."

"That's hot."

"The next scene is even better."

"Cool."

Curtis didn't glance at Danny when he spoke. He gaped at the sexual metronome ticking before him. Danny reached for Curtis's shoulder but let his hand drop before reaching him. In elementary school, these men learned about "good" touch and "bad" touch. He decided to wait for Brandon to finish bathing to make his exit. Brandon had promised Danny righteous penetration at some point that early morning; doubting him required too much effort. Until then, he watched porn from the doorway.

Still, he could hear the chorus, the voice cajoling him to join an unknown kingdom, but he focused on the loud hum inside his head, instead.

On the laptop, the blond now jammed himself down the bearded man's throat while the brunette continued thrusting himself inside the man's ass. Danny fell with relief into the textbook couplings on the screen. The porn required he focus only on the image before him, wilfully ignorant of what might follow. There was no past and no future; it was an oasis of flesh in this desert of a house.

The image flickered.

"What was that?" Danny asked.

"What was what?"

"Didn't you see it?"

Again, the screen cut to darkness. This time, however, a figure emerged from the black, the head of a stallion. Its wide, muscular neck sprouted from the bottom of the screen. Its dead white eye stared directly at Danny and Curtis. Its luxurious mane fanned as if caught in a breeze. The porn did not return. Curtis stared dumbly as if he'd accept whatever the laptop wished to show.

Danny, meanwhile, inched toward the screen, mystified. The quiet, steady crackling in his head grew louder.

Their fathers never expressed interest in what they said, or what remained unsaid.

The horse's image reared back its head and let out a guttural scream. It was a cry of alarm, of sudden recognition. Throughout the house, it echoed until finally slipping beneath the bumpy dance track. You can't stop the music—as the old song goes. The three copulating men reappeared on the screen. The blond shot a stream of semen onto the bearded man's face, into his waiting mouth.

"What the fuck was that?" Danny cried.

"That one guy just came on the other guy."

"Girl, didn't you see what happened?"

Curtis's limp penis drooped between his thighs. "You're fucking tweaked."

"There was a horse, and it was screaming. It was right fucking there."

Curtis looked at Danny through half-shut eyelids, like a sly drunk. "I told you not to fucking smoke so much," he said. "Tina can be one cruel bitch."

Danny backed away from the laptop. "But I saw it…"

From rear of the house, Brandon shut off the shower. Danny froze in the doorway, his mind too electric with frenzied life to plot an escape. He'd desired escape for so long that he no longer recalled what trapped him. The chant bubbled from the speakers in the living room, more clearly than ever before.

The time is now, the time has come

Join us in the high kingdom

He looked at Curtis' empty eyes and slack limbs. Panicked, he hustled from the bedroom, through doorway after doorway, until he reached the closed bathroom. He slammed his fist and the door rattled in its frame.

A low, casual voice greeted Danny from inside. "Nobody wants to fuck a dirty boy."

"Brandon, get out here."

"Still drying off, sweetie."

Danny tried to tell his host about the chant, about the stallion, but he never spoke. The words sounded stupid in his head. Brandon always had good shit, and he was a terrific fuck, so Danny was torn about being branded a tweak freak. When removed from the judgment of society, this subculture of men instantly judged one another. Still, Danny couldn't bear standing helpless, waiting for a new bizarre signal to reveal itself. He mustered all his calm and inched his face into the door's opening. "I should take off, sexy."

"Fuck that, it's only three o'clock."

"I'm totally jacked. I need somewhere quiet."

Danny heard Brandon scrub a towel across his back. "Wait a second," his host said. The door swung wide and a nude Brandon fixed Danny with a slight downward gaze and tilted chin, a pose of concern. "You were fine when I jumped in the shower."

Danny didn't reply. To his horror, red splotches glowed where Brandon's eyes should have been, shapeless like splattered cherries. Their bewitching brightness mesmerised him. His host was a small, compact and muscular man—or that might have been someone else, some other weekend.

Brandon, meanwhile, continued in his mild, surprised tone. "If this is about Curtis, don't twist your knickers. He gets like this every time. Stuff enough tweak up his nose, and he checks out." Danny's helpless gaze filled a silence longer than he'd expected. "You didn't do more shit by yourself, did you?" Brandon asked. "I hope Curtis didn't fucking talk you into slamming."

"What…what happened to your eyes?"

"I ran out of Visine."

Brandon seemed to add snidely that Danny had been smoking dope long enough to know the side effects—except he didn't say that. Among these men, condemnation was never expressed directly.

Danny said nothing, staring into Brandon's red eyes. He backed, step by slow step, away from Brandon and through the doorway, into the kitchen. His head pulsed and his stomach clenched. His mind couldn't string all he'd seen together. They remained isolated horrors, each a graveyard spook bolting out from behind a headstone. Danny yanked a chair from underneath the small dining table. He collapsed into the seat, clapped his hands over his face. The unexplained sounds and images were less terrifying than the unceasing menace beyond Brandon's front door. Perhaps the morning would release him, as it typically did these men, demanding their silence in return. The moment a man admitted he wished for numbness, he lost access to that very thing. Danny wanted to cry but couldn't remember how.

The chorus repeated itself with no end, now almost as loud as the dance track. Danny covered his ears, squeezed shut his eyes. If he could just wait out the hallucinations, he'd be okay. He believed this like a schoolboy believes in the goodness of candy.

Brandon walked into the kitchen. A ramshackle tower of dirty cups and dishes reached the faucet. Brandon rearranged them and placed a glass beneath the tap. He twisted a knob, and the screech was so horrible Danny snapped out of his cowering state to look. Holding the glass, Brandon's forehead creased with worry. The red splotches obscuring his eyes shimmered before Danny.

A thick ooze of brownish blood sputtered into the drinking glass. The metallic shriek that accompanied the sludge rang out, as if the room were festooned by wind chimes composed of lead. Brandon didn't seem to notice any of this. He absently rubbed the small of his back. "Might do you some good to take a shower, too," he said.

Danny shook in his seat, his feet drawn beneath him, hands folded beneath his chin as if in prayer.

Brandon continued, perfectly reasonable. "If you want, I'll find a way to ditch Curtis. I mean, if that's why you're freaked. He's so dumb, he won't know I ditched him till he walks out the door."

Finally, Danny managed to speak. "I—I just need to go somewhere quiet."

Yes, quiet. Danny couldn't speak for other men, not even those he claimed to have once loved, but he himself knew that's all he desired from life: the din of advertisements and gossip and ridicule to one day stop, the silence like the first hollow moments after a jackhammer finishes its duty.

"I can turn the music down," Brandon said. "I'd rather not turn it off. You know how silence fucks with your head."

Danny's fingers twisted into a useless, gnarled tangle. His eyes jittered in their sockets, bewildered searching for something safe to view. The glops of putrid blood continued to seep into the glass. Brandon glanced back and swiftly twisted the knob. The blood ceased, and he took the glass to Danny, set it in front of him.

"You haven't drunk anything since we started," Brandon said. "You're dehydrated."

"The time is now," Danny replied absently. "The time has come."

Danny gaped at the glass of congealed blood as if he could will it out of existence. He cut his gaze to see Brandon standing over him. His eyes still glowed a horrible red. Danny's clothes, where were they? He needed to get dressed. He needed to leave. It was the middle of the night. He could handle the sporadic oncoming cars and the brief, fluttering headlights. If he stayed here, he would lose his mind. Worse, someone might take it from him.

He leapt from the dining table, knocked Brandon in

the chest. Brandon wobbled back to his feet, but Danny was already past him. The host shook his head and sighed. He took a long sip from the glass of blood.

Danny stumbled to a stop in the living room. He searched wildly along the floor. His clothes, as well as those of Curtis and Brandon, were tangled into a large knot. He clawed through it, tossing skimpy briefs, shirts and jeans. The inescapable chant skipped about the room, now dominating the track, rendering it as incidental as elevator music.

The time is now, the time has come

Join us in the high kingdom

As he jammed his legs, his arms, his head through his clothes, the chant echoed in his imagination. Time for what? Where the hell was the high kingdom? Who lived there? And why speak to him and no one else? Danny rammed his feet into his loafers and dug into his pocket for his keys, hurrying for the door.

Brandon appeared in the doorway at the opposite end of the room, his arms braced against the top of the frame. His long, muscular body arched out from the frame with the good-natured ease of a high-school athlete. "Call or hit me up online when you're feeling better, okay?" his host instructed. The red splotches in his eyes glistened as he spoke. "I wish I'd gotten to sample that boy pussy."

Danny quickly nodded and slammed the door behind him. In his haste, he nearly collided with Curtis perched on the porch's railing. "Girl," he purred, "you have got to chill the fuck out." He wore only a flimsy blue bathrobe, the fabric threadbare at the elbows. Danny realised he'd been forgetting what either Curtis or Brandon looked like the moment they left his sight. Some men would consider this a gift.

"I'm sorry," Danny sputtered. "I gotta go."

"The will of the high kingdom cannot be escaped," Curtis said.

Danny stopped in the front yard after hearing those words. He stood motionless, unable to tame the overwhelming static in his brain and decide his next move. "What did you say?"

"The high kingdom, my fellow heathen. The time has come."

Danny noticed the sky was impossibly bright for this long before dawn. Pale greys, lavenders and soft pinks floated up from the horizon, crawling higher by the moment. The neighbourhood was too quiet. No passing cars, no barking dogs, no comforting swell of a nearby party. Danny turned to watch Curtis light a cigarette.

The emptiness filling his eyes now conceded to purpose and malice.

"I come to these gatherings. I offer my flesh. Each time I hope to expand the kingdom. We corrupt our minds so we can't acknowledge it. We corrupt our bodies so we can't welcome it. But the high kingdom, Daniel, it can demolish any obstacle."

An immense cloud of smoke surged from his thin lips. Danny couldn't help the stirring he felt in his gut, recognizing how the cloud was dense and bright like a cloud from a meth pipe. There was a thickness in his hands and feet, a force pulling him to the ground like a marionette minus its manipulator. Of course, he'd always known the men not like him believed his kind to be corrupt, foul, beneath contempt. They had sent Curtis to collect him. He could've been riding Brandon or calling his dying mother. He backed closer to the curb, his parked car.

"You're totally fucked up," Danny stammered.

"We will be saved," Curtis replied. As he crossed the grass toward Danny, the sky continued to blossom with softer colors. A ring of stark, brilliant bone-white circled the horizon. Danny ducked his head, the brightness was so stunning.

"We need not waste our bodies and minds ever again."

The harsh sea of white raced through the heavens.

The whole atmosphere glowed with a punishing dazzle. Danny fell to his knees, his hands thrown over his head. Curtis stopped before Danny as he cowered at the curb. He placed a hand atop Danny's head, raised his other as if signalling a congregation. He lifted his chin, and there, underneath the blank eternity, Curtis intoned in a voice firm and rich, "Our whole lives we have waited. We knew You'd come. We were naked and corrupt, but now we are Yours."

Danny was paralyzed with terror, his heart pounding like a gong. He couldn't believe that such a meager memory would choose to resurface now, but it did: Three or four months ago, he'd scurried downtown in the early and dark morning. The bathhouse stood between an abandoned church and used truck lot, no lighted sign or streetlamps illuminating the way. After leaving through the heavy swinging door, its ominous click signalling his return to legitimate society, he spied an elderly couple across the street. Even with her cane, the old woman poked down the sidewalk, her husband gingerly holding her elbow. Surely, they both knew this would do little to prevent a fall, but the warmth and intimacy of the gesture moved Danny to tears. A moment later, both the man and woman turned to face Danny, realizing he was watching them. Danny waved and the couple's faces drew tight with distaste. They shuffled away. They knew, he had thought. They wanted me to know they knew. He felt like a child too gangly and sensitive, a child cast adrift. He had spent the next five minutes hiding in his parked car, hitting the pipe. He didn't remember how to cry then either.

"I'm going home," Danny announced, his voice hard.

"Yes, my brother, we're going home."

"Not with you, asshole."

"My brother, we soon must leave. Others in crisis need me."

Danny sprang to his feet and strode purposefully back onto the porch. Curtis gaped at him. Something inside Danny hardened like amber inside a tree, his soul the ancient insect forever trapped inside. He reached for the doorknob.

"My brother, please! I cannot come back!"

Danny's tone was flat and hard. "Brandon promised he'd fuck me." He fixed Curtis with a blank gaze. Danny's mouth went slack as he leaned against the front door, confident Brandon's eyes had lost their red fire, and confident he would hear no more about any kingdom. Not all the holy pyrotechnics unfurling in the sky would make him erase who he was.

The muscles in Curtis's neck stretched tight. "How long must your sorrow last, Daniel?"

"I'll make that decision." He opened the door to Brandon's house. "Right now, I have a dick to suck."

Little Man of Apartment No 1610

by Tristan Drue Rogers

Within a dark and damp corridor of sour stenches and very small amounts of horror rested a tiny boy with a brave heart. The cave filled throughout with many unknown relics of a forgotten age; bright colours were peeking out from within the shadows as the boy readied himself for a great battle, the likes of which the boy could only begin to imagine.

To help you understand a bit more about the boy, I suppose that I should have started from the beginning. Please excuse me, as I am a bit slow for my age and not near as young as I used to be… Now, the boy of this strange little story was brought into this world with very little potential to succeed. Sadly, he has had very little influence from his caregivers as well. His mother was forever busy with her attempts to keep her son within a "steady environment" as she and her reading material had put it. And the tale concerning his relationship with his father is one that I would rather not speak of.

One day, while mother was at work, the boy began his usual ritual of tuning in on whatever was blasting from the television. Searching for something with a great deal of lunacy, I'm sure. He then would climb atop a large and vast structure of perilous heights in search of the fabled cereal box. While eating, he soon grew tired of the channels, which were at his disposal and elected to step outside and play, as children often used to enjoy.

While off on his adventure he found his way to the lone swing set of the apartment complex, hopping onto it. The child soon became afraid of thrusting too far from the ground; the swing came to a slow and steady stop as a man appeared next to him. The man's voice was of a devastating sound to the child, he felt as if he had swallowed his own heart upon the forcefully filling vibration. The man looked directly into the boy's eyes while feverishly scratching his neck as flakes of his skin floated down upon the dirt below them. The boy soared out of the swing, gliding toward his door with the numbers one, six, one, and a zero held onto it, never opting to look back behind him.

His mother seemed to have shown up in just the nick of time as the boy hid inside, spying out from the window. The scary man grabbed his mother with a great show of anger. It was at this moment that the boy, without a drop

of hesitation, grabbed his towel for wearing around his neck; a boy was of great speed while wearing his cape. And summoned "Bonk-Da-Bonk," his red baseball bat of unlimited strength and resources to help in his struggle.

The hero of our story rushed toward the villain as the wind pushed down against his tiny frame. Once he finally climbed past the breeze to reach the bad man, he took Bonk, slamming it onto the man's leg. The man threw mother to the floor as he deliberately stepped to the young boy. The hero stood proud while protecting his mother just before the police came, answering the mother's call before she gracefully took on the role of damsel.

Now here is where things get interesting, I've honestly been struggling to stay awake up until now.

As the policemen approached the abuser, shadows quickly surrounded and engulfed his body. Furiously, he broke free from his shell, revealing a beast of immeasurable form. Strangely, as he did this, only the boy reacted. The mother was tightly holding her boy, telling him that everything would be okay. The two badges didn't even seem to realise that he broke free.

The boy prepared to escape from his mother's warm embrace as the shadowy figure abandoned him; he knew that mom needed him now more than she ever will.

A few days sped by, and the boy had yet stayed

forever vigilant in his pursuit to find the beast that attacked his family. Each night had increasingly become more difficult for the child; the branches would brush against his window like tendrils taunting prey. Sounds from the television that he previously welcomed now screamed his name from below his room.

And let us not forget the dark! I very much despise the night, very enigmatic. I would believe our hero agrees.

Bonk… Yes, I forgot about its part in this story. Let me explain a bit about him. Now, the kid loved to run around in the sun and play. Or he used to. He would go out and meet new people to go on adventures with daily. One of these days his mother brought him a red-coloured baseball bat as he had recently gotten interested in playing the sport. The boy was very excited, so much so that he actually named it! Who knows what that means, right? But the boy only rarely unleashed the mighty Bonk-Da-Bonk's power for sports. He would often imagine himself in an epic landscape in an unknown world, battling hundreds of monsters and beasts. All of this was to save the girl of his dreams, who, at his age, happened to be his mother.

Bonk was there for all of this and more; he once saved the boy's life from expiring at the hands of the horrible Mud Face. And again from a vegetative state by

Ninja Broccoli's terrible tasting lair. You might not have heard of them—their dastardly crime sprees didn't exactly get too far from the apartment complex, if you know what I mean. As of yet, the boy had found multiple reasons to rely upon his mighty Excalibur.

The boy had every single gosh darn light in his room turned on as he did not plan to sleep. He tried earlier, but he now understood that this is not the time to do so. He heard something coming from below, from downstairs. Not the usual screech from the snowy static of the television, it was something more meaningful and less repetitive.

Our hero slowly stepped down every step in his stairway, trying to breathe less and less so as to not wake anyone or disturb the origin of the scary sounds. Once in the living room, the boy shut off the snowy static and assumed the shadows. He scanned the room to find the creator of the noises. An unknown figure scratched at the window, its form boldly announcing its devious intentions. As the boy slowly stepped toward it, a monstrous force somehow pushed him back, slamming his body against the wall behind him. That force was that of the villainous deformity who the boy had prepared for. The ogre pushed itself through the window and into the house of a mother's guardian.

It crept toward the hero. He ran up the stairs to his mother, screaming for her to wake up and run as fast as she could. Right before she had finally awoken from her slumber, it grabbed the boy, carrying him into his room, but not before wrapping him up in his own blanket. I assume, to slow him just that small little bit. The boy fought as best he could, but couldn't break free quick enough. The grotesque creature must have somehow blocked the door. There is no other way out than from that very door. The grotesque noises added to the boy's anxiety about his mother's safety, especially as the sounds grew louder.

This child is not wearing any underwear outside of his pants. This child does not have an emblem to represent his powers. His apparel barely matched and yet this little one would learn what it took to become a true hero.

One must act fast in any situation that should arise in the event of fear. The boy, surrounded by a forest of socks, books, and, well, I'll call it a forest of many obstacles. He struggled as he acted as if a hurricane ignited within his own room, destroying everything in his path, all in search of an exit: the window. It is the only option. The boy, realising he was too small for reaching such a height, stacked up anything and everything that he could carry. He climbed the tough terrain. He stumbled, but didn't let it wither down his determination. The child reached the glass blocking his exit. He yielded the great Bonk-Da-Bonk. The neighbour's lights flared as they heard the sound of glass breaking from inside of that nice single mother's apartment. The boy escaped onto the edge. He searched for the quickest route to his mother's room. He leapt toward the window to the right of him. He scaled the building slowly, but surely. There was no time for screw-ups. He must be perfect in his execution.

He was closing in onto the damsel's window. He heard both pain and joy coming from within the room. No time to question it: the hero tossed his bat at the window with a fantastic amount of strength. This was his only chance. He must leap for the window, no worrying about cuts and other such nonsense.

The boy wildly plunged into the dimmed room. Sirens blared. The tragic sight of his mother crying as the demon ran in his direction. The boy was strong; he ran without even thinking and screamed a roar so loud that it awakened mother from her trance. The monster clashed with the child, overpowering the little one. A hero cannot be so easily defeated. The boy kneed it where it always counts, grabbing the sheets from the bed, circling around the creature until it lost visibility. Its left claw was all that was bare. The boy stomped on it as red splashed all around the room.

The beast had given up, but one must know never to assume. It took its beaten claw, flapping it about. It grabbed the boy's foot and knocked him to the floor. The hero saw the door in front of him fly open as the police kicked it in. They did what they do best, yelling and pointing their weapons at it. It seemed more affected by this that all of his effort combined. It was then unravelled out from the sheets that the boy had put it in before the police had caged its shivering wrists.

The boy's mother crawled to him, wrapping her arms around him as she had many times before. Her tears have yet to grow tired. Our hero tried to calm her, but to no avail. Seeing his mother so distressed convinced his own tears to escape.

As mothers often find themselves doing, her instincts took over as she tried to console him. She praised her son for his bravery, calling him her "little man of the house."

She then whispered to her son that his father will never be able to hurt them again. And I'm sure she believed it. But the beast was soon released on bail. He rarely did ever terrorise our hero and his mother again, though. Within months he had found a new family to distress with far more satisfactory results, I'm sure. Nevertheless, that boy was courageous, yet filled with an infinite kind of fear. Realising that I haven't been selfless since the night that I ended my mother's torment, maybe it's high time I changed that. I should give her a call. I miss her.

What Hears your Prayers

by Wondra Vanian

Another tedious day, another long, lonely night. Lori turned off the light and climbed into bed with the same enthusiasm she showed the rest of her life…none.

The arms that reached out to surround her as she lay her head down brought such comfort that, for a moment, Lori forgot she lived alone. Realisation came with a rush of terror. A hand clamped over Lori's mouth before she could release the scream lodged in her throat.

"Hush," a voice whispered, low and deep, next to her ear. "There's no one to hear you. Save what little breath you have left."

Her heart rose and fell in a swift, sickening spiral. The faceless voice was right; even if Lori screamed at the top of her lungs, the nearest neighbours were too far away to hear. Hell, even if they weren't, she doubted they'd bother. Lori had lived on the street nearly four years and not one of her neighbours had ever so much as stepped foot on her porch.

Save what little breath you have left.

Oh, God. She was going to die.

"Yes," the voice said. Lori felt movement on the pillow behind her as the dark figure nodded its head. "Yes, you are going to die."

He—the voice, the weight holding her immobile, were unmistakably male—could read her thoughts. The moment the realisation struck her, Lori's thoughts became an uncontrollable whirlwind. The harder she tried to control them, the wilder they became. All Lori's most terrible, disturbing, embarrassing thoughts pushed their way to the front of her mind, despite her best attempts to repress them.

The intruder chuckled softly against her ear. His breath was an icy wind that chilled her straight to the bone.

"Calm yourself," he said. "I already know everything you would hide from me."

The hand on Lori's waist slipped under the oversized tee she slept in. It was impossibly cold against her skin. Sliding upward, his touch left a frosty trail that made Lori shiver.

"I know you despise your friends for their perfect, oblivious lives."

His relentless hand cupped her breast and his thumb

flicked her nipple negligently. Lori was ashamed of her body's reaction. Even as fear squeezed her chest so tightly, she could barely draw breath, her nipple hardened in response to his touch. Even as she struggled to come to grips with the death that held her in his vice-like embrace, desire trickled through her veins.

"I know your family resents your intelligence only slightly less than your independence."

He squeezed her nipple between two fingers, drawing a weak gasp from her.

"I know you allow your coworkers to take advantage of you because you're so desperate to be liked."

The hand over Lori's mouth slid down her throat, along her arm, to her waist. She didn't even consider screaming. There wasn't enough air in the room. Every ounce she could drag into her body was too precious to waste.

Save what little breath you have left.

"I know you lie awake at night, begging, praying someone, *anyone* to give you what you've been missing. What you…crave."

His hand dipped under the waistband of her panties.

No, Lori wanted to say. She wanted to beg him to stop, to release her; wanted to shove his hand away. Wanted to, but couldn't. Lori could do nothing but cling helplessly to his forearm. Lori was unable to move yet felt like she was falling, farther and farther. Faster. Harder.

"You should have been more careful with your prayers."

Icy fingers slipped between her legs, seeking the folds of her womanhood and, finding them, delving deeper. Lori cried out as long, talented fingers found her core and plunged mercilessly inside. A deep rumble of laughter met her ears as she arched into his touch. Tears of shame pricked her eyes.

"Not everything that hears your prayer is a god."

The mysterious man worked Lori mercilessly; cold, impersonal hands drove her to breaking point without asking a thing in return. He made Lori writhe against him; made her pant and moan; made her wild with a passion she'd never known—with no reaction on his part but a dark, cruel chuckle as Lori shivered on the terrifying edge of oblivion.

"Some are demons."

With that, the unseen figure twisted to hover over Lori, eyes bright as hellfire in the darkness. He lowered his head. Rows of razor-sharp teeth bit hard into her flesh as his cold thumb hit the tiny nub at the heart of her desire. The pleasure and pain were linked so closely, Lori couldn't tell where one ended and the other began. She threw back her head with a cry, letting them take her.

Satisfaction pulsed lazily through her veins as Lori slowly came back to herself. It took a long moment to realise the man's—the demon's—hungry mouth was still clamped to her throat. The moment Lori became aware of it, pain chased away the last ripples of her orgasm. His sharp teeth worried her flesh, his forked tongue greedily lapping up the blood that flowed free from the jagged tear. Panic gripped her.

Yes, you are going to die.

You should have been more careful with your prayers.

Maybe the demon was right. Maybe she should have been more careful. Should have tempered her prayers. Should have been less desperate, accepted what she had.

But...maybe not.

Her fear ebbed, receding like waves from the shore of certainty.

Nothing the dark figure had said was untrue—and that was only the tip of the dark, horrible iceberg lodged in Lori's heart. Maybe she'd always known the only way to free herself from that iceberg was to find something colder, something sharper. Something like her nighttime visitor.

Maybe the cruel, unseen creature was the answer to

her prayers, after all.

At least he made Lori feel alive once before she died.

Lori's breathless "Thank you," was too soft for a human to hear, but not too soft for the demon at her throat. He smiled against her flesh as the last drop of life seeped from her body.

The Fallen Lust of the Dragon

by Zoey Xolton

Lucifer studied God's precious creations of Earth, intently. Holy angelic wards barred him from entering the Garden of Eden in his Fallen form, but his keen eyesight meant that even at a distance his vision was without fault; and his celestial ears heard every sound as if he, too, were sitting right there in the garden.

The Man called Adam was male, and created, he observed, with the Archangel Michael in mind; the creature might have been made in God's spiritual image, but Adam—with his deep blue eyes and his hair the colour of spun gold—could have been the Archangel's offspring, if such a thing were possible.

He sat beneath a vibrant, laden tree, biting into the succulent, juicy flesh of a downy, sunset-coloured fruit, his eyes trained upon his mate; the female who would be his wife. Lilith was her name, raven-haired, with eyes the colour of stormy skies. She luxuriated in a sparkling stream, delighting in the refreshing, cool waters under the midday heat.

The Fallen angel watched from his vantage point with disdain. What had these mortal beings done to earn such peace and freedom? *Nothing*, he thought sourly. He had Fallen for his right to control his own destiny, to be something more than a pawn of the Creator. He had paid the ultimate price. Severance from the Source carried with it a tangible pain, one that manifested as grief of the very soul, and could be felt by all those who had chosen to Fall with him.

With a sigh, he mulled over many schemes. He would, one way or another, ruin God's little paradise. He would inject chaos into its harmony, like poison into the vein. And then it dawned upon him, and the perfect plan was formed. He smiled from beyond Eden, the clouds darkening around him. Adam was haughty, and righteous—dominant to a fault, but had no mind of his own—nothing more than a *flesh puppet*. Lilith however, was contemplative and intelligent; he longed to covet her. He saw the fires of rebellion in her beautiful stormy eyes each time Adam forced himself upon her. All he needed to do was stoke that precious fire, that spark, and fan it into an unstoppable, unquenchable inferno.

Lilith moaned in her sleep as she was assaulted by uncannily vivid dreams. A deliciously dark stranger beckoned to her, and she found that she could not resist his charisma and allure. He had stunning feathered wings of midnight, and silver-blue eyes the colour of glittering stars. His beautiful mouth whispered her name and teased her with promises of carnality beyond her wildest dreams.

He took her into his arms and he felt like fire and ice, all at once. His soul sang to hers in a way that she could not understand. *Who was he?* He never gave his name. All she knew was that he was her secret, and that Adam must not know. Her mind was her own, was it not? What right did he have to her dreams, anyway?

That night she experienced pleasures she had never known. As Adam slept beside her, her back arched and she bit her lip to stifle the cries of ecstasy that threatened to escape her. There was a fire in her belly, a gnawing, growing, unrelenting intensity the likes of which Adam had never ignited within her. Her hands trailed the length of her hot, sweat-slick body until they came to the soft nest of hair between her legs. She was wet with desire, and it was all the doing of her phantom lover. She felt him as if he were truly there—and yet he remained maddeningly intangible.

When the waves of her release finally subsided and her breathing relaxed, she rolled over, spent, staring off into the night. "Who are you?" she whispered? "*What* are you?" before sleep claimed her, and she drifted soundly into oblivion.

For more days than she could count, the sweet, rapturous torment went on. Night after night her invisible dream lover came to her. Sometimes they were alone together, other times she was loved and pleasured by many beautiful, strange, starry-eyed men. On occasion, even strange women, females, just like her, but of otherworldly beauty—and possessing that dark inner fire of her silver-blue-eyed secret—joined in.

With each sunrise that passed she felt the flame of her soul flicker with anger and indignation. It grew, and grew, until she felt trapped within the confines of the garden and its perfection; trapped with Adam and his pathetic, unsatisfying rutting. *She yearned for more.* "What have I done that I should be forced to endure this?" she asked the wind. "What lies beyond Eden? This garden seems little more than a gilded cage. Does God not love me as dearly as he loves Adam? Why must I lay beneath him, and submit to his every whim?" The wind tousled her long black locks in response, but had no answers for her.

Lilith sat beneath the one tree in Eden that they were forbidden to partake of. She peered at its glossy red fruit, wondering. Moments later the bright green leaves rustled gently and she watched intently, expecting to see a small bird, or a scurrying mouse. A creature she had not seen in Eden before emerged from the foliage; its black iridescent scales shimmering, its forked tongue flicking. Wise golden eyes regarded her as it wrapped its length around the branch directly above her.

You have many questions, it said, though its mouth had not moved. *Are you afraid?*

Lilith stood, her face but an arm's length from the never-before-seen visitor. "I am not," she answered honestly. "Where have you come from?"

Beyond Eden, it replied.

Lilith's eyes widened in shock and awe as a smile spread quickly across her face. "Beyond Eden? Tell me, please, what lies outside of this garden? I long to know!"

There are realms beyond imagining, Lilith. I come from one such place.

Lilith reached for the branch with one hand, closing the space between them. "Can you take me?" she asked.

I cannot take you, Lilith, you must leave of your own free will.

Dismay painted Lilith's features. "How? I have walked these meadows tirelessly, there is no end! Whichever way I turn, all paths lead back here."

You cannot leave in that manner. You must defy God, upset him—so that he casts you out, only then will you truly be free.

"Upset God? How?"

The slithering creature held her gaze for a time before retreating into the greenery. *You must defy Adam, it whispered. If you defy him, you defy God.* And then the beautiful, foreign beast was gone. She searched the branches, but found no trace of it. For a moment she felt crestfallen, but a surge of excitement and rebellion buoyed her spirit just heartbeats later. "I have the power," she realised. "I cannot be taken. I am my own, and I will be free!" She grinned to herself beneath the Forbidden Tree, gloating in the knowledge that the evening would bring her heart's desire.

From beyond the garden, Lucifer smiled.

"What is wrong with you, woman?" muttered Adam as he tried to mount his mate.

Lilith fought him, denied him, fending off his advances as best she was able, but he was stronger and overpowered her, pinning her slight frame to the soft grass, annoyance and anger clear upon his face. "Submit to me, as is God's will!" he demanded, before moving between her thighs.

"Adam, please, stop," Lilith beseeched him. "I must tell you!"

Adam's brow furrowed in consternation. "Tell me what?"

"Lean closer so that I may whisper it to you."

Perplexed and irritated, Adam lowered his ear. "What is it, woman?" Lilith did not wait for a second chance. His throat within reach, she strained forward with all her might and sunk her teeth into his flesh. Blood filled her mouth as Adam's howl filled the night. She rolled out from under him as he fell to the side, clutching at his wound. Lilith stood, chest heaving, rage and exhilaration fuelling her, blood dripping to her breast.

"I will not submit to you! I will not lie beneath you," she swore. "I am not yours to claim!"

Above them, the dark sky thundered, and lightning rippled through the heavens as the clouds parted. A blinding white light saturated the Garden. Even wounded as he was, Adam clambered to his knees in fear, head bowed. "Kneel, you fool!" he hissed at Lilith. "You have invoked the ire of God!"

Lilith looked to the sky, but held her ground, equal parts thrill and terror coursing through her.

A voice alike the thunder spoke, "You have sown discord within Eden, my daughter, and forsaken your purpose."

Flicking hair from her face, she shouted back. "What is my purpose?"

"You were to bear the sons and daughters of Adam, and fill the Earth with my children. It was your duty to raise them in fear of my name."

"I will not!" she cried. "I do not want his children, or *yours*! I do not fear you, and I want my freedom. You say that you have gifted us with free will, yet I am not free to do as I will! I am trapped here, naught more than his slave, and your servant!"

God shook the earth and a break in the perfection of Eden was revealed. A gateway leading into a vast expanse of nothing stretched before her. "If it is freedom you so desire, then freedom you shall have. You are banished from Eden, Lilith, and your womb will never bear fruit of your own kind. You have caused chaos within my vision and I will look upon you no more."

Every fibre in Lilith's being was on fire. The blaze

within her soul consumed her. Stormy eyes flashing, her smile darkened. "You need not banish me, oh *Lord,*" she scoffed. "For I go willingly!" Stepping through the gateway, the false dream of Eden glittered and faded behind her, no more than a mirage. When she looked next to the barren and desolate landscape, she gasped, and a delicious, black hope sang from her soul.

Her midnight-winged, silver-blue-eyed lover awaited her with open arms.

"My name is Lucifer Morningstar," he said, placing a lingering kiss upon her hand. "Would it please you to live your dreams for all eternity? To offer God the greatest insult of all?"

Lilith's heart raced. "Yes," she breathed, heart racing. "But how?"

"Stand with me, and rule by my side, as the Queen of Hell."

"With you…as your equal?"

"Yes, my beauty," he purred. "If you will have me, and swear allegiance to our fight for freedom against our Father."

Lilith returned his obscenely deviant smile and allowed him to take her hand as he guided her into an embrace. "He is no father of mine," she said with venomous defiance.

"Then come," he whispered, enclosing his black wings protectively around her. "Let me give you a taste of the sweet freedom you so yearn for."

Lust

Author Biographies

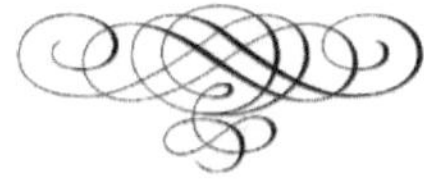

A.L. KING

A.L. King is an author of horror, fantasy, science fiction, and poetry. As an avid fan of dark subjects from an early age, his first influences included R.L. Stine, Edgar Allan Poe, and Stephen King. Later stylistic inspirations came from foreign horror films and media, particularly Japanese. He is a graduate of West Liberty University, has dabbled in journalism, and is actively involved in his community. Although his creativity leans toward darker genres, he has even written a children's book titled "Leif's First Fall." He was raised in the town of Sistersville, West Virginia, which he still proudly calls home.

A.R DEAN

A.R. Dean is a dark and twisted soul. Dean has spent their whole life spreading fear with the tales from their head. Best known for stories that terrify and show the evilest side of human nature. So, look for Dean haunting your local cemetery or under your bed, because they're here to spread the fear. Turn off your lights and enjoy a scare. Dean is being published in Black Hare Press's Beyond and Unravel Anthologies. Keep a lookout for more stories.

Facebook: <u>A.R. Dean Author & Ghoul</u>

A.R JOHNSTON

AR Johnston is a small town girl from Nova Scotia, Canada. She is known to write mostly urban fantasy, though she goes where the muses lead her and you never know where that may be. She is a lover of coffee, good tv shows, horror flicks, and a reader of good books. She pretends to be a writer when real life doesn't get in the way. Pesky full-time job and adulting!

Facebook: arjohnstonauthor
Website: arjohnstonauthor.wordpress.com

BLAKE JESSOP

Blake Jessop is a Canadian author of sci-fi, fantasy and horror stories with a master's degree in creative writing from the University of Adelaide. You can read more of his historical speculative fiction in "Battling in All Her Finery: Historical Accounts of Otherworldly Women Leaders" from DefCon One.

Twitter: @everydayjisei

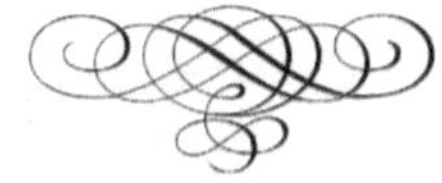

CATHERINE KENWELL

Catherine Kenwell is a Barrie, Ontario, mediator and author. After 30 successful years in corporate communications, she sustained a brain injury, lost her job, and joined the circus. She writes both horror/dark fiction and inspirational non-fiction. Her works have been published in Chicken Soup for the Soul, Trembling with Fear, Siren's Call, and HellBound Books.

Website: www.catherinekenwell.com

CINDAR HARRELL

Cindar Harrell loves fairy tales, especially ones with a dark twist. Her writing is often fairy tale inspired, but she also loves mystery and horror. Her stories can be found in various anthologies from publishers such as Black Hare Press, Iron Faerie Publishing, Dragon Soul Press, Blood Song Books, Soteira Press, Fantasia Divinity and more. Traveling is a passion for her as it inspires her imagination to run wild, especially in places that have a mystic presence in the air. She regularly moonlights as another human, but no matter who she is, she is always writing. Her novella inspired by The Snow Queen is set to release in 2020 as well as her debut novel, Lithium, and short story collection, Perchance to Dream.

Facebook: CindarHarrell

CLINT FOSTER

Clint Foster lives with his herd of four cats, beloved Basset, Zero, and wonderful wife, Nik. He loves to tell stories just as much as he loves to read them, and is excited to share his work. A longtime consumer of media of all kinds, he enjoys giving back what he hopes everyone else thinks are good stories.

Facebook: ClintFosterAuthor

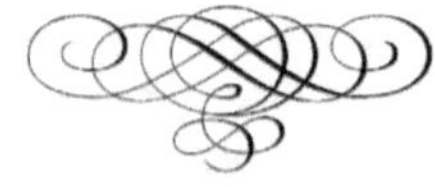

D.J. ELTON

D.J. Elton is a writer living in Melbourne's west. As a child she came from England to Australia, on the last boat down the Suez Canal, where she underwent a sacrificial dunking ritual in the court of King Neptune, and has never looked back. She likes creating speculative micro fiction and short stories, as well as random essays. Her work has been published in several anthologies, and she has written a historical fantasy novella, 'The Merlin Girl.' When not playing with a pen, she likes most of all to go to the green country.

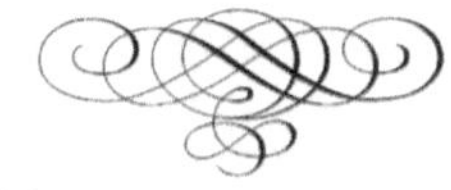

DANNIELLE VIERA

Dannielle Viera has been involved in the Australian publishing industry for over 20 years – first as a copywriter and then as an editor, project manager, proofreader and author. She has worked on over 100 non-fiction books, writing about subjects as varied as the history of Christianity, Native American mythology, vampires, knights and the death of Hollywood film stars. Some of the books for which she is credited as a contributor include Outside In Gains a Soul (ATB Publishing, 2019), A Christmas Cornucopia (Christmas Press, 2019), and Fire Burn, Cauldron Bubble: Magical Poems Chosen by Paul Cookson (Bloomsbury UK, 2020).

Facebook: DannielleVieraAuthor

DAWN DEBRAAL

Dawn DeBraal lives in rural Wisconsin with her husband Red, two rat terriers, and a cat. She has discovered that her love of telling a good story can be written. Published stories with Palm-sized press, Spillwords, Mercurial Stories, Potato Soup Journal, Edify Fiction, Zimbell House Publishing, Clarendon House Publishing, Blood Song Books, Black Hare Press, Fantasia Divinity, Cafelit, Reanimated Writers, Guilty Pleasures, Unholy Trinity, The World of Myth, Dastaan World, Vamp Cat, Runcible Spoon, Dark Christmas, Siren's Call, Iron Horse Publishing, Falling Star Magazine 2019 Pushcart Nominee.

Amazon: amazon.com/Dawn-DeBraal/e/B07STL8DLX

EDDIE D. MOORE

Eddie D. Moore travels hundreds of hours a year, and he fills that time by listening to audiobooks. When he isn't playing with his grandchildren, he writes his own stories. You can find a list of his publications on his blog or by visiting his Amazon Author Page. While you're there, be sure to pick up a copy of his mini-anthology Misfits & Oddities.

Website: eddiedmoore.wordpress.com
Amazon: amazon.com/author/eddiedmoore

EDWARD AHERN

Ed Ahern resumed writing after forty odd years in foreign intelligence and international sales. He's had over two hundred fifty stories and poems published so far, and five books. Ed works the other side of writing at Bewildering Stories, where he sits on the review board and manages a posse of five review editors.

Twitter: @bottomstripper
Facebook: EdAhern73

ERICA SCHAEF

Erica Schaef worked as a Registered Nurse for many years before becoming a stay-at-home parent. Her short stories have been featured most recently by: Visual Verse (Vol. 06- Chapter 09), Blood Moon Rising Magazine (Issue 77), and HellBound Books ("The Toilet Zone"). More of her short stories will be in featured in upcoming anthologies by Fantasia Divinity ("Isolation"), and Jitter Press (Issue 8), as well as in the forthcoming issue of Still Point Arts Quarterly. She lives in rural Tennessee with her husband and two children.

G. ALLEN WILBANKS

G. Allen Wilbanks is a member of the Horror Writers Association (HWA) and has published over 100 short stories in various magazines and on-line venues. He is the author of two short story collections, and the novel, When Darkness Comes.

Website: www.gallenwilbanks.com
Blog: DeepDarkThoughts.com

GABRIELLA BALCOM

Gabriella Balcom lives in Texas with her family, loves reading and writing, and thinks she was born with a book in her hands. She works in a mental health field, and writes fantasy, horror/thriller, romance, children's stories, and sci-fi. She likes travelling, music, good shows, photography, history, interesting tales, and animals. Gabriella says she's a sucker for a great story and loves forests, mountains, and back roads which might lead who knows where. She has a weakness for lasagne, garlic bread, tacos, cheese, and chocolate, but not necessarily in that order.

Facebook: GabriellaBalcom.lonestarauthor

HARI NAVARRO

Hari Navarro has, for many years now, been locked in his neighbours cellar. He survives due to an intravenous feed of puréed extreme horror and Absinthe infused sticky-spiced unicorn wings. His anguished cries for help can be found via 365 Tomorrows, Breachzine, AntipodeanSF, Horror Without Borders, Black Hare Press and HellBound books. Hari was the Winner of the Australasian Horror Writers' Association [AHWA] Flash Fiction Award 2018 and has, also, succeeded in being a New Zealander who now lives in Northern Italy with no cats.

Amazon: amazon.com/Hari-Navarro
Tumblr: harinavarro.tumblr.com/

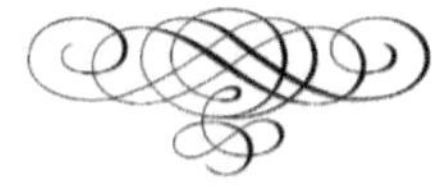

J.L. ROYCE

J. L. Royce lives in the northern reaches of the American Midwest. He is a published author of science fiction, macabre, and whatever else strikes him. From time to time he may be spotted lurking in the North Woods, searching for the elusive psychological moment.

Amazon: amazon.com/author/jlroyce
Twitter: @AuthorJLRoyce

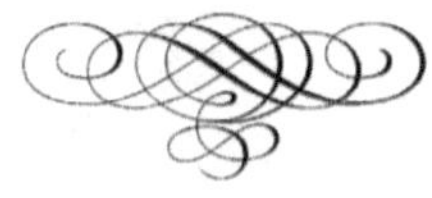

J.M. MEYER

Jacqueline Moran Meyer is a writer, artist and small business owner living in New York, where she received her master's degree from Teachers College, Columbia University. Jacqueline enjoys writing speculative fiction and mysteries. Her favorite author is Alice Munro and her favorite film…is…anything horror related. Jacqueline also enjoys hiking with her dog Molly and the company of her husband Bruce and daughters; Julia, Emma and Lauren. Jacqueline's Mantra lately; there's no such thing as failing, it's called learning.

Website: jmoranmeyer.net
Amazon: www.amazon.com/author/jacquelinemoranmeyer

J.W. GARRETT

J.W. Garrett has been writing in one form or another since she was a teenager. She currently lives in Florida with her family but loves the mountains of Virginia where she was born. Her writings include YA fantasy as well as short stories. Since completing Remeon's Quest-Earth Year 1930, the prequel in her YA fantasy series, Realms of Chaos, she has been hard at work on the next in the series, scheduled to release August 2020. When she's not hanging out with her characters, her favourite activities are reading, running and spending time with family.

Website: www.jwgarrett.com
BHC Press: www.bhcpress.com/Author_JW_Garrett.html

JAMES DORR

Indiana writer James Dorr's THE TEARS OF ISIS was a 2013 Bram Stoker Award® nominee for Superior Achievement in a Fiction Collection. Other books include STRANGE MISTRESSES: TALES OF WONDER AND ROMANCE, DARKER LOVES: TALES OF MYSTERY AND REGRET, and his all-poetry VAMPS (A RETROSPECTIVE). His latest, from Elder Signs Press, is a novel-in-stories, TOMBS: A CHRONICLE OF LATTER-DAY TIMES OF EARTH. An Active Member of HWA and SFWA with more than 500 individual appearances from ALFRED HITCHCOCK'S MYSTERY MAGAZINE to XENOPHILIA, Dorr invites readers to visit his blog.

Website: jamesdorrwriter.wordpress.com

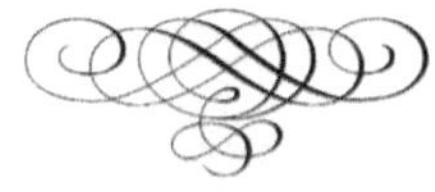

JAMES LIPSON

James Lipson's debut book, Fallen and Other Stories, was published in 2019. His short stories have appeared in Black Hare Press Anthologies, Teleport Magazine, Inner Circle's Writers Group Anthologies, and others. With a background in art, James has naturally turned to illustrating as he writes, bringing many of his short stories to life not only with descriptive detail, but also detailed visual imagery.

Website: www.jameslipson.com
Instagram: jameslipsonart

JASON HOLDEN

Jason is a human. He lives here and there in the UK, always with his wife, daughter and fur baby. His primary goal is to raise his daughter to adulthood without any major damage. When he can, he writes. He thinks he does it well, but you can be the judge of that. He has been published in a few anthologies here and there, has been praised and put down for his writing. You can find and follow him on Facebook, although he asks you only follow him on Facebook and not through the streets. That's just creepy.

Facebook: Jason Holden-Author

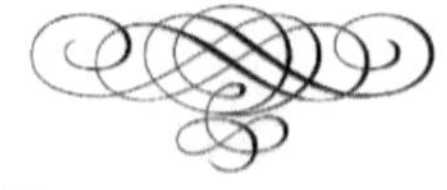

JESSICA CHANESE

Jessica Chanese is a speculative fiction writer living in Upstate NY with her husband, two forces of nature masquerading as their children, and their Boston Terrier, Max. She's written several as-of-yet unpublished short stories and a full-length contemporary fantasy novel, and has too many other pieces in the works.

Website: www.jesschanesewrites.com
Twitter: @JChanese

JO SEYSENER

Jo Seysener is a mum of three crazies, a scatter of chickens, a decrepit kelpie and a rambunctious GSD. She lives with her husband near Brisbane, Australia. When she is not exposing her kids to cult story books from her childhood, she can be found in the kitchen experimenting with new flavours and pairings. She adores alpacas.

Facebook: joseysener
Website: www.joseysener.com

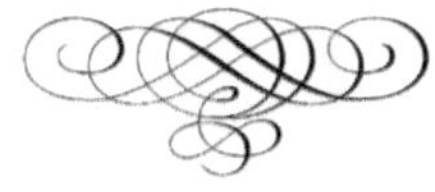

JODI JENSEN

Jodi Jensen, author of time travel romances and speculative fiction short stories, grew up moving from California, to Massachusetts, and a few other places in between, before finally settling in Utah at the ripe old age of nine. The nomadic life fed her sense of adventure as a child and the wanderlust continues to this day. With a passion for old cemeteries, historical buildings and sweeping sagas of days gone by, it was only natural she'd dream of time traveling to all the places that sparked her imagination.

Twitter: @WritesJodi
Facebook: jodijensenwrites

JOHN H. DROMEY

John H. Dromey was born in northeast Missouri, USA. He enjoys reading—mysteries in particular—and writing in a variety of genres. In addition to contributing to the Black Hare Press series of Dark Drabbles anthologies, he's had short fiction published in Alfred Hitchcock's Mystery Magazine, Martian Magazine, Mystery Weekly, Stupefying Stories Showcase, Thriller Magazine, Unfit Magazine, and elsewhere, as well as in numerous anthologies, including Chilling Horror Short Stories (Flame Tree Publishing, 2015).

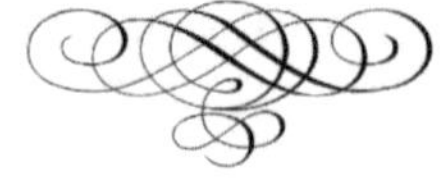

K.B. ELIJAH

K.B. Elijah is a fantasy author living in Brisbane, Australia with her husband and three cockatiels. A lawyer by day, and a writer by...also day, because she needs her solid nine hours of sleep per night (not that the cockatiels let her sleep past 6am). K.B. writes for various international anthologies, and her work features in dozens of collections about the mysterious, the magical and the macabre. Her own books of short fantasy novellas with twists, The Empty Sky and Out of the Nowhere, are available on paperback and Kindle now.

Website: www.kbelijah.com
Instagram: k.b.elijah

LYNDSEY ELLIS-HOLLOWAY

Lyndsey Ellis-Holloway is a writer from Knaresborough, UK. She writes fantasy, sci-fi, horror and dystopian stories, focussing on compelling characters and layering in myth and legend at every opportunity. Her mind is somewhat dark and twisted, and she lives in perpetual hope of owning her own Dragon someday, but for now she writes about them to fill the void... and to stop her from murdering people who annoy her. When she's not writing she spends time with her husband, her dogs and her friends enjoying activities such as walking, movies, conventions and of course writing for fun as well!

Website: theprose.com/LyndseyEH

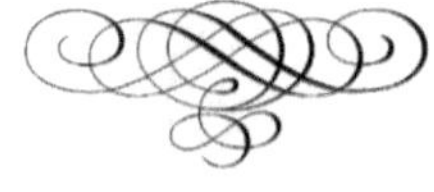

M. SYDNOR JR.

M. Sydnor Jr. is an author of novels and short stories. He began his career in writing in 2005 after trading in his basketball sneakers for a pen and pad, and the desire to create worlds took off. Early in his writing journey, he learned there was more than just putting an idea to paper, you had to read. He lives in Northern California collecting an unhealthy number of movies, books and graphic novels. The characters of his fantasy series, The Legends of the World, take most of his time when he's not coaching high school basketball.

M.J. CHRISTIE

A writer of novel-length fiction, short fiction and poetry. M.J. Christie recently became addicted to writing shorter fiction - the shorter the better - and poetry. The UK's Lincolnshire Coast provides the backdrop and inspiration for M.J.'s writing, giving focus and meaning to everyday life. M.J. has had 100 word drabbles and one poem published (so far) in online magazines.

Website: www.mjchristie.com

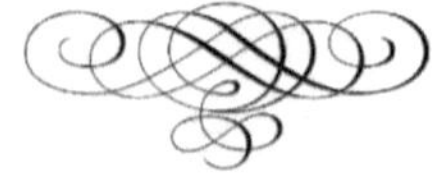

MARK MACKEY

Mark Mackey is the author of various self-published books. In addition, he has had various short stories published in charity anthologies. They include such captivating titles such as Christmas Lites, No Sleeves and Short Dresses: A Summer Anthology, Painted Mayhem, and Grynn Anthology, among others. A long time resident of Chicago, when not writing, he spends time reading various genres of books.

MAURA YZMORE

Maura Yzmore is a writer and science professor based in the American Midwest. Some of her darker fare can be found in The Molotov Cocktail, Aphotic Realm, Coffin Bell, and elsewhere.

Website: maurayzmore.com
Twitter: @MauraYzmore

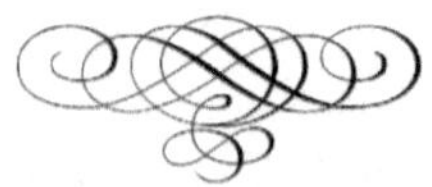

MAXINE CHURCHMAN

Maxine Churchman lives in Essex UK and has recently started writing poetry and short stories to share. Her interests include learning to improve her writing, reading, knitting, walking and teaching yoga. She is also planning a novel.

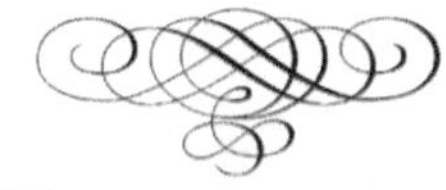

MICHAEL D. DAVIS

Michael D. Davis was born and raised in a small town in the heart of Iowa. Having written over thirty short stories, ranging in genre from comedy to horror from flash fiction to novella he continues in his accursed pursuit of a career in the written word.

N.M. BROWN

Since N.M. Brown made her first post to a popular Internet forum, she's taken the horror community by storm. Her ability to create, terrify, and drive home her stories is insurmountable. N.M. Brown's published works can be found in multiple anthologies for all to read, but be forewarned, if you do... you may want to call your therapist after, her stories are terrifying, disturbing and devilishly unsettling. She is not only a fright visually, but also has a creepy tentacle in horror podcasting as well. Sinister Sweetheart writes, voice acts and is the media director of the Scarecrow Tales podcast.

Website: Sinistersweetheart.wixsite.com/sinistersweetheart
Facebook: NMBrownStories

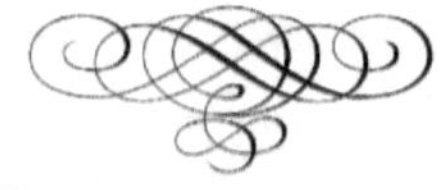

NERISHA KEMRAJ

Nerisha Kemraj resides in Durban, South Africa with her husband and two mischievous daughters. She has work published/accepted in various publications, both print and online. She holds a Bachelor's degree in Communication Science, and a Post Graduate Certificate in Education from University of South Africa.

Amazon: amazon.com/author/nerisha_kemraj
Facebook: Nerishakemrajwriter

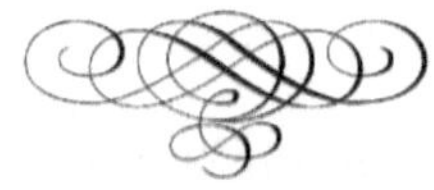

NICOLA CURRIE

Nicola Currie is from Cambridge, UK where she works in educational publishing. She has published poetry in literary magazines, including Mslexia and Sarasvati, and short stories in various anthologies. She has also completed her first novel, which was longlisted for the Bath Children's Novel Award.

Website: writeitandweep.home.blog

RAVEN CORINN CARLUK

Raven Corinn Carluk writes dark fantasy, paranormal romance, and anything else that catches her interest. She's authored five novels, where she explores themes of love and acceptance. Her shorter pieces, usually from her darker side, can be found in Black Hare Press anthologies, at Detritus Online, and through Alban Lake Publishers.

Twitter: @ravencorinn
Website: www.ravencorinncarluk.com

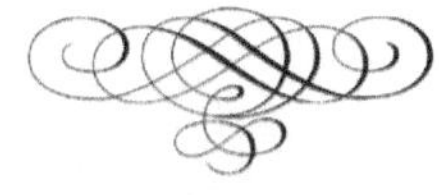

RHIANNON BIRD

Rhiannon Bird is a young aspiring author. She has a passion for words and storytelling. Rhiannon has her own quotes blog; Thoughts of a Writer. She has had 4 works published. This includes 3 short stories and 2 poems. These are published on Eskimo pie, Literary yard, Down in the Dirt Magazine and Short break fiction. She can be found on Facebook, Instagram, and Pinterest.

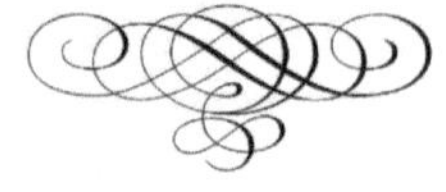

ROBIN BRAID

Robin Braid writes stories of the mysterious and macabre. A resident of Fife, Scotland, he graduated from Dundee University with a degree in English Literature. When not working in his regular job he can often be found rambling over hills and glens in search of inspiration for further tales.

Twitter: @robinbraid

SANDY BUTCHERS

Sandy Butchers is an author and an artist, known for her elaborate fantasy worlds and creature designs. After living in Scandinavia for a year and traveling throughout the world, she now settled in the countryside, along with a variety of pets and maps on which X marks the spot.

Website: www.sandybutchers.com
Facebook: AuthorSandyButchers

SERENA JAYNE

Serena Jayne is a graduate of Seton Hill University's Writing Popular Fiction MFA Program. Her short fiction and poetry can be found in Switchblade Magazine, the Drabble, Crack the Spine Literary Magazine, 101 Fiction, the Oddville Press, and other publications.

Website: www.serenajayne.com
Twitter: @SJ_Writer

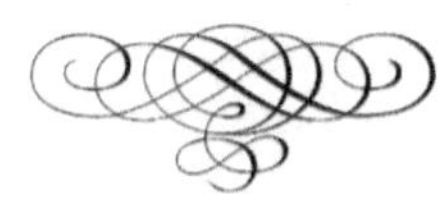

STEPHANIE SCISSOM

Stephanie hails from Altamont, TN. She works nights in a tire factory and plots murder by day. She's currently working on a twisted apocalyptic trilogy starring Lucifer and his tortured wife.

Facebook: stephaniescissom2019

STEPHEN HERCZEG

Stephen Herczeg is an IT Geek based in Canberra Australia. He has been writing for over twenty years and has completed a couple of dodgy novels, sixteen feature length screenplays and numerous short stories and scripts. His horror work has featured in Sproutlings, Hells Bells, Below the Stairs, Trickster's Treats #1 and #2, Shades of Santa, Behind the Mask, Beyond the Infinite; The Body Horror Book, Anemone Enemy, Petrified Punks and Beginnings. He has also had numerous Sherlock Holmes stories published through the Belanger Books - Sherlock Holmes anthologies.

Amazon: amazon.com/-/e/B07916SQQS
Facebook: stephenherczegauthor

SUE MARIE ST. LEE

Born in Chicago, Sue Marie St. Lee currently lives in Oklahoma with her husband and Manx cat. A storyteller since learning to talk, her wild imagination caused reprimands from her Mother. Her imagination persevered. Retired from Finance Management, Sue began ghostwriting until 2019, choosing to have works published internationally, in print and online, under her own name. Black Hare Press, Fantasia Divinity, and Spillwords Press are some of the publishers to feature Sue's work to date.

Blog: suemariestlee.home.blog
Amazon: amazon.com/Sue-Marie-St.-Lee/e/B07WJFRF1L

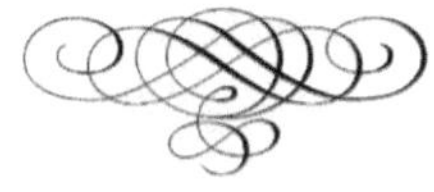

TERRY MILLER

Terry Miller lives in Portsmouth, Ohio. His work has been featured in Sanitarium Magazine, Devolution Z, Jitter, Rhysling Anthology 2017, Poetry Quarterly, Sirens Call Ezine, The Horror Tree's Trembling With Fear, SpillWords, Organic Ink Vol. I, Curses & Cauldrons Anthology from Blood Song Books, Forest of Fear from Blood Song Books, the Dark Drabble Anthology Series from Black Hare Press, 100 Word Zombie Bites from Reanimated Writers Press, Scary Snippets, Guilty Pleasures & Other Dark Delights, 100 Word Horrors 3, and O Unholy Night In Deathlehem from Grinning Skull Press.

Facebook: tmiller2015
Amazon: amazon.com/author/millerterry1

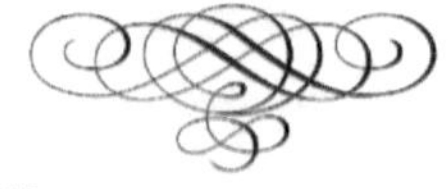

THOMAS KEARNES

Thomas Kearnes graduated from the University of Texas at Austin with an MA in film writing. His fiction has appeared in Gulf Coast, Berkeley Fiction Review, Timber, Hobart, Gertrude, A cappella Zoo, Split Lip Magazine, Cutthroat, Litro, PANK, BULL: Men's Fiction, Gulf Stream Magazine, Wraparound South, Night Train, 3:AM Magazine, Word Riot, Storyglossia, Driftwood Press, Adroit Journal, The Matador Review, Pseudopod, Underbelly Magazine, Black Dandy, the Best Gay Stories series, Mary: A Journal of New Writing, wigleaf, SmokeLong Quarterly, Pidgeonholes, Sundog Lit, The Citron Review, and elsewhere. He is a three-time Pushcart Prize nominee and three-time Best of the Net nominee. Originally from East Texas, he now lives near Houston and works as an English tutor at a local community college. His debut collection of short fiction, "Texas Crude" is now available at Lethe Press, Amazon and Barnes & Noble.

TRISTAN DRUE ROGERS

Tristan Drue Rogers has had his writing and poetry featured in literary magazines (such as Vamp Cat, Genre: Urban Arts, Weird Mask, and more), and horror anthologies (such as 100 Word Horrors Book 3 & 4 and Twenty Twenty). Tristan lives with his lovely wife Sarah and their son Rhett in Texas.

Website: www.tristandrue.wordpress.com
Twitter: @RogersDrue

WONDRA VANIAN

Wondra Vanian is an American living in the United Kingdom with her Welsh husband and their army of fur babies. A writer first, Wondra is also an avid gamer, photographer, cinephile, and blogger. She has music in her blood, sleeps with the lights on, and has been known to dance naked in the moonlight. Wondra was a multiple Top-Ten finisher in the 2017 and 2018 Preditors and Editors Reader's Poll, including the Best Author category. Her story, "Halloween Night," was named a Notable Contender for the Bristol Short Story Prize in 2015.

Website: www.wondravanian.com

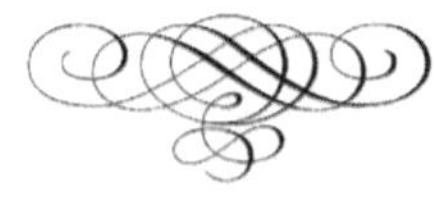

XIMENA ESCOBAR

Ximena is writing stories and poetry. Originally from Chile, she is the author of a translation into Spanish of the Broadway Musical "The Wizard of Oz", and of an original adaptation of the same, "Navidad en Oz", both produced in her home country. Since 2018 she has published several short stories in various anthologies and online platforms, and is now slowly working on her own collection. Ximena has a degree in Arts & Communication Science and lives in Nottingham with her family.

Facebook: Ximenautora
Twitter: @laximenin

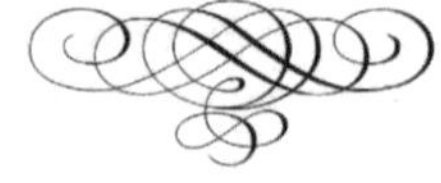

ZOEY XOLTON

Zoey Xolton is an Australian Speculative Fiction writer, primarily of Dark Fantasy, Paranormal Romance and Horror. She is also a proud mother of two and is married to her soul mate. Outside of her family, writing is her greatest passion. She is especially fond of short fiction and is working on releasing her own themed collections in future.

Website: www.zoeyxolton.com

Lust

482

Acknowledgements

When we embarked on our Black Hare Press journey back in late 2018, we never envisioned the huge support we'd get from the writing community. We have been truly humbled by the number of submissions we've received (around 3,000 over our first eight publications!) and have loved reading every single one.

So, thank you to everyone who crafted tales just for us—from the tiny tales in our Dark Drabbles series to these sinful tales you have read here in Lust—we thank you from the bottom of our hearts.

To our families and friends, collaborators, random strangers who took pity on us, and everyone who has helped us on the way: we couldn't have done it without you.

And to you, our discerning reader, we and these talented writers did it all for you. We hope you enjoyed these tales, and if you did, don't forget to leave a review.

Thank you all—see you next time.

Love & kisses
Ben & Dean

www.blackharepress.com

Lust

Lust